*The Mathematics
of Jane Austen*

The Mathematics of Jane Austen
and other stories

Elizabeth Smither

For Irene

Published with the support of
Creative New Zealand Toi Aotearoa

Published by Godwit Publishing Limited
15 Rawene Road, P.O. Box 34-683
Birkenhead, Auckland, New Zealand

First published 1997

© 1997 Elizabeth Smither

ISBN 1 86962 008 9

Cover design: Sarah Maxey
Printed in Hong Kong

Contents

Francophilia 7

Rose Madder 23

Cricket 43

A Turkish Proverb 57

The Mathematics of Jane Austen 68

The Ladies Chatterley's Gardener 84

Big Bertha 99

The Pulley 114

Genealogy 123

Money 139

Jesu, Joy of Man's Desiring 155

The Lark Quartet 167

Abraham, Edward Ernest, Jacob and Nina 182

Milly-Molly-Mandy 194

Six Sisters from Ouse 206

Acknowledgements 223

&

Francophilia

Pascal Gerrard, his long frame bent like a half-opened Swiss army knife in his economy class seat, tried and failed to sleep as the Singapore Airlines 747 droned above the mountains of Turkey. He had consumed two brandies, one at a gulp and the other slowly, but the net result had been a ball of resentment or throwing fuel on a fire.

This time it's certain, Simone had faxed. *I've spoken to two specialists and though they can find no overwhelming symptom all the indicators are there. About a week. So use up those free air miles you've been hoarding.*

Simone had a knack of making him feel cheap but she didn't appreciate how far it was from Paris to Sydney. Simone had moved only as far as Sydney: the French names their mother had bestowed as babies had hurt her less. Whereas Pascal had scuttled under nicknames or invented false names on the spot until he had eventually, by being mistaken for French by his bank's head office, been set down in his rightful country, full of Jean-Pierres and Claudes, Guys and Andrés, even his occasional namesake.

Jean Gerrard had wished to be transferred to Sacred Heart hospice before her son landed at Kingsford Smith, but on Friday she was still in a medical ward and not even a private room. She had rallied a little during the night and the improvement in her vital signs was noted on the chart at the foot of her bed. As if realising this, she refused breakfast.

From under her pillow Jean withdrew a small hand mirror. It was impossible to see her entire face in it, just a cross-section of fine lines and deeper wrinkles. A topographical map in which her features — nose, eyes, brows — were a peak, lakes, rising ground. But Jean did not worry too much about her face: her eyes, the lakes, were still dark and glimmering, and her luxuriant hair which surmounted her skull like fleecy clouds was remarked on almost daily by ward minions. At the last visit of the hairdresser Jean had asked for a more modern style and the young woman, terrified of the corpse-like appearance of her client, had produced a thick upsweeping wedge and even shaped a point at the nape in line with the vertebrae of her spine.

As she returned the mirror to its hiding place Jean thought of Colette, the writer who had started her on the road to becoming an ardent Francophile. It was not merely the heroines she had identified with as a girl, Gigi or Claudine or Annie, but the older mysterious women, like Lea, so versed in the ways of the flesh. Long before she had a sexual life Jean knew Colette kept a powder compact under her pillow so as not to alarm a waking lover with a morning's déshabillé. Jean could not expect a lover but her daughter would undoubtedly appear and before another nightfall her beloved Pascal.

Finally, above the Indian Ocean, Pascal slept. An awkward limb-twisted sleep, in which he imagined he was an old tree. Below him he could hear voices — as a boy he had been a great and nimble tree climber — recommending the tree be felled. Except the voices spoke French, which puzzled him, since he had hidden in the topmost branches because his name was French. *Pascal, Pasha, Pansy, Pastille.* What had possessed his mad Francophile mother to burden her children with her obsession? It was not as if she had changed her own name. Sometimes he thought of names for her, the ugliest he could find. Noémie, Aceline, Galatée. Simone, his sister, had fared better. Simone de Beauvoir was practically a bible and Simone Signoret a seductress. When he woke the stewardess was bending over him and the man in the next seat was offering to accept an airline breakfast on his behalf.

Simone, meanwhile, was driving across the Harbour Bridge in the shimmering morning sun. She wore huge tortoiseshell sunglasses behind which she imagined her thoughts were concealed: would her mother die; had she summoned Pascal for nothing? In her linen sheath she bore a faint resemblance to Simone Signoret in *Room at the Top*. But Simone Signoret would have been decisive, dismissive, whereas Simone Adams often took action at the wrong time or leapt to a conclusion for cathartic reasons of her own. Her mother's doctor and the ward nurse had been so certain her mother was dying two days ago when she had faxed Pascal. They were to move her to a side room that very afternoon and the nurse had offered to contact the hospice if Simone thought that was her mother's wish. Instead Jean had rallied — how many rallies, Simone wondered — and the bed had stayed put. 'Someone else needs it,' the nurse had said snappishly to Simone's inquiry. 'Someone on life support.'

Simone had felt herself floundering: she no longer knew what expression to wear when she entered the ward where her mother's bed was against the window. The ledge was piled with cards, ever-changing flowers and bottles of mineral water. Simone's twins, Anne and Peter, had made posters of their grandmère: a rubicund balloon-like head with curls was taped to the wall above her head to be sighted by the nurse when she picked up her chart. Would Pascal bring yet more flowers? Simone could see him striding through the corridor, long elegant coat flapping because it would have been cold in Paris, holding a cellophane cone of carnations.

At 6.15 a.m. Pascal landed at Kingsford Smith. He was dog-tired but the relief of stretching his limbs outweighed his desire to prop his eyelids open with matchsticks. He forbore to phone Simone; instead he asked the taxi driver to find him a decent motel in walking distance of the Prince of Wales hospital. After inspecting two — treating the proprietor each time like a concièrge — Pascal settled on a unit with a kingsize bed and bath he could stretch out in on Belmore Road. Surroundings, part of his maternal heritage, were important to him. He had also noticed a small writing desk in the living area which would be useful since he intended to write frequently to Guy. Already he had a handful of postcards from the airport: koalas, platypus, a line of kookaburras. He had already posted one, of a Boeing 747, with a scrawling note from the *Pensées: Our nature consists in movement. Absolute stillness is death.* At the bottom he had added: *Absolute stillness would be better. See you before too long. Au revoir, Pascal.*

Luckily the motel was close to a suburban shopping centre, a rather superior one, if the appearance of the shops was any indication. They were of an almost medieval smallness and dimness but their interiors glowed with pyramids of hand-picked fruit, fine china, rustling dresses, liqueur-filled chocolates. Selecting a few items for his pint-sized fridge — wine, bread, cheese, grapes, tomatoes, a few slices of ham and a head of lettuce

— Pascal added four stems of golden lilies. Only a few of the buds were open: he would have the pleasure of watching them bloom on his motel table. He did not consider them for Jean who had forced him like a hot-house plant. Besides, wasn't there something about the dead hand of lilies?

Simone, standing at the workbench of her pine-walled kitchen in Waverton, buttered doorstop sandwiches for the twins and thought of the Earl of Sandwich. Surely if he hadn't been a gambler he could have been a hospital visitor? Onto the thick slabs she laid slices of luncheon sausage, ketchup, tomatoes, cheese. Then she pressed her palm on the bread and cut off the crusts. Anne and Peter took their plates into the garden.

Pascal had still not phoned. Perhaps he was already at the hospital, sitting in the visitor's chair, concealing, because Pascal concealed everything, his surprise at their mother's appearance. Perhaps they would speak in French, a few words that were like a game. Chère Maman . . . ma pauvre petite . . . Simone had abandoned French, though it was her mother's wish and possibly the cause of their rift. For who can tell what tiny decision opens a wound? The name is enough, she had told her mother, and it had been taken as an insult. Whereas Pascal . . .

Simone walked into the spare bedroom, freshly made up, just in case, though she knew Pascal would not stay. She might never learn where he was staying, any more than she could visualise his Paris life. A flat on the rue Boileau shared with someone called Guy. Guy de Maupassant whom Simone had read in translation: a girl crippled for life leaping from a window to spare a lover; a woman washing floors to replace a paste necklace. Pascal and her mother were welcome to it.

But in the event, Pascal did show Simone his motel. They met in the corridors of the Prince of Wales. Simone could see the tall lanky figure, coat slung over one arm, advancing with the gait of a giraffe.

'We must talk,' Pascal said, as they came alongside. 'I won't detain you now. Here's my address. It's not far. Say in about an hour or so?'

Simone, not expecting an embrace, only nodded.

'Au revoir then,' Pascal called over his shoulder, resuming his stride.

At her mother's bedside, Simone instantly recognised a change. Her mother was sitting up, had more pillows, almost a tower. Presumably Pascal had fetched them down from the top of a wardrobe or charmed a nurse with his accent. The pillows were criss-crossed in the manner of plaits. White plaits against which her mother, in an exotic Chinese bedjacket of ming blue, reclined.

'What a nice colour combination you make,' Simone offered. But her mother hardly returned her gaze. Her eyelids closed as if holding an image in, as the eyes of the murdered are supposed to reflect the image of their killer.

The lilies were the first thing Simone noticed at the motel. In a glass jug, the buds as prominent as the striking yellow flowers, they gave the room a gracious air. Pascal always bought flowers, Simone knew. Flowers and then books were his idea of furniture. The coat lay across one of the easy chairs, a pile of books occupied the seat. The titles seemed to be all in French.

'Shift them onto the floor, if you like,' Pascal said. 'So . . . now you've got me here.'

'I apologise if the crisis disappoints you,' Simone replied. 'All the indicators were there and on Thursday there was a distinct loss of will. If you don't believe me . . .'

'Of course. It's not a question of belief. It may even prove convenient. Better to love the living than mourn the dead.'

'Let the dead bury their dead, you mean,' Simone replied, on a rising anger. 'You think I am suitable to cope with that.'

'Of course you will have my support whenever that occurs. I may not be able to be present, that's all.'

Simone foresees herself cutting sandwiches, elegant ones this time, chicken or cucumber, and handing around plates. Pascal will outdo himself with flowers. A huge sheaf of white lilies probably, enough to sink a coffin or obliterate a dining table. Oh why is her brother such a cad?

Simone's father had tried to impress on her three things about their mother. Pascal was in Paris by this time and John Gerrard was dying of liver cancer. He was not in pain, but day by day he grew yellower. He had wished to die at home but Jean had had him moved to the hospital. When Simone visited, tears running down her face, he explained that her mother was mortally afraid of sickness, and having hardly ever experienced any, it sent her into a depression.

'It's one of the three things you need to know about her. The other two are that if you do something for her she demands something else straight after, and she saves resentments up, sometimes for years.'

His sufferings on all three weaknesses had been extreme, though there had been happiness as well. Perhaps the physical passion they had enjoyed even had its origin in these failures. He had never prevailed on Jean to allow him a pause after something completed. 'Praise is not enough,' he had snapped at her once. 'I want a rest.' But already she was putting catalogues in his lap about a rose-trellis and working out which roses to grow on it. The resentments, stored like some exotic pickle in dark jars, he had become used to, because he knew in her heart she was ashamed. Not that Jean ever apologised or imagined the words could be undone. He would find a book he wanted on his pillow and once, after a particularly violent outburst, tickets to a fishing lodge. The depressions, he thought, would be the worst for Simone to deal with.

'Like hauling treacle out of a well, honey,' he said, laughing at the idea of skeins of it, looping over the arms and falling in coils. 'Your mother just doesn't understand being ill.'

When Simone asked why her mother was so besotted with everything French, her father could not account for it. Jean spoke the language in a halting rudimentary way and certainly not colloquially; she could probably get the gist of a French newspaper. He had protested at the naming of Pascal, less so Simone. He had insisted on Pascal's second name being William.

'But you don't mind Simone, do you?' he asked, holding her hand, turning his yellow face towards her.

'No, I'm simply a suburban mother,' Simone replied. 'When the kids leave home I can be a late-blooming Simone Signoret.'

She bent over her father and kissed him on both cheeks, wiping a tear from each eye against his cheekbones.

One thing Simone and her father were correct about was *Paris Match*. It lay on the newly vacated café table, still with its coffee cup and water glass, a few golden crumbs from a croissant. The waiter was approaching, his haughty aristocratic face and long girded apron which reminded her of a priest. Jean set her face into what she hoped was a mask of ennui. She didn't dare light a cigarette in case the match went out. The waiter glided with the look of a master of the Alexander technique. *Stand as if you are poised at the edge of a cliff.* Well she was.

'Café au lait, s'il vous plaît,' Jean said, as quickly as she could.

She thought speed might indicate familiarity.

'Coffee, Madame?' he replied, mocking her with dark eyes.

When he returned she had her phrase book out and her dark glasses on, but she removed them to acknowledge his service. She made the tiny cup last as long as she could while she worked out what to do.

Marcy had been overcome by stomach cramps on the ferry. At first Jean had thought it was seasickness. Marcy had eaten a hot dog as they strolled around Dover. 'Say goodbye to English unsophistication,' she said, throwing the stick at a seagull.

They took a taxi to the room they had reserved at the Hôtel Michel in the rue d'Odessa. Much scanning of guides and visits to different travel agents had foreshadowed each decision. Marcy wrote the information in a notebook she carried with her. On the departure day she had added the Paris forecast, 20° overcast.

Marcy's temperature soared to 102° as she lay doubled up in agony on the double bed in their room. There had been a mistake: they had asked for two single beds but with Marcy's pain and their small French they could not explain. Perhaps there is a bolster, Jean thought, pressing the mattress which felt unpromising. She wrung out her face flannel and placed it on Marcy's forehead; she tried to induce her friend to take an indigestion tablet. 'Au secours,' Marcy said in a faint voice, to prove her humour had not deserted her. 'Go to the desk and get an ambulance.'

The young Frenchman had picked Jean up in the Louvre, in front of Boucher's 'Diana Resting After Her Bath'.

'Je trouve toujours que celui-ci c'est sous-estimé, n'est ce pas? La facture c'est tellement délicate, les couleurs si fines . . .'

'Pardon,' Jean replied, crimsoning.

'Ah, the fine pale skin with the blood rising, like a rose that does not bloom.'

Jean dared not risk another 'Pardon' or ' Je ne parle pas français.' The last tatters of her schoolgirl French fell off like gossamer. She was in love with the language, a language that changed its skin colouring as you spoke, and that love prevented her from advancing through thickets of cases and tenses, 'Je regrette, Monsieur . . .' she began.

'Charmante. We shall speak English then . . .'

Jean had been happy to go with him that afternoon, that night.

Sneezing absorbs all the functions of the soul just as much as the sexual act, Pascal read in the *Pensées*, opening them at random and letting his eye alight where it would. He thought of Guy who would be expecting to hear from him. Guy was probably at this moment cleaning the gas cooker, which he had been threatening to do for weeks. 'It'll give me a chance,' he said when he heard the news. Pascal hoped he wouldn't do anything foolish, like getting a dog. Guy, though he worked as a draughtsman, had an impetuous side. He regarded life as small parcels to be seized: a beautiful morning, temporarily smog-free; a tarte Tatin from the patisserie; a line of barges on the Seine. He would be scouting out new restaurants for them to try, consulting the Michelin guide and perhaps planning a country weekend since most of the best restaurants were now in the country.

If I had been called Julien, he thought, not Pascal. And Simone, Elisabeth. Though for Simone it hardly mattered. She needed the French name to lift her above complacency. Simone was more than a little boring. Still they would meet this afternoon at the hospital.

FRANCOPHILIA

When Simone knew she was having twins she rejoiced: it was Donald who went into shock and had to be consoled. Two birds with one stone, she thought; their very closeness would set her free. Whereas she and Pascal had never been free. Their mother had no idea of the taunts Pascal would face, insisting on difference. Différence. Vive la différence. Well, Pascal had experienced that gay sophisticated phrase to its depths. He had come out in Paris, a non-event. Honeymooned in Amsterdam. Moved in with Guy. Simone would never visit la Belle France; she would skirt it, if necessary, a large green square on the map like a tablecloth at a country picnic.

'Do you want to go across to Paris?' Donald had asked, the year before they had the twins.

'No, Pascal is away. I'd rather go to Florence,' she had replied.

But she had thought of Pascal every day. There were even perfect little corners, undespoiled medieval streets, where she thought she began to understand her brother.

'She is stable for the present. Another attack could occur at any time. You know she has asked for no intervention?' the doctor explained to Pascal. No, he didn't know; felt, against his will, it was a stirring of nobility. *Noblesse oblige.*

His mother was sleeping when he got to her ward. There were fresh flowers on the ledge, a mixture of daffodils, yellow as eggs, and blue irises. On her bedside table he picked up the newest Brookner, *Incidents in the Rue Laugier*, with a bookmark at the second chapter. All these details about one whose life, it seemed to him, had been governed by a vast unassuaged longing, a vagueness like falling in love with something in a shop window, an artful arrangement without substance. *There are some vices which only have a grip on us through other ones, and which, when we take the trunk away, are dispersed like the branches.* It was a piece of Pascal he had memorised once, applying it to his own case, sifting and sifting it for meaning.

His mother stirred suddenly and opened her eyes. At first she didn't seem to recognise him.

'Dr . . .?'

'No, it's me.' He regretted the childishness of the words as he spoke them. He lifted one of the limp vein-festooned hands, their backs polka-dotted like a veil. Her hands were almost as large as his own, swollen by tasks. There was no returning pressure; he could not tell if his own slightly urgent pressure was cruel.

Simone appeared in the doorway, her arms full of more flowers. It gives her something to do, he thought, as she bustled away to find a vase or a bottle in the sluice room, then returned to fiddle at the handbasin. 'There,' she said, making a space for them on the window ledge, displacing a few cards which closed up like some sea creature.

'So,' she said to Pascal.

'She's asked for no resuscitation,' Pascal said, then remembered that hearing was the least-impaired sense.

'Perhaps she was pressured,' Simone said as they walked along the corridor towards a coffee machine.

'This is disgusting,' Pascal protested, tipping his back into a plastic bowl. 'Let's go for a walk in the grounds.'

The grounds had a desiccated look, like the grounds around a crematorium, only those were likely to be more fertile: dust to roses.

'She wants to be buried with father,' Simone observed.

Pursuit even in death, Pascal thought. Would Guy wish to be buried with him? Unlikely they would last so long.

They walked in silence, searching for a bench.

'What drew her to France, do you think?' Simone asked. 'All

those cloying Colettes she forced on me birthday after birthday, inscribed *Pour ma chère Simone*. You did better, at least you went to France.'

'Having suffered so much for my name I wanted to find other Pascals. Actually the name's not all that common. Did you know I was called Lozenge at school?'

'You never told me.'

'Simone sounds more exotic. I wonder if mother intended you to make use of it?'

'In which case I have failed. I gave up French, never went to France, avoid French movies even today. A pretty violent reaction on the whole. Whereas you, who suffered more, have assimilated more.'

'Father once said she practically seduced him,' Pascal remarked.

'A little OE can go a long way. I wonder if she conceives a *la belle France* in heaven?'

For the first time in his visit a comradely look passed between them.

'Shall we try speaking in French? I mean myself. You can be the French native, the Parisien. Not that we shall get far. Is it true the Parisiens are rude to non-speakers?'

'Mais non, Madame. On vous a mal renseignée; une nouvelle étude indique que les Parisiens deviennent plus polis.'

'Pardonnez-moi, Monsieur. Je ne parle pas français. Je parle seulement un petit peu. Je vous en prie de . . .'

'S'excuser c'est le mot qu'il vous faut, je crois, Madame. Ne vous gêrez pas. Nous autres Français, nous sommes cosmopolites. Quant à moi, j'avoue que j'admire beaucoup le teint anglais. Si vous me permettriez . . .'

'Certainement, Monsieur. Vous êtes . . . too kind,' said Simone, breaking out. 'Pascal, what is the word for too kind?'

The phone rang in the early hours of the morning and Donald got up to answer it. Simone came rushing out of their room and laid her hand on his shoulder, as if this way she would receive the message.

'We'll come at once,' Donald said. 'About fifteen minutes.'
'We'll need to pick up Pascal,' Simone cried.
'I expect they'll have notified him.'
'I don't think so. I'm next-of-kin. I signed all the forms.'

There was a light burning outside Pascal's unit but no response to their knocking. The proprietor, summoned by the night bell, said he thought Mr Gerrard was out for the evening.

'At this hour?' Donald remarked. 'What can he be doing?'
'Don't ask,' snapped Simone.

Their mother was sleeping again when they arrived, but there were more tubes. The oxygen tent had been taken away. Her pulse was weak, but it had been fluttery. It was a new young night nurse who had summoned them.

'I'm very glad,' said Simone, looking down at the not-yet-defeated form.
'We'll know more in twenty-four hours.'

Pascal was at a jazz club, drinking beer from a bottle. The walls of the club were black, the patrons mostly wore black, the clarinet disappeared into the darkness, as did the amps of the electric guitar. Smoke from individual glowing cigarettes rose towards the mirror ceiling and hung there like upside-down mist. A blues singer in a sequined sheath shimmered like a fish. He remembered how he had once hugged the name Pascal Roget to himself, as if it was an escape route. By 2 a.m. the smoke had descended from the mirrors and caressed the shoulders of the patrons. Instead of speaking, everyone swayed or rocked, arms raised over their heads or pressed tight against sides. There was no need to smoke; Pascal could simply inhale. He shouted in the ear of a blond man with a nose stud, but left alone.

'How could you?' Simone wailed down the phone. 'Drunk *and* dancing.'

'The further off from England the nearer is to France / Then turn not pale, beloved snail, but come and join the dance,' Pascal quoted, hiccupping faintly.

'I'll see you at two o'clock. Be sober.'

'Mother will hang on like the Maginot line,' Pascal states as they sit on their bench again.

They have sat, one on each side of her bed, one hand each.

Can she distinguish? Simone wants her healthy blood to flow into her mother's; she wants to operate on her with psychic surgery in which a chicken's entrails are hidden in a little bag underneath a table. Pascal's aim is the opposite. He thinks of his mother as a French field. *O make haste to light up the green fields of France.* He realises, unlike many Frenchmen, he is terribly afraid of the Maginot line.

'I've booked to go the day after tomorrow. I've sent Guy a fax. I've decided, if I can, to be in France when she dies.'

'Are you mad? It could be any time. It could be tomorrow.'

'If it is tomorrow I shall be here, shan't I.'

'And what will you do in France? Lay a wreath at the Tuileries, tie a ribbon to a plane tree on the Champs Elysées?'

'Calm down,' Pascal tells Simone. 'At least she's produced one Francophile.'

He thinks he and Guy will go to Père-Lachaise when he gets back and visit the grave of Colette. Or it doesn't have to be Colette. George Sand or Héloïse. It can be an unknown woman. It will be misty in Paris now and Guy will have laid some of those crystals that absorb damp. He will have shaken the mothballs from their winter coats. They will be sober but not too sober, with a bunch of roses between them. Or even a wreath. Guy will know a florist. Then they will repair to Les Deux Magots. Who knows, his mother might have been there before them.

Jean Gerrard dies when Pascal is once again jack-knifed into a seat over the Indian Ocean. He sleeps fitfully as she comes fully awake. Simone too is asleep, having railed for hours about Pascal's selfishness. As she sleeps she sniffles and moans.

But Jean Gerrard is clearly awake in the ward at 3 a.m. Around her three other women sleep in postures that indicate sleep is their release. One holds a hand in the air, as if attached to an invisible sling. Jean stretches out her two hands and strokes the counterpane with small movements, like grass. Pascal and Simone have been, she knows. Her eyes open wide before she falls back a final time. A tiny smile responds to her last memory: how bold she was on the bed in the rue Pouchet.

&

Rose Madder

THERE ARE TWELVE blooms on the Trumpeter bush: twelve vibrant red roses, flamboyant and yet open, in the way some people's faces are 'open'. Annie picks them at the last, when the tall Agee jar and the weighing stone, the rubber gloves and the little phial of weedkiller, the book to read aloud, are all stowed in her wicker basket.

The Trumpeter roses are the colour of arterial blood, and she has to brace herself to cut the three stems — three roses, four, and then five — for like the sound of trumpets the roses are prodigal, air and ear piercing. Annie knows she will miss them; her eye will travel to the space they occupied and it will be weeks before fresh buds open. She knows too that flowers left on graves are mostly for the backward glance of mourners, that the dead are debarred from their sight, though she holds there is something in the notion of 'someone just walked on my grave' and infrequent visits may be known. But the compulsion to sacrifice them, to lay them over arterial blood spilled, as if those two could meet, to read a poem that has consoled her: these are greater than reason can countermand.

When she is still streets from the cemetery, driving past a retirement village and restored railway workers' cottages, Annie has a vision of herself, kneeling, lightly brushing her lips to the roses as she arranges them. And a sound, like the announcement of a trumpet, echoing underground.

William had died in the spring and today is his thirty-fifth birthday. Annie adopts the present tense by decision: she has become an existentialist. Only this way can the minutes of her and William's life have proper weight. And the cemetery — newish, well preserved, full of floral tributes, photographs and lately miniature windmills in the shape of daisies — reinforces this heavy timelessness. Annie has watched William sink, as the mound of bisected turfs over him subsides like swelling after healing. She has watched, with a pitying irony, small grave gardens grown over the length of a loved one's body, blazing in a rage, gradually falter and fall back. One evening in summer she had come upon a man weeping over a trowel and gazing into the setting sun. William lies next to a baby and a former mayor. What can they have to say to one another, Annie wonders, for she retains lines of Emily Dickinson, images of bones loosening and wandering, Death in a carriage, and green mould creeping like vines. Will William comfort the baby while he berates the mayor about the rates? William always thought ahead: he will be on the baby's side.

And so, as Kinsmen, met a Night —
We talked between the Rooms —
Until the Moss had reached our lips —
And covered up — our — names —

The rose Trumpeter has very sharp thorns and Annie pricks herself as she arranges them in the large Agee jar with its stone at the bottom. At first she had brought proper vases, even a favourite one, but these disappear between visits. William will not care, and besides he always liked her way of arranging flowers, plunging them in carelessly and allowing them to shift for themselves like someone settling into clothes.

But when she stands back Annie has to admit the twelve Trumpeters are her best arrangement yet. Against the grey mottled headstone with its rough uncompleted edge — to suggest William's incomplete life — the roses do more than blaze: they dominate and bless; they seem as if they could draw William back to life again. Annie takes out her camera — their camera — steps back and takes a photograph. Then she walks down the line of graves, past the baby whose porcelain flowers are sealed in two glass domes, past a photo of a man raising a glass of beer to his lips, a motorcyclist whose wooden headstone has been carved by his friends. This is her method of reconnoitre, of feeling at home. Then she will turn and walk back to William as though she is coming to a door.

From the old part of the cemetery where flowers are less and moss more, Annie can still see William's grave and its blazing roses. She takes a few shots with a zoom lens. As she returns she reads a few inscriptions. It amazes her that not one inscription has words like 'feared spouse of . . .', 'disagreeable child of . . .' The word love seems so debased here, but not for William. William should be an obelisk, a mausoleum, an Albert Memorial, for William was so loved. Annie had enquired about an angel: there are several in the old cemetery, pointing heavenwards or bending over a child's cot with a pebble coverlet, but limited lawn cemeteries prohibit angels. Tactfully the stonemason enquired if she wished to leave space for another name? She could tell he was thinking: she is young, she will re-marry. Yes, she answered firmly. She would marry again or be someone's mistress or simply keep a cat, but she would return.

Annie quickens her pace towards William to reassure him. A

red sports car roars into the cemetery and a young man in dark glasses leaps out, seizes William's roses and roars way. Annie just has time to raise her Leica and shoot.

'Dear husband' Annie had the stonemason inscribe. 'Dear child' she had read somewhere and its simplicity moved her more even than *Cover his face, mine eyes dazzle. He died young.* For William had taken to husbandry the way some people take to swimming or amateur dramatics. It was as if he surprised himself in it and since he could not wait to pass anything good on, Annie was to be surprised too. Bunches of flowers, a chocolate fish wrapped in foil, once a book of poems by Rita Dove, because he liked the name, were conjured for her pleasure. The week before his death he had paid a deposit on air tickets and a luxury hotel by a lake. Annie only heard of it when the travel agent phoned.

All these things are in Annie's mind, are in her mind perpetually, but especially when she walks amid headstones, every single one of which reads *Beloved* or *Dearest* or *Sorely Missed*. It makes her want to scream. It makes her want a beam of light to come from behind a cloud and glow around William's grave, for a Moving Finger to point to *Dear husband* while these fake inscriptions are burned with a brand.

How dare William's roses be taken. Annie has never felt such rage. She feels it in her whole body: a fiery heat that rises and consolidates. Unknowingly she has pressed the shutter three times, so there are three photographs to study. The first is a blur but the second and third prove more useful, especially when Annie uses the magnifying glass at Langwoods. The number plate can be read: XZ099F. The Trumpeter roses are a blur, like Jacqueline Kennedy starting to move over her slain husband. Here is the young man's arm, grasping the door. In the third photograph number plate and flowers are gone but the thief is clearer.

'As big as you can get these two,' she instructs the girl at the counter. 'And please take good care of the negatives. They may be needed for evidence.'

The painted face registers its first flicker of interest.

There is a phone number for prospective buyers to check car registrations. Pen poised and ready, Annie dials.

'XZ099F.'

'Make and year?'

'I'm sorry I don't have all the details.' Annie's voice becomes helpless, suggesting mechanical incompetence. 'It's a red sports car. A Porsche, I think. I saw a For Sale sign as it zoomed past. But I did get the number. My husband would be interested . . .'

'Registered to a Mr Tony Dillimore, 49 Milmoe Avenue, Hamilton.'

'Thank you very much,' says Annie, her voice firmer. 'Thank you very much indeed.'

The day William died he was driving from Auckland. Annie had suggested he fly, but their new car, bought after exhaustive visits to car dealers and long conferences between them — each Tuesday evening they sat down together at the dining table and went through their cheque butts together — still needed running in. Annie, though she didn't say so, secretly enjoyed these financial reconciliation sessions, as they were called. She thought of herself as a chatelaine, keys hanging at her belt and a long skirt trailing in the rushes on the floor. Her financial management was prudent and cautious and it was William who urged her to the occasional splurge.

'Buy a hat,' he would say. 'Or gloves, books, anything you fancy. Don't let money restrict you.'

'What would I do with a hat?'

'I could take you to the races and you could be the best-dressed lady.'

'And win $1000,' she laughed, throwing her cheque book at him.

In the event William's journey started late. The medical supplies firm he was visiting had insisted on lunch. Then he had driven across the city on a colleague's recommendation to buy a special leather steering wheel cover. It was fringed and had the look of a buckskin shirt. He was anxious to try it out on the drive home. Before he left he phoned Annie but she was studiously looking in a bookshop window. William instructed one of the secretaries to try later, handing her the number on a piece of paper.

Soon he was beyond the city, considering how hills substituted for buildings, listening to the words of The Eagles as they floated out through the open window.

And I want to sleep with you in the desert tonight
With a million stars all around . . .

The car approaching him wavered slightly and he noticed it was old and from a low-slung box-shaped period. There was no indication as The Eagles reached *Because I'm already standing on the ground* that it would suddenly cross the centre line and aim straight at him.

The denuded Trumpeter rose bush, with only one tight bud, all its vibrant colour drained from the air, strengthens Annie's resolve. From registration to name to street is easy. She drives past Tony Dillimore's residence and is angered by its opulence. Or gentrification. Whether by Tony Dillimore and his paramour or by some previous owner, 49 Milmoe Avenue is superbly restored. Beautifully and professionally painted. Gleaming in fact. White finials, dove-grey walls, a door of aubergine. Annie parks her car and walks back, Leica in hand. The wide lens scoops up a velvet lawn, beds of phlox and lavender.

But she doesn't feel like entering, not yet. She is thinking of a dossier, something like the glossy bound book that is presented to victims of *This is your Life*. Should she find a baby photo of William, naked on a sheepskin? No, but there must be William. An enlargement of herself and William dancing at the last staff party? Someone had shot a streamer at them and it twines over their shoulders and down William's back like a spider web. Then there are the Trumpeter roses in the Agee jar with the weighing stone visible below the stems. William's name and *Dear husband* enmeshed in blooms. How long had she pored over Emily Dickinson —

Wild Nights — Wild Nights!
Were I with thee
Wild Nights should be
Our luxury!

or

Their costume, of a Sunday
Some manner of the Hair —
A prank nobody knew but them
Lost, in the Sepulchre —

— before being turned away by the stiff archness of it, the endlessly knowing look she imagined Miss Dickinson to wear, drifting down the stairs in a white dress. Descents that had nothing casual about them, timed to a bird call or a visitor.

In the end, though, an album seems too pretentious and she simply adds the photographs of herself and William dancing to the evidence. The packet fits neatly into her handbag. But first she needs to phone.

'Mrs Dillimore?'

'What's that to you?'

'Am I speaking to Mrs Tony Dillimore?'

'You'll need to identify yourself first. Anyway it's not Mrs.'

'My name is Annie Plover. It's about your husband.'

'Thick, aren't you? If I'm not Mrs I don't have a husband.'

'I wonder if I could call. It's rather private.'

The phone is slammed down.

Annie decides to contact one of William's friends, their best man, if fact. She phones and asks him to lunch. Hugo is a punctilious creature and will tell Isobel, his wife. But he can be trusted to fudge the nature of their conversation. Hugo, Annie realises, is utterly scrupulous with the quality of the truth, like Portia, but not the quantity.

'How's things?' he says, as they seat themselves.

'Why do people always say things when they mean the opposite? Things are the least likely things at a time. . .' Then she laughs.

'Things you hold to, I suppose,' offers Hugo. 'Filofax, car keys, cheque book, have I paid the mortgage.'

'Perhaps it would be better to say "How's the dog?" Make it a halfway house. Not too human, but not inanimate.'

'How's the cat/dog then, Annie?'

'No fleas to speak of, a bit off its food, I'm tempting it with a few gourmet tins.'

'That's the spirit. Shall we order? The open sandwiches are particularly good.'

'I presume there was something. . .' Hugo says after a while.

'Yes,' replies Annie. 'A matter of roses hoisted from a grave, William's of course. What other would I grow roses for?'

'Here, take this.' It is not the serviette that Hugo passes but his elaborately folded, breast pocket handkerchief.

Sympathetically Hugo elicits the story and gives it his full attention. An inner voice ranks it not high on the human catastrophe index, but Hugo's facial muscles are as far from his mental processes as an inland city is from the sea. He listens while Annie extols the aggressive-sounding rose and suggests the thief may have sustained a few scratches. He ventures that such behaviour may not be unknown to the police who unfortunately are unable to investigate, roses coming somewhere lower than missing bicycles or hub caps. He visualises (privately) a team known as the Rose Squad and a Rose Maria. A dark blue constable winched up under a helicopter's searchlights, his arms full of roses. It is when Annie produces her photographs and the one of William falls out that a chill seizes him. He bends over the cleared table, apart from coffee cups, to admire.

'Is it wise?' is all he can find to say. 'Annie, is it wise?'

Annie knocks at the aubergine door of 49 Milmoe Avenue and holds herself very straight. A stanza of Emily Dickinson buzzes in her head

I heard a Fly buzz — when I died —
The Stillness in the Room
Was like the Stillness in the Air —
Between the heaves of Storm —

When there is no answer Annie strikes the knocker, a satyr's head. After a long pause she hears footsteps, odd soft dragging footsteps, a pause, and then a faint thud before the footsteps resume. The door opens a crack and a dark eye, matching the door, looks out. The latest in make-up, Annie thinks, like black fingernails or black lips. But no, the eye is genuine.

With a resolve that surprises her, Annie pushes the heavy door with her left hand and with her right presses the shoulder blade of the crumpled figure against the wall. She almost commands 'Stay'. With her left foot she kicks the door closed. She feels like an octopus; no, she feels good. She had not realised how good action feels. Should she now hoist the woman over her shoulder in a fireman's lift? Swiftly she calculates the woman's weight. Instead she sets her handbag with its packet of incriminating photographs on the hall runner and leads the woman along it. Towards the back of the house is a dining room. On a large polished table surrounded by tapestry-covered chairs sits a modern slab-glass vase. In it, as though signalling for help, are William's Trumpeter roses.

Two hours have passed and Annie is driving home again, her handbag, recovered from the hall runner, on the seat beside her. The photographs have not been produced: the woman's eye was still swelling and when Annie left it was about to close. Annie has bathed it and looked for a steak in the refrigerator. The refrigerator is crammed with delicacies: pâté, foil-wrapped quiche, a custard tart topped with glazed strawberries. In the milk compartment crowd bottles of bubbly.

Annie has offered to call the police, rejoicing that the roses could perhaps be included in an inventory: she sees herself accosting a police constable and drawing him into the dining room.

'The roses, constable . . .', and 'roses' will be added to the notebook.

The woman, Julia, has sworn she will visit her GP but Annie has little faith in this. She should have asked for the GP's name so she could phone and ask him to call. But Julia has said hardly anything; neither of them has: Annie has acted and Julia has received. Going to the fridge and finding the steak, holding it against the eye, finding disprins in a bathroom cabinet, setting two to dissolve in an elegant glass, finally making and turning back the disordered king-size bed in which, if Julia and the rose thief were not speaking, there is the vastness of a plain between. Julia lies against the propped pillows, steak held to the damaged eye until Annie relents and takes it to the kitchen. Such a steak can never be eaten, but is there a cat or dog who would be glad? On cue a thin grey cat emerges and Annie cuts it into delicate pieces.

Why does everything in that house require delicacy? Annie wonders as she stops at lights. Julia's eyes were closing so she had slipped the tripillow gently from behind her shoulders and tiptoed to the door. If only she had thought to uplift the roses she could have gone straight to the cemetery and given them back to William.

Tony Dillimore works for a firm of stockbrokers in Cutfield Lane. On the afternoon that Annie phones he has a pounding headache on which two paracetamol have hardly begun to work. The flickering of his PC causes him to raise one hand over his eyes. Still hangdog looks are not unusual at Terrill & Jane, and pallor is often put down to a drinking bout or a business lunch. Wisely the scene at home is well suppressed, though the occasional idea of a peace offering flickers and dies. Then he recollects the roses were intended as a peace offering for a previous fight.

It was Douglas's idea. Douglas the great embroiderer, the novelist manqué. It had happened in Milan, at a fashionable cemetery. The dark cypresses, the widows in weeds and yards of veiling — like lingerie on their heads, as Douglas described it —

the huge bouquets, formal and stiff, laurel wreaths studded with jewel-like blooms. The thieves who swooped after the mourners had departed had to unpick them before they could present them to their mistresses.

'Try it,' Douglas had urged. 'The dead don't need flowers. The living do.'

The way Douglas presented it, the act was practically a mercy mission. The dead had the advantage of a fresh gift but before the innocent flowers could imitate the recipient they were whisked away and revived. That someone else was cheered by them was a small point. 'Let the dead bury the dead,' Douglas concluded, going for another round of drinks. There was something wrong with the logic, Tony perceived, because the roses he had stolen had been freshly placed in water and there was even a stone in the jar to withstand wind.

But there is another phrase that appeals to Tony as he turns his Porsche through the cemetery gates: the quick and the dead. His Porsche is quick, though it idles now, and the flowers: is there still quickness in them? Just in time, he thinks, leaping out and snatching at a bunch of long-stemmed blood-red roses. The Porsche roars into life, even the blood on his fingers that drips on the steering wheel pleases. Red and quick. The quick red fox. . .

'A woman to see you, Tony.'
'Who is it?'
'She wouldn't give a name.'
'Then say I'm not here.'
'She saw you come in. She's waiting in reception.'
'Good-looking?'
'Determined-looking.'
'Bring me a coffee and show her in in ten minutes. Buzz me first.'

'It's probably a relative of Julia's,' Tony thinks. In which case he'll be icily polite. Trudy will call him after five minutes with a bogus incoming call. All the same he goes and peers at himself in the washroom mirror, dashes some water on his face, washes his hands. His cuffs cover the rose scratches.

'Do you recognise this rose?' Annie asks, holding out the final Trumpeter rose which has opened this morning. Does the bush know something?

'A rose is a rose is a rose,' says Tony hopefully.

'I think you can do better than that.'

'In what way?'

'Are you or are you not the owner of a red Porsche. Licence number XZ099F?'

'I am. What's it to you? Are you a car spotter?'

'Not in the normal course of events, no. But I have a particular interest in that particular car. Possibly you can guess what it is?'

'It's not for sale, if that's what you're thinking . . .'

'I'm thinking of a car that sneaks into the cemetery and lifts roses laid on someone's grave. When the person who laid the roses is equipped with a powerful camera and is within range.'

'You mean you were still in the cemetery . . . that they are your roses?'

'I have the photographs here. Not the negatives. They are somewhere safe.'

Tony rises hastily to his feet and shuts the office door. Then he buzzes Trudy and tells her to hold all calls. Let them think what they like, he thinks angrily. An affair pales beside grave robbery.

'I suppose you consider me a grave robber?'

'Of sorts. The hygienic sort. But every bit as bad. William, my husband, chose that rose bush. They were his roses, for his grave. Their name is Trumpeter.'

The photographs Tony peers at are amazingly sharp. He reaches for them with a derisory smile on his lips, prepared to say, This, dear lady, could be any sports car, this athletic dark-suited man any man. Then he sees the clarity: XZ099F in sharp focus and himself gangling and furtive. Next, his face: flushed, smirking. He picks out the tie he was wearing that morning, a regimental imposter.

'A fair cop,' he says. 'But I can explain. It was Douglas's idea. I'll introduce you to Douglas. He's great on history, precedent, that sort of thing. It's not a new idea. It could have been done from a carriage, not a Porsche. Douglas will explain.' Keep it above the ground, he thinks. Everything above board.

Home again, Annie opens Emily Dickinson's *Collected Poems*, William's last birthday present to her; closes her eyes and points a finger. Emily Dickinson is to be taken in small doses, like a liqueur, but William would be surprised at her pin-sticking method. Yet it is surprising how often Emily acts the prophet. When Annie opens her eyes her finger points to:

I've heard it in the chillest land —
And on the strangest Sea —
Yet, never, in Extremity,
It asked a crumb — of Me.

What is Emily talking about this time, Annie wonders. But then like any accomplished crossworder her eyes seek the top line where the poet usually disposed of the subject as if, if something required naming, it was best to get it over with. '*Hope*' *is the thing with feathers*. Annie tucks the marker ribbon in the place and props the book on the mantelpiece to look at from time to time. '*Hope*' shall have its week of public viewing until she turns the page. Annie considers Emily a violent woman, barely contained by an upstairs room, an obligatory white dress. Her ornateness hides something very iron-like. What would Emily do if her designated roses were filched? Bring down a curse in four lines?

Two nights later there is a knock at the door and a thickset red-haired man with amazingly white skin stands on the doorstep.

'Douglas Devine,' he introduces himself. 'I work with Tony Dillimore. I wonder if I could have a few words.'

Annie leads the way into the dining room where now the last single Trumpeter is gallantly bearing up in a slim glass vase. Annie notices Douglas Devine glance at the rose.

'I've come to explain about Tony and the part I played in it, I'm afraid. Tony is very suggestible, you see. He doesn't really own that house or the car. He's hopelessly in over his ears. Everything's been going wrong for him, including your roses.'

'I don't see that personal circumstances excuse actions,' Annie says firmly, in what she hopes is the tone of Emily Dickinson dealing with an admirer who has broken into her garden. 'Or that I cannot dispose of my own roses as I please.'

'But it's my fault for putting the idea in his head. I'd been reading a book about grave robbers getting bodies for dissection and how the students at Guy's used to dissect the maggots that crawled out of them to amuse themselves . . .' Then his hand, as freckled as his face is pale, goes over his mouth. 'I'm so sorry. I should be blaming myself, not Tony. Your roses were intended for . . . ?'

'William,' says Annie. Just the bald word. William and no maggot. Sweet William sometimes. William, her favourite name. Willpower.

'Please leave,' she hears herself saying. 'I've had as much as I can bear.' And she begins to walk down the hall, her head held high. She opens the front door and stands beside it and the young man stops, level with her.

'Can I make it up to you?' he asks. 'Can I send you some roses?'

Driving away in his silver Daewoo, Douglas Devine is shaken by the offence he has caused. It's a wonder he hasn't enumerated the colours cadavers can turn: blue, green and black. He sees them tumbling out of earth-stained sacks on to the tables of un-hygienic dissection rooms in old hospitals. He sees young men affecting bravado finish a mouthful of pie and porter before advancing with a scalpel. And he sees the hastily re-covered graves, dented because the soil is not sufficient, the flowers flung aside and trampled. Perhaps a bunch is caught up in a grubby hand or put for shelter under a coat. 'Thanks for me buttonhole, guv.'

What he has not foreseen are the returning widows, wailing, and running for the sexton. Why in his fantasies does he never reach the aftermath? The sexton would undoubtedly wring his hands and pass the woman on to the parson. Who would have some well-worn words about a double resurrection. It might even become a matter of snobbery. A body secure in the ground would be a cachet.

Annie too feels self-disgust. From the moment of seizing the Leica and shooting the number plate, the black suit cradling a circlet of red, she has envisaged inexorable consequences. The telephone call, the office interview — but like Douglas her vision has faltered. 'You need to have an aim,' she hears William say, as though he is standing beside her elbow. She imagines him sitting opposite: cheque books spread out, bank statements, bills. And the big ledger in which, because it amuses them both, she writes in black ink. The pages of the months to come, where the bills to come are neatly set out. 'See what the electricity was this time last year,' William instructs, and Annie is pleased to follow his command.

Annie gets in her car and drives to the suburb where Tony lives. She takes the Leica with her, for no reason she can think of. She finds a park and walks towards the house. But her footsteps slow as she nears the gate. O William, she thinks. And then, *A rose is a rose is a rose.* As she turns in at the gate she sees the FOR SALE sign sunk into the lawn. The house has a closed, vacant look. Annie takes a photograph of the sign and writes the name and number of the land agent in her pocket book.

The land agent is a vivacious woman who is nonetheless wary. Annie can see over the house at 11 a.m. the following morning; another viewer is expected at 11.30. Annie suspects she has not sounded convincing. Surely, as a widow, she should be buying down not up? As she waits outside the gate Annie decides she will suggest, in a rather vague way, that she is thinking of a joint purchase with another female friend, one who is divorced with small children. That would account for some of the bedrooms. Though the rose thief and his black-eyed consort seem to have been on their own.

Annie feels irritable, almost aggressive. The land agent seems distracted, and beyond requiring her to sign a visitor's book and pointing out the main rooms she is free to wander. She pretends to inspect the kitchen, and opens one or two cupboards, still full of china.

'The previous tenants left in rather a hurry. They were renting,' the land agent says. 'Now the owner wishes to sell.'

In the bedroom where Julia had lain against the pillows, the bed is tautly made. In the dining room the emptied vase stands in the centre of new polish. But Annie spies something on the carpet. She stoops and picks up a red rose petal.

Exceedingly depressed, Annie opens Emily Dickinson again, closes her eyes and stabs with her index finger.

Did Our Best Moment last —
T'would supersede the Heaven —
A few — and they by Risk — procure
So this Sort — are not given

Apposite Emily, she thinks. Really she is far worse than the Bible. Slipping knife-like poems in a drawer. '1835' it says at the bottom of the page; Emily could cut the year like a wrist. Annie stuffs the rose-heist photographs in a drawer where she keeps string and rubber bands. What shall I do, William? she thinks. What *can* I do? Wait for Trumpeter to grow more roses? Find some mausoleum-like china flowers in a glass dome that no one would steal? Sit on your grave and have a picnic? Take out a book of spells?

The phone rings and at first Annie can't make out the caller. Then she recognises the grave-snatching authority, Douglas Devine.

'Tony's leaving town. He's asked for a transfer. I wondered if I could take you to lunch or a coffee?'

'Funeral baked meats,' says Annie. 'I expect they lay in state in a complementary fashion to the dead. Then in an equivalent way they broke down and the remnants of the cold cuts were minced. Very symbolic really.'

'Sorry again,' says Douglas.

'Coffee will be acceptable,' says Annie.

Douglas Devine is determined to be factual. Waiting at the coffee shop he goes over in his mind the few facts he knows about

Tony Dillimore. When Annie Plover is late he takes out a notebook and writes them down.

competent at his job but inclined to take risks
likes to impress people of higher status
exceedingly impulsive

Then his mind, typically, begins to wander. Doesn't impulsiveness equal immaturity? Something to do with marshmallows? The child that can refrain, unsupervised, from consuming one marshmallow will be rewarded with two? It sounds like a biblical tract. The Book of Postponement. Carried down the mountain on tablets of marzipan. Pull yourself together, he thinks. Tony was simply besotted by a passive spoilt girl from a rich family. Hence the house rented from a family connection, the Porsche with crippling repayments, the free roses.

Annie is coming towards him. Her expression is severe, almost inquisitorial. He has a bet with himself her first word will be 'Well?'

'Well?' says Annie. 'I think you owe me an explanation.'

'Would a backgrounder do?'

'A backgrounder to what?'

'A tale of two brokers, one in dire straits, the other affecting an over-fertile imagination. A dastardly act brought about by improvidence.'

'You mean you were attempting to get him to economise?'

'Something like that. Though he was more taken by the impetuous part.'

'I suppose the black eye was part of it?'

'From the same fabric, I'm afraid.'

'I found a rose petal on the dining room carpet.'

The talk turns to rose bushes and the amount of care it takes to grow a rose.

Annie takes the pocket edition of Emily into the cemetery and sits on William's grave. She takes a bunch of yellow roses and a stone in her pocket. She walks slowly between the graves, lingering, reading inscriptions, peering at the photographs she abhors, disks covered in some weather-protecting material like seeing through a glass darkly. She ponders the avoirdupois of a young blond man with a very flushed face, the leathery lean man raising a golden glass of beer.

I will not dip into Emily again, she says to William, talking inside her head like silent reading. I'll read her properly and do the accounts. I'll read Emily every Tuesday when I write the cheques. That's what she is really, a financier.

The yellow roses glow against the stone, tighter furled than Trumpeter. Did William hear anything? The screech of tyres, her shouting voice, the tiny click of the Leica? A few sobs. The Trumpeter petal is safe now on her dressing table, pressed under a sheet of glass.

Then Annie climbs the little rise behind the graves and settles herself against a tree. She opens Emily deliberately now at

Because I could not stop for Death —

and reads steadily on until she reaches *Eternity —*

&
Cricket

Poseur that she sometimes acknowledged herself to be, Victoria Beauchamp recognised the great ground by instinct, nothing more. As the double-decker bus on which she had an upper-deck seat moved sedately through north London, her eye caught the oval shape, the high curving walls of the fabulous Lord's. What nonchalance, not recognising it, she would have had to maintain among a bus full of the chaps.

The park has man-made grass terraces. A grassy Mayan temple, Victoria thinks, climbing up what seems a wall of grass to take a seat on her favourite terrace, the northern. This is the terrace of the rowdies, of aficionados, unlike the eastern terrace which boasts shade umbrellas and hampers. On the northern terrace they consume lager from cans and hot dogs and pies. There is a beer tent close by and someone barbecuing sausages. On the southern side where the scoreboard faces the sight screen a rabble of small boys lie in the grass, being directed by a face in an aperture. The numbers they carry and climb a ladder to slide against players' names are the size of their upper torsos. The eastern terrace, near the gates, is abbreviated, since the road curving past it leads to the cricket pavilion in which white figures can sometimes be sighted. Directly opposite, a gap in the white boundary fence allows the cricketers entrance. It is a very short walk compared to other cricket grounds and recognising this few children attempt autographs. Sometimes waiting batsmen sit on the eastern terrace under blue umbrellas reserved for them. It was on the northern terrace, about half-way up, that last summer Victoria had watched Merv Hughes work the crowd like Herbert von Karajan. Three terraces below her a Merv Hughes clone wearing a huge moustache and a straw hat with corks bowed to the fast bowler and he had bowed mock-seriously back. And when Hughes began some limbering exercises the northern terrace had responded to a man.

Today Victoria, eyes lifted to the tops of the terraces, north, east and west, admires the tapering Norfolk pines, superior to any umbrella. When it gets too hot on her terrace she will climb to the top and cool herself under one.

Victoria was the only member of her family who liked cricket excessively. Like edging into love the way a drive edges past cover and reaches the boundary. The family, like many, listened to the radio but not religiously. Victoria has been told of the apocryphal afternoon her parents went to a 5 o'clock movie. The MCC had just gone in to bat. When they returned the whole side had been bowled out, mainly by the 'chucker' Meckiff. Meckiff is a name that stays in her memory from then on.

'The killer instinct,' Victoria's father offers, and she puzzles about that too. She still looks for the killer instinct every time she focuses her binoculars, high-quality birdwatching variety, on the wicket. Between batsman and incoming bowler a palpable tension, unshared by the fielders — at deep extra cover Merv Hughes is signing his name on a miniature bat — rises like dust or a tumbleweed. The expression on the face of Martin Crowe, partly obscured by the bars of his helmet, is as intense and concentrated as her father could wish. Which is the killer? Or are they both?

Victoria who often goes to cricket matches on her own is soon, settled on her favourite row, back sinking into the warm springy grass, part of a group. There is an endless passing to and fro of bodies, and soon the discreet gaps between groups fill up. In no time Victoria is being offered a can of beer by a young man with shoulder-length hair and green zinc on his nose. She declines the beer but proffers instead her binoculars. Someone further along has a transistor and it is singularly pleasant to listen to the commentary as it allots names to the various strokes. Crowe is performing at the crease. Through her binoculars, when they are passed back, Victoria can see the distinctive headband and its ties, like a Presbyterian minister's collar in reverse. Later she will make her way down the grassy slopes to the barbecue tent or the beer tent next door. There is agony in picking the right time, however. Even the most settled periods of play pose danger. How often has she been fumbling in her purse, back to the wicket, when the shout has gone up and someone has gone. Then the sausage curled in its slice of doughy white bread with its stain of blood-red sauce seems a poor substitute.

The bus trip to Lord's is advertised in both William Goodenough and London House, Victoria recalls, or is she mistaken? William Goodenough, which is largely women, has apartments for families and some of these might wish to visit the famous cricket ground. The Cathedral of Cricket, as Victoria knows full well. The cathedral, the dreaming spires, the pavilions on which players come out as though taking tea or walking — except it is too high off the ground — in a private English garden. But the notice of the tour is definitely in London House (men) where there always seem to be a great many men in blazers in the foyer. It is at London House that the Commonwealth graduates and post-grads go to dine on subsidised meals under portraits of benefactors. Whereas William Goodenough, with its courtyard garden in which a few late roses are straggling and leaves beginning to pile up, has the bar.

Victoria seems to stand amid a great many colours, blue and green and maroon, collars and cuffs contrastingly piped, pockets emblazoned with crests, as she approaches the warden's desk. She is not sure if she imagines hockey sticks, golf clubs. No, it is only scholars checking in or out, getting their room keys, paying their toll bills. Each room, though Spartan, has a private phone. Victoria hasn't been able to think of any significant use for hers, apart from friends.

'The bus trip to Lord's,' she says to the warden. There is panelling behind his desk: the whole area, apart from the blazers, is very dark.

'Yes,' says the warden. 'The notice is on the board. 1400 hours in front of the entrance. Room for thirty. Includes guided tour and commentary.'

'Wonderful. I'd like to go.'

'No women. Sorry.'

'Why? Why are there no women?'

'There just are. Sorry.'

'Can I appeal? Send a note to the head warden?'

'Please yourself. It won't do any good.'

In the *Who's Who of New Zealand Cricket* Victoria notices that under *Favourite Drink* a surprising number of cricketers say *Water*. And gratified that *Pukekura Park* is so often the favourite ground. Martin Crowe puts it alongside the *Adelaide Oval*. Victoria, sharing binoculars and beer with a group of young men, has watched Martin Crowe through most of an afternoon, stroking with such deliberate and elegant grace she thinks of a great ballerina. Not only does Crowe, scrutinised through the glasses for signs of angst, seem to have time to think, he also seems to have time for amusement, as though each delivery is creating its own stroke. The boundaries at Pukekura Park are shorter than most and it is easy to get fours. There is a steep ditch at the edge of the field and the ball drops into it in a satisfying manner. And though you can glimpse the whole park as you come in at the main entrance — the multi-coloured terraces dotted with umbrellas, the lines of brown legs hanging over, the transistors and cicadas, the crowning trees — there is no way of knowing how it must appear to a player. It must be like being in a jar of Smarties.

Victoria wishes there was a third umpire she could appeal to: a green light that would glow above the warden's desk where the dark wainscoting rises to dark ceiling but the warden is adamant.

'Can I see the head warden?' Victoria asks, recognising a Bailey-like stand.

'It wouldn't get you anywhere.'

'But you could take in a note.'

'If you insist. But again . . .'

'Very well. I'll just be a minute.'

The warden, who doesn't even offer pen or paper, goes on serving someone else while Victoria fumbles in her handbag, tears a page from her notebook and leans on the counter to write:

Dear Warden,

I have a deep affection and good knowledge of the game and would like to go to Lord's. Can an exception/exemption be made.

Victoria Beauchamp

She almost writes 'good knowledge for a woman' but controls herself. One day, she is sure, there will be women priests.

By late afternoon there are long shadows on the ground as though the trees have sent them down. It is more comfortable on the northern terrace now. For the last overs before lunch she had sat on the grass, dangling her legs, tempted to lie flat on her back. At lunch when the players went off Victoria spread out her lunch, two lettuce, cheese and tomato sandwiches, like a school child. She wondered what Martin Crowe was eating inside the pavilion. Cold meats and salads and something vegetarian. Did cricketers eat quiche? Victoria finished off with a small red apple, shook the crumbs from her skirt onto the terrace below, got up stiffly and went for a walk.

Sorry. Not possible the warden had written at the bottom of Victoria's note. *Why?* she wanted to add. *Why not? Please explain.* They could go on all day. Should she have called him 'My dear old thing', said she was a relative of Blowers? Not true, of course. But at least Blowers would have explained. What was the female equivalent of a dear old thing?

Tony Blain is wicketkeeping. Victoria remembers his favourite ground is *Pukekura Park*, his drink *Water* and he likes *honest laughter*, *clean smiles*. Victoria thinks of him as workmanlike, honest, fair, open. What he does is clearly visible, like an illustration in a textbook on how to keep. Wicketkeepers have a way of finishing off each gesture like a conductor, going to the limits of each move and then a little beyond, to draw your attention to what you are seeing. Blain certainly shows his team he is to be depended on. Here I am, each gesture of the gloves seems to say. And he praises the bowler, asserting they are in it together. Well bowled and well taken. Through the afternoon Victoria develops a healthy liking for Tony Blain. 'People who fix things,' her father would say, 'are superior to those who simply buy something new.' But liking is not love. Her favourite wicketkeeper will always be Ken Wadsworth, whom she saw play only once. It must have been one of his last games. His exuberance was so great, his gloving so splendid, his gestures to the sky and the umpire so operatic and boyish at the same time. Victoria can still picture him. The ends of his gloves seem to glow, each gesture sets a particle field, a kirlian girdle around him. The night she heard he had died, Victoria was at a pub where a band was singing M I S S I S S I P P I. If she hadn't been crying into her drink she would have shouted NELSON, CANTERBURY, anything but a foreign river to remember him by.

Where did this love of cricket come from? Not the games played with her two brothers, one older, one younger, in the back yard with a slim apple box for wickets. When someone was clean bowled it fell over. Victoria doesn't remember any passion then. She was hardly ever allowed to be wicketkeeper. Her bowling, when she got a turn, was sneered at. Girls' underarm, her brothers chanted. If other boys joined in she was relegated to the boundary, near the laburnum hedge. It begins, she thinks, the day she held a real cricket ball in her hand — a Christmas present, not hers, naturally — and twisted her fingers about it, tucking the thumb under, parting the fingers. The day she bowls her first spin delivery and sends the wickets splaying like the outline of a harp.

Later there is beach cricket, cricket at high school. It is a distinguished school but no one regards the cricketers who practise on a field called the Annexe. It is totally unadorned except for a small white pavilion. Victoria is neither good nor bad, like the rest of the team. Practically no one turns up to watch their matches: when a ball hit high over long leg falls towards her cupped hands, she almost lets it go. Her hands have learned to catch the hard ball, anticipating its trajectory and becoming part of its motion. Her body feels like a shield but she is aware she is too soft. Even when she is batting — her highest score is 33 — she feels like one of those insects deceptively armour-plated. She adopts an aggressive stance, she addresses the ball — jargon for advancing on it — but inside she remains uncertain. Besides, she has already heard Blowers' mellifluous delivery on the radio. She decides she wants to be a cricket commentator.

'Pushed it close to Martin Crowe in the gulley. Martin Crowe with that leg brace he has to wear.'
'That's found the gap. No third man.'
'And gone. Dion Nash has struck.'
'*That's* a good ball.'
'When he got down to Lord's he looked as though he could become a good exuberant fast bowler.'
'That's a fine shot. On the up, nicely through the covers.'
'New Zealand needs a man to polish off the tail-enders.'
'Short arm jab. Unveiling all the shots now.'
'That's the great thing. If you really fling the bat at the ball the edge is going to go a long long way.'
'The wheels are coming off as far as the New Zealand bowlers are concerned.'
'My dear old thing . . .'

Victoria Beauchamp meets Peter Van Der Poel at a party when she steps out on to a balcony for a cigarette. Victoria carries three cigarettes (three stumps?) to each party in case she feels desperate or bored. It is very cold on the little balcony, but at her back the room feels like a heater. Peter Van Der Poel who works for the Met office approaches with a shawl.

'Where did you get this?' Victoria asks as he offers it. 'It's not mine.'

'A detail,' he answers her. 'Can't you feel the frost?'

Drawing smoke deep into her lungs, watching the speech breath issue from the mouth of this serious square-jawed man, Victoria wants to laugh. Smoke issues from her nostrils and a puff of breath from her mouth. 'I must look like a dragon,' she thinks. Truly, she doesn't feel cold. The air is dry, so dry she could crumble it between her fingers. Nonetheless there is an energy there, something moving in the frost.

Anyway, persuaded by the seriousness of Peter Van Der Poel, Victoria allows herself to be led indoors where, in her estimation, the party has not improved. She decides to leave and looks around for the hostess. Peter Van Der Poel escorts her to her car, an elderly Austin, and produces from his pocket a little scraper which he uses to remove ice from the windscreen. They exchange telephone numbers — is this in exchange for the use of the scraper? — and Victoria drives off.

The next day Victoria has a sharp pain in her chest when she breathes, and the doctor diagnoses pleurisy. She feels pleased, pleased that she had seen something mysterious from the balcony: the air about to pounce. The frost running from tree to tree like those Norwegian commandos on skis, dressed in white. The doctor is not so pleased, however, and orders her to take a week's leave from her job at the local paper where she is feuding with the sports editor about being allowed to cover local cricket matches.

'I could just sign my initials,' Victoria protests. 'V.B.'

'And what good would that do? Your initials mean nothing and have no status.'

'What about H.B. then? Short for Henry Blofeld.'

'As if Henry Blofeld would cover local cricket matches.'

'I don't see why not. He's played at The Valley of Peace.'

'Where no member of the fair sex is allowed,' booms the sports editor triumphantly. Not that he considers Victoria a member of the barred sorority: he's always been suspicious of redheads.

Half-delirious in bed, Victoria dreams she is in The Valley of Peace at the foot of the Cashmere Hills. She wears a white belted dress, a white hat and gloves, and white shoes with tongues. She has arrived with Jeremy Coney, who has dropped her at the start of a winding lane. She walks on the grass verge like Virginia Woolf crossing the Fellows' Lawn at Cambridge. Any minute a Beadle like a black beetle will appear. Or Blowers himself will come out from the log pavilion and say, 'My dear young thing.'

'But I have a cinema ticket,' Victoria hears herself protest. 'This is the Christchurch Cinema Club, is it not? Why can't an usherette play?'

Victoria falls asleep, so she never learns the outcome. Perhaps Henry Blofeld will lead her to a deckchair under a great elm tree, discreetly out of sight. No, it is more likely he will arrange transport and escort her from the ground.

When the head warden's note is delivered to her with *Stet* scrawled across it and an illegible signature, Victoria turns on her heel and walks stiffly out of London House. She is wearing flat shoes, and this strikes her as perfectly in keeping with her image of the abashed Virginia Woolf creeping back on to the gravel. So what if the hallowed dressing rooms of the Home of Cricket are denied her — 'They'll probably take in the dressing rooms, you see,' the sub-warden tells her after he has delivered the folded note, to soften the blow a little.

'Thanks for trying,' is all she says.

Peter Van Der Poel does not dislike cricket. He's like a neutral umpire: a diagnosis on romance. He quite enjoys one-dayers, which is all they are likely to get at Pukekura Park. There must be many people here, he reflects, who don't like the game. It's a chance to sit in the sun and have a picnic, watch the passing parade which includes women in bikinis. But Victoria is quite scathing about one-dayers. They are designed for the spectator, she points out, handing Peter a small carton of 100% orange. For the batsmen they pose an impossible dilemma: to stay in and yet score as rapidly as possible. Privately she finds it bullish, not to say mulish. It is the philosophy of the five-day game she loves. The time Ian Meckiff bowled the whole England side out when they were at the movies: that was a one-dayer inside a five-dayer. All that space on either side: time to be redeemed in or to fail. Defeat from the jaws of victory, that sort of thing. Naturally she keeps some of this to herself.

'This is the flight and loop of the spinner we've been talking about.'

'Never really got it in the gloves.'

'He's swotted it away in the same manner one might deal with a troublesome mosquito.'

'A very good innings when you consider New Zealand had England by the throat at one stage . . .'

Victoria, standing on the pavement outside London House, sees the bus take off for Lord's. It is not quite full: there would have been room. She wants to do something violent, like sending a folded note to the head warden with a single swear word on it.

Instead she walks slowly back to William Goodenough House and then along the track that crosses Coram's Fields. Perhaps she will walk it at night when it is reputed dangerous. The warden will hear of it and her last note to him saying 'I love cricket' will be found crumpled in her fingers.

On one side of Coram's Fields is a high mesh fence around a playing field of artificial grass. Its unnatural green hurts the eyes. On the other, in the kindergarten enclosure, are rabbits and a sheep, ducks and geese. A squirrel shoots up the fence suddenly and climbs down towards her. It hurts her that she has nothing to give.

Victoria and Peter go to several cricket matches: New Zealand versus Pakistan, Central Districts versus Zimbabwe. After a while it becomes clear that Peter will not go to a full test match. He will come for an innings — when Crowe is batting, for instance — or part of the final day. He simply cannot spare the time, he tells Victoria. 'What did I miss?' he asks later and she cannot tell him. That Greatbatch went out while she was buying a can of Steinlager, that nothing happened for hours and then there were two run-outs. It is impossible to explain the philosophy of cricket to Peter, who now he has engaged her interest in himself listens less. In future she sees he will regard it as a peccadillo. 'Victoria is crazy about cricket, you know. And not the one-dayers either. Those dreadful five-dayers where nothing happens.'

Nonetheless, over dinner, Victoria does try to convince him for the last time.

'It's not that nothing happens,' she begins.

'Compared to other sports,' he interrupts.

'True,' says Victoria, biting her lip.

'We're talking of five day tests here,' he confirms, like a man checking his watch.

CRICKET

'How can I make you understand,' Victoria groans. 'You're already prejudiced against them.'

'White men on a green field. Leather on willow,' he goes on, taking some of her best lines.

'Damn you,' says Victoria.

'Well?' says Peter.

'I feel as though I am watching my life unfold. The present, past and the future. I've been here before, I think.'

'You assuredly have,' says Peter.

'Don't interrupt. When I watch cricket I think of my future plans and what might become of them. I consider fate, which is something I don't normally do. I think of my chances and I adjudicate them rather slim.'

'What chances?' Peter asks impatiently.

'Any chances. My chances of anything. My chances with you, for one thing.'

'I'll ignore that,' Peter replies. 'I consider that settled.'

'But don't you see, thanks to cricket, I can't. I could if it was one-day cricket. You could bowl me out or vice-versa. It wouldn't matter much one way or the other. I could always bowl you out the next time. A simple contest. Any fool could cope with that.'

'I never realised you took cricket so seriously.'

'It's not cricket, it's life itself.'

Peter thinks Victoria, wearing his sapphire and diamond ring on her finger, is exaggerating of course. He dimly recalls speech days at school where life is compared to a game and conduct to sportsmanship. Life is a game of tiddlywinks. Victoria has been overcome by philosophy, he decides. Five days sitting on the terraces is unnatural for a woman. When they are married he will restrict her to one-day matches.

But when Peter attempts to suggest this, he's met with a

surprising ultimatum. Victoria intends never giving up the five-day game, and what's more she won't marry him unless they can honeymoon in Melbourne where the MCC are playing Australia for the Ashes.

One hope Victoria has consigned to oblivion: she will never be a lady cricket commentator. She will leave that to Blowers and lesser men. Blowers understands that 'It isn't cricket', with all its meanings, is still important. And that 'Cricket has always had something to do with all that is decent in life'.

As for herself and Peter, they are still negotiating. Two days at the MCG is all he will allow so far. But Victoria is determined.

'Everything will be all right, you'll see,' he says, but already he sounds slightly weary, as if he has doubts. How many seasoned test cricketers have felt the same?

'My dear old thing,' says Victoria.

A Turkish Proverb

When you tell the truth keep one foot in the stirrup
Turkish proverb

JANE SHIPLEY dreams she and a man she was once interested in kiss so passionately at a restaurant they topple off their chairs and continue their embrace on the bare wood floor. Renee, Jane's amazingly popular friend, is with her and she attends to the noise of falling chairs, upset cutlery, and tries to hush a rising murmur. But Jane's and the man's lips remain pressed together like two fish she has seen on television. The outer rim of the fishes' lips is transparent and banded like the neck of a condom.

This dream disturbs Jane considerably. It is with her as she pulls out weeds in her rose garden, taking care to judge the distance of eye-level thorns. She thinks not just of the man in the dream, Neil Harris, whom she has hardly thought of for years, but of other men. And why her and her friend's normal roles are reversed. What comes after the kiss in the dream is uncertain, though Jane has a hazy recollection of another setting, a river bank perhaps. Some kind of explanation is taking place and her friend is listening solicitously. But the passion engendered by the kiss is real, as though some deep well inside her has been located by a dowser.

THE MATHEMATICS OF JANE AUSTEN

Later that afternoon, when Jane is sitting propped up in her double bed reading a story by Mavis Gallant — the wind has risen and it is too cold to mow the grass — she thinks of a genesis for that warmth. It is the warmth that puzzles her most: the all-pervasiveness of it, so the fall to the floor and the chaos are rendered oblivious. Jane is used in an amateurish way to analysing her more striking dreams, those in which there seems something to face. She has a friend who is an analyst, whose conversations can resemble consultations but which are very flattering; she also has an embryonic notion of Black Bears in life: difficult passages that require confronting and going beyond previous limitations. Jane now locates the warm slow smiles she had exchanged with a man at a neighbour's slide evening the night before the dream. The slides are of the Lake District and the Arctic: two vastly different regions. In each there is a concentration on landscape where Jane would prefer buildings, people. She wants to peep into the tiny-paned windows of a stone hotel or glimpse the tearooms at Windermere where a rooster and then a pet sheep had helped themselves to afternoon tea at outdoor tables. Instead there are dry stone walls and sheepfolds on the sides of barren hills, like wedding rings cut off a finger. In the Arctic there are rows of tents, caribou and snow hares. The snow hares give birth to camouflage-coloured young which they race away from after a minute's feeding; they return exactly eighteen hours later to the selfsame spot and repeat the process. They separate themselves from the birthplace to distract predators. The man with whom Jane exchanges slow matched smiles does not see Windermere or the snow hares: he simply calls to collect a relative. Jane sits opposite him at a potluck supper. They smile, perhaps because they are the youngest in the room by a considerable margin. Or because they are both direct gazers into eyes. Or their mouths — both mouths curl up slightly at the corners — curve in unison.

Renee, Jane's friend, is immensely popular with men, which makes her subservient role in the dream disconcerting. Each cell in Renee's body is more energised than a normal cell belonging to anyone else. She doesn't merely bounce back, she pogo-sticks back from any setback: flu, broken heart, a day that refuses to live up to her expectations. She reminds Jane of 'Up Guards and at them', repeated charge after charge, day after day. Renee surmises that men like confrontation of a soft underbelly kind: a confrontation that both parties know will yield. Whereas Jane believes, stubbornly, irreducibly, in equality, though she has never found it, never even come near. Except in a dream. She must ask her analyst friend if dreams are the tearing away of veils, revealing real motives, raw bedrock hopes, primeval non-negotiable bargaining stances.

Because she knows the man in the dream, Jane forces herself to go back over their ill-considered encounter. As a fresh history graduate she had been engaged for a year to write the history of a textile firm. The commission was generous and there was no shortage of staff lists, board members, minute books in copperplate or interview time with the various managers. Jane had fallen in love with the back of the neck of the marketing manager as he stood by the tea urn in the staff cafeteria. Why this had happened she could not say. Was she a secret fetishist? Neil Harris had curly brown hair, a few tendrils of which hung down where the barber had shaved, creating a margin between hair and skin. He wore fashionably loose suits under which Jane suspected his frame was rather slight; the hair which circled his head like a Giotto angel whose halo is about beret-height issued a conflicting statement. On the subject of the old family firm, Ffaringtons, Neil Harris was both forthcoming and reckless. Nonetheless the history of the firm, once Jane had sketched in a time-line, was far from ordinary. The Ffarington family who still retained the major shareholding were both thrifty and philanthropic. One of the younger sons was a poet who had founded a literary magazine — like the firm, still in existence. The sons and grandsons were Oxford educated, and expected to bring back a freight of culture to be dispersed not merely through the firm but through society itself.

Jane Shipley and Neil Harris discovered they shared a philosophic bent. Questions such as tradition versus innovation, old money and new, slow progress against a hare-like dash were debated, along with the history of the firm and its current diversification. Jane and Neil dined out to continue their discussions; their mutual liking for argument seemed insatiable.

Jane's first draft showed an alarming tendency to meander: she forced herself to walk around the venerable two-storeyed wood building, freshly gilded in new paint, which had housed Ffaringtons for ninety-nine years. And she sat at the feet — actually she occupied a small stiff-backed chair — of white-haired Felix Ffarington Snr while he expounded the family history with a great many digressions.

Jane and Neil kissed one another on the cheek, both cheeks, when the final draft was accepted and Ffaringtons' cheque was safely in her handbag. Jane felt Neil wanted to hug her when their minds exhibited moments of amazing accord, when their synapses linked and burned out together.

'It's been great, truly great, working with you,' Neil said on Jane's last day when the Board had invited her to afternoon tea.

Jane returned to her home town where she worked as a private secretary to the general manager of an oil company. She blamed herself for not throwing her arms around Neil Harris's neck at the moment of synaptic concurrence: at the very least she would have been rebuffed. Or did he suspect Jane would be incapable of that fading technique used by movie directors to close a scene after which something mundane or prosaic is required to allow it to set? Jane seemed not to grasp that revelations are exceedingly tiring and need bringing down to earth. Her desire to weave something out of insight recalled the bowerbird or one of those spun-sugar confections at a Vietnamese restaurant.

Nevertheless the book, when it appeared, won a small prize in the regional history section of the National Book Awards. The title, *The Philanthropic Fabric: A History of the Family Firm of Ffaringtons*, was Jane's idea because she thought it deserved a wider audience. Felix Ffarington Snr sent a handwritten letter saying they were well satisfied. Later she heard Neil Harris had left the firm and gone overseas.

The experiences of Jane's life were largely the same as others. It was her mother who had imbued her with romantic ideas, meeting Jane's father on a blind date arranged by a friend whose fiancé brought a friend: a common enough pattern, as her father would point out. There are many people in the world you might fall in love with, he instructed Jane: all it takes is a certain age, proximity, a reasonable degree of attractiveness. Perhaps it also took the question: 'Tell me about yourself.'

Jane married a pipeline engineer, learned to cook and garden. She took a course in French conversation with a friend whose life was almost parallel. Later they studied pottery, with small results. When she was widowed young, Jane turned again to writing the histories of firms — they were now corporations — and small towns commissioned by amalgamated city councils. She wrote Mission Statements at the head of glossy reports — the information came supplied like a dress pattern — and, once, a brochure outlining the importance of the Treaty of Waitangi which had the words 'founding document' attached. Sometimes she exceeded her brief and made suggestions which were politely ignored. Her sentences appeared among the sentences of other copywriters so she could never claim them.

The Philanthropic Fabric had been out of print for a decade, or stored forgotten in the basement of Ffaringtons, when she received a letter from Felix Ffarington Jnr. The firm would be pleased to pay her airfare and a few nights' accommodation if she found herself free to call on them at her convenience.

Jane replied asking if she could stay at the Montrose, a hotel whose interiors were illustrated in a travel guide, offering to pay the difference if they considered the room rate excessive. She asked if they could extend her booking for a week, with the extra days of course being charged to her.

It was a crisp dry autumn week, perfect for exploring a city with a main street based on the Royal Mile and a street plan so stubbornly Edinburghian that some streets rose almost vertically into the air like bristles on a porcupine. The meeting with Felix Ffarington Jnr was for the middle of the week.

On the first day Jane took a bus tour and discovered that, while the Royal Mile might be as straight as a spine, real quality equals elevation. The bus panted up impossible inclines to reveal mansions in moon-shaped crescents looking down through long windows at the street below as if it were a pool. Others were glimpsed from winding drives and dry stone walls softened by rhododendrons. Finally the bus eased into an old cemetery lost in drifts of leaves. They stopped before graves angled for panoramic prominence, and Jane squinted at an inscription that seemed to read

Dedicated to the memory of
Hamish McDiarmid Wombwell
(Menagerist)

'Old Felix has gone to the great textile mill in the sky,' said young Felix, showing her to a chair. 'Retirement did for him as it does for so many others. He insisted on starting as a delivery boy all those years ago, though his father would have promoted him. I think he imagined himself sleeping under the counter at night and having a quick wash at the pump.'

Jane reflected this was hardly the style of his successors.

'There were some others here when I was researching the book,' she replied casually. 'Neil Harris, for one. Did you hear what happened to him?'

'Ffaringtons' one black sheep, I regret to say. Bit of a playboy, I gather. I expect you guessed that though.' Felix Ffarington Jnr's eyes were lowered and he seemed to be scrutinising his blotter.

'I seem to recall I had dinner with him a few times,' Jane said. 'Working dinners I suppose you would call them now. Though I believe they are usually working breakfasts. There was a good deal to discuss . . .'

'Quite,' said Felix Jnr.

'Mr Harris had a good many theories . . .' Jane's voice trailed away.

A simple denial and no embellishments, her father had always advised. Refuse, no need to explain. Still there was an odd silence in the room; she felt Felix Jnr was fighting an impulse to straighten his tie.

'Tea,' he said suddenly. 'Or coffee if you prefer. Then we can chat about the new updated edition. A whole new chapter may be required. If you feel up to it . . .'

The little colonial cottage was very close to the street, one remove from a front door that opened on to the pavement. Jane had always rather liked that: the windows swathed in thick layers of lace curtain, the sound of feet passing as you lay in bed. Heavy feet, some as light as mice.

Half a dozen steps — she wished there were more to collect her thoughts in — took her to a low wooden verandah painted dove-grey. There was a door knocker and a bell: she chose the bell and heard it chime inside the house, two notes like a footfall along the hall runner.

The door opened suddenly and a man stood there, a short glowering man with a shock of white hair and narrow eyes. Jane had involuntarily stepped back.

'Scared you, did I?' the man said sardonically, and in that instant Jane recognised Neil. He had said that once coming up behind her in the cramped little room Ffaringtons had allotted her.

'Jane,' she said haltingly. 'Jane Shipley. You've probably forgotten.'

'Little Jane Shipley. No I haven't forgotten. Not likely. The bitch that caused my divorce. Oh not forgotten at all.'

'I beg your pardon,' Jane stammered.

'I'm sure you do. Do you want to come in? For old time's sake. Celebrate the auspicious occasion with a cup of instant. I don't think it warrants more.'

'I'm not sure,' Jane faltered.

Whatever scene she was expecting, it was certainly not this. Nonetheless she found herself following Neil Harris along the passage and into a long kitchen at the back of the house. Widowed, alone in the world, who can tell what awaits? Still she knew it was a mistake. If the coffee was intended as an insult there must be worse to come.

'You mentioned a divorce,' Jane began. 'I had no idea you were married.'

'No idea when you were making sheep's eyes at me. Asking

for a little after-hours help with your pet project. Come on . . .'

'Neither of us discussed our personal circumstances if I recall. I didn't think it was your business then or now.'

'Oh no, the whole business was Ffaringtons, its noble history, its shining personages, its genteel greed so cloaked in propriety it was practically a pillar of the church. And you swallowed the whole lot of course. Just like Moby Dick.'

'I wasn't paid to do otherwise,' Jane retorted. 'What did you expect? The fall of the Romanovs, the last days of Nero? It was hardly intended for general circulation.'

'Any more than you were, in spite of appearances.'

'I think you are absolutely odious,' Jane cried, putting her untasted coffee down on the table. 'I thought you were genuinely interested in what I was writing. But your theories were just a lot of hot air. As for your divorce, it was nothing to do with me.'

'Nothing to do with you! That's rich. That was the week my wife was having me followed. The expression on your face was enough to do the trick. In flagrante delicto. A rich irony. Missed the woman I was really involved with because she was out of town and lighted on you.'

'That's enough.' Jane ran down the passage, fumbled with the door handle, ran the few steps to the pavement. Never had pavement seemed safer: a river, an escalator to bear her away. She didn't look back.

When you tell the truth keep one foot in the stirrup is an old Turkish proverb. Jane forgets where she has heard it. Or read it. It appeals with its image of the balanced body, one foot seemingly dismounting, the toe hovering over the ground but in truth ready to fling itself over the steed's back in a motion like a gym vault, the other foot squeezed in its metal holder like someone wrestling with a too-tight shoe.

The truth of herself and Neil Harris cannot be this kind of truth, she thinks. She has not told him any kind of truth because she has been afraid to. He has not followed her along the passage, as far as she is aware. She definitely had one foot in the stirrup then. The sight of his angry eyes, all the personality she had remembered stripped away to reveal this resentment, is unnerving. 'A black sheep, a bit of a playboy,' Felix Ffarington Jnr had said, and he'd looked at Jane as though she'd known and perhaps even succumbed.

Jane goes back to her hotel room at the Montrose, all latticed panes and heavy Burgundy velvet drapes as if the city has a pact with tartan. She runs a deep bath and soaks in it for an hour. She applies fresh make-up and walks along George Street.

I used the word odious, she thinks, stopping finally at a student café where ragged students in op-shop coats are consuming vast trenchers of pasta. She orders a volcanic-looking muffin and a cappuccino. I must have been mounted on an animal about the size of a gerbil with stirrups the size of teaspoons. Whereas truth, real truth, requires at least a Berber clutching a scimitar. The word to be flung must be known in advance.

It is another kind of truth she must face. A lesser kind to do with self-analysis and the falling out of things. With perception and the serving of summonses. With giving — and here is the real nub — the wrong impression, of not explaining herself. Had she, on those evenings when they continued their discussion of Ffaringtons, been signalling something else? She had come home and looked into the mirror and seen her eyes shining. Could the machinations of an old family firm be responsible for that? It is this that hurts as Jane dismounts from her gerbil, licks the last froth from her teaspoon. Her idea of love has been damaging.

Tomorrow she will ask Felix Ffarington's secretary what really happened to Neil Harris. She will say something like, 'I thought I caught sight of him in the street. But I couldn't be sure.' What she won't say is, 'He seemed horribly changed by some conversation we had years ago.'

The Mathematics of Jane Austen

JANE AUSTEN must have been very fond of the number 2. Have you never noticed it? Two proposals by Darcy; two good sisters (and three foolish ones); two ill-mannered matriarchs, Mrs Bennet and Lady Catherine de Bourgh; two unsuitable suitors, Mr Collins and George Wickham. Two attempts to reside at Netherfield; two friends, Darcy and Bingley; two attempted elopements, Lydia and Georgiana Darcy. Oh there are countless others. Jane Austen even admitted it was unlikely a man would propose a second time. Two brothers-in-law: Darcy and Wickham. Everything has a pair, a shadow in psychoanalytic terms. Miss de Bourgh (sickly) and Georgiana (sickly but saved). Even Elizabeth is caught between the twin scales of Jane (universal benevolence) and Charlotte Lucas (everyone has her price).

A variation of these thoughts — and a new example of twoness: the marriages of the Gardiners (soundly based) and the Bennets (short-lived lust) — occurred to Irene Fisher as she crossed the quad between Direct Marketing and Zoology where a trailorload of dead white chickens were parked. But could she work it into a suitable proposal, one that would impress her supervisor, crusty and conservative Professor Mordaunt, who practically regarded Jane Austen as his own child?

No she would not mention it at today's meeting: she would listen and nod, act the acolyte, because this is what Professor Mordaunt preferred. She would be as self-effacing as Jane faced with visitors.

'Just *Pride and Prejudice*,' Irene says to Professor Mordaunt. 'I just want to use *Pride and Prejudice*.'

'And when did you come to this decision?' Professor Mordaunt asks. His face is deeply marked and some of the lines are fatigue.

'Over the last month,' Irene replies, thinking it best not to say while she was crossing the quad.

'You will severely limit yourself, you realise that,' Professor Mordaunt says, not raising his eyes from Irene's face, as if he attempts to solicit a blush. 'You are abandoning the altogether more ferocious *Sense and Sensibility*, *Emma* with its delightful female jealousy, *Persuasion*, I need not go on.'

'I realise *P & P* has been thoroughly analysed in the past.'

'And by those — excuse me, dear lady — more esteemed than Miss Irene Fisher. Scholars of impeccable credentials.'

Irene flinches a little at this and the professor looks as if he has scored a hit. But having reduced her — for such is his mechanism — he instantly relents.

'There, there,' he says patting her hand. '*P & P* is my favourite as well, in spite of the charms to the aged of *Emma*. I'll be your batman, if you like.'

'I should like it a good deal,' Irene replies, thinking if her thesis can get through this minefield it will be marked elsewhere.

'Well then,' says Professor Mordaunt, sinking into his cavernous old chair with grubby cushions. 'We need a detailed outline.'

No, thinks Irene, rising finally, we need those cushions washed. She can see Cassandra bustling about, saying to Jane, 'I'll just do the cushion covers if you'll make a suet pudding.'

Irene slips into the university library and goes to the section of the occult. It is a small section: numerology, palmistry, witchcraft. Some of the tomes on witchcraft are impressively dense, as if lending an air of respectability. Irene takes down a book called *The Key to the Universe* and makes some notes. *The number 2 is the symbol of Duality. It is the number of Differentiation, the 'fall into matter'. By the Pythagorians it was called audacity.* Of this only *audacity* pleases, though Irene considers Jane Austen greatly concerned with financial security. But surely first impressions, pride or prejudice, count for more? If they are unresolved there will be no Pemberley, no phaeton with a nice little pair of ponies to go round the park. She is simply a real writer, Irene muses, as her own pen scratches away at the nonsensical vague mysticism. *The Number 2 is, therefore, the Number of Contrasts and the 'pairs of opposites', good and evil, truth and error, day and night, heat and cold, health and sickness, pleasure and pain, joy and sorrow, male and female, etc., and because of this it is called by some 'the beginning of evil'.*

Irene skims some comments on Adam and Eve and alights on *2 representing the marriage made in heaven. But before such a marriage can be consummated on all planes it must be confirmed on earth according to the legal requirements of the country in which the ones so united dwell.* Is this the beginning manoeuvre of Mr Darcy's letter, to size up the respective statuses: Elizabeth's mother and father against the Gardiners; Lydia, Mary, Kitty against the counterweight of Elizabeth and Jane?

Irene buys a carton of orange juice and a sandwich sealed in a little plastic container like a tomb, and goes to sit under a beech tree in the park. Perhaps, a small voice of reason suggests, two-ness is nothing more than the unquenchable optimism of a spinster, a free-ranging romanticism above an unvaried existence. Large parts of Jane's life were ordered and even the occasional cataclysmic move ironed out. A spinster may well be more optimistic than a married woman. Yet how does Jane understand so well the tremor caused by a letter, a sighting, a stiff visit ending in bows? What a young heart leaps inside Elizabeth Bennet and how truly decent is Fitzwilliam Darcy.

Irene is usually home by 3.30 p.m. in time for Ben's return from school. Sue, Ben's mother, with whom Irene boards, assures her this is not necessary, that Ben will fling his satchel on the floor and find his way to the fridge. But Irene, since she has decided to have no children of her own, endeavours to greet Ben. Sometimes, like *The Simpsons*, they arrive at the driveway together.

Sue works in broadcasting, as a research assistant to a famous female broadcaster. Her days are an endless adrenalin rush of bringing details together, soothing interviewees, soothing the star, sweet-talking at the height of panic. Sue drinks too much coffee, as does the star. When she gets home around 6 p.m. she falls into an oversized chair and kicks off her shoes. Irene pours two large gin and tonics. Sometimes she provides a shoulder massage.

'So, how did you get on with the professor?' Sue asks, after a big gulp of g & t.

'So-so,' says Irene, nibbling on an olive. 'I think he'd prefer the full canon instead of just *P & P*.'

'And what about your theory, did you discuss that?'

'No, I chickened out. It needs development. I can't very well go to him with a book on numerology.'

'Numerology? That's something we might use on the programme. Particularly if we could find a scandal attached to it. Or am I thinking of Scientology?'

They eat lasagne and salad and Ben takes his ice cream and peaches into the den to watch the *X-Files*.

Irene hesitates to mention two-ness to Sue but then she reflects Ben is their two-ness — Ben and Fleet the red setter that Irene walks each night while Ben and Sue have time together. Fleet is part of Sue's marriage settlement: once they lived on a lifestyle block. Still, Fleet has adapted well enough to city life, lolloping by her side as they stride through the suburbs; it is her chance to walk fast and Fleet's to slow down. They can let him run only at weekends when they go to the beach or drive into the country.

Two is also the number of friendship, Irene reflects, as Fleet trots beside her. She thinks of Elizabeth Bennet crossing field after field in an English drizzle to comfort her deliberately drenched Jane. Surely her petticoat, trailing in the mud, is a sign of passion. Passion not yet fixed on its proper object, but perhaps passion must first be illustrated in an unconscious manner. Mr Darcy is required to witness the petticoat and draw his own conclusions. Then Irene thinks of another perambulating two-ness: Elizabeth and Caroline Bingley walking in the great room after dinner, to display themselves to Mr Darcy. Has Jane Austen turned every coin over for this purpose? Was she a player of heads or tails?

If Jane Austen permitted in her novels an undue use of the second chance — 'undue' as compared to its prevalence in real life — is it simply a plot device which she found effective or does it represent a more profoundly held belief, a personal philosophy or wish? This thesis will concentrate on her best known novel, Pride and Prejudice,

THE MATHEMATICS OF JANE AUSTEN

published in 1813 and originally titled First Impressions, *but examples of second chance abound in all her works and may be readily discovered by the reader.*

Did Jane Austen herself wish for a second chance, a return of suitor? But Irene will not say that. However, she will say something about romanticism. She writes *Romanticism* on a fresh page in her exercise book and then a question: *Is Romanticism an essential element in the notion of a second chance?*

'I want ten examples,' Professor Mordaunt says to her when they meet and Irene finally introduces her theory. She is careful to keep her voice lowered and measured, for Professor Mordaunt likes feminine girls, smart girls with brains whom he can encourage. He likes to feel he has made them smarter than men. It is very warm in Professor Mordaunt's room and the air outside is heavy and still. In the quad below Irene can see students walking singly and in pairs and a couple embracing under a tree.

'Take care whether you mean duality, the twice-repeated event or simply a closure into which you read something that is not there.'

When Irene looks surprised at his acquiescence, a sly smile spreads over his face.

'Get along then. What are you waiting for?'

Irene is almost inclined to bow like Elizabeth beginning a set at the Netherfield ball.

The ball at Netherfield (two balls) is the first item on Irene's list. She will explain that her examples are not in any order of significance, nor are they to be equally regarded. An insult at a ball is not to be placed alongside a second proposal.

> 1. Two balls at Netherfield. The refusal to dance by Mr Darcy, then the seeking (unsuccessfully)

of Elizabeth's hand.
2. Mr Darcy's two proposals.
3. Mr Darcy's pivotal letter explicating two problem areas: Jane and Wickham.
4. Two exemplars of foolishness: Mrs Bennet and Lady Catherine de Bourgh.
5. Elizabeth makes two journeys (both involving Darcy), to the Collinses (Hertfordshire) and Pemberley (Derbyshire). Jane Austen never travels without a purpose.

There is something haphazard about these entries and Irene feels dissatisfied. Didn't Jane Bennet also make two journeys? The one where she is surrounded by the Gardiner children and the second to Gracechurch Street? Suddenly the world seems full of purposeful carriage journeys. Irene herself feels a great need to stretch her legs. Besides, five examples is enough for one afternoon. She closes her door, clatters (sound of hooves?) down the stone stairway and emerges in the rose garden.

That evening when she walks Fleet, Ben comes with her. He wants to ask her something, and the dusk and the anonymous streets are a good place to ask. If only Irene wouldn't keep pointing out things: the way some colours stand out as if they are waiting for darkness or how Fleet only goes ahead a certain distance before he looks back.

'Some kids at school think you and Mum are lesbos,' Ben says finally, as they pause to cross Eden Avenue.

'Lesbians,' Irene corrects. Not one of Jane Austen's worries. 'No, darling,' she says, putting an arm around the thin shoulders. 'It's natural people should think that, but we are just good friends. We went to school together, about the age you are now.

Then when you were born and the marriage broke up, your mother needed a boarder. I was just back from overseas, so I came to stay. We thought you might like two mothers. Don't you?'

'Most of the time. Yes. But they don't understand at school.'

'I expect some of their parents are secret cross-dressers, or drag queens, or into child pornography, or fantasise about sleeping with sheep. Or wear false hair or have their noses straightened or their bums tucked. Ignore them, Ben. Just say to them, "Are you sure about your own set-up? My mothers could take a lie detector test any day".'

'Thanks, Irene.'

'Call me Number Two Mother.'

'Race you home.'

Jane and Cassandra. So close. The original two. Undoubtedly Cassandra is the model for Jane. A sweetness fine and ungrained. Unyielding in its hope of Bingley. Jane Bennet is practically a cosmologist, imagining the globe as an ever-evolving kindness. Whereas Jane Austen, alias Elizabeth, perhaps wrote down and thereby dispersed those observations that allowed her to remain a loving sister and aunt. How therapeutic it might have been to make a suet pudding in the kitchen. How far from the materialism that underpins marriage. *The number two is the foundation of marriage, the reunion of 2 expressions in 1 soul. Any couple looking upon marriage in this light would naturally recognise their duty to the community as to themselves.*

Still there is another week to go before her next meeting with Professor Mordaunt. Examples of two-ness will come to her as she walks in the park. There is no example of two dirty petticoats, but everything turns on its obverse. Perhaps Lizzie Bennet's toilette is exceedingly scrupulous thereafter. Did she think while she was crossing stiles and fields . . . *I never could be so happy as you. Till I have your disposition, your goodness, I never can have your happiness.* Or did she simply drift and ruminate, as active minds often do, subsumed in nature?

Sue is making beefburgers when Irene gets home. It is Thursday night, Ben's night for ordering dinner. He writes his order at the beginning of each week on the kitchen whiteboard so it can be included in the weekly shopping. Lately Sue and Irene have been taking him with them, under protest, to calculate the cost of what he eats. He carries a pocket calculator and hesitates between two sizes of Coke. Sue swears she's not trying to make him feel guilty, like Elinor Dashwood over meat.

'The second step,' Sue argues, 'is to teach him to cook what he buys, carefully, and without waste.' So tonight Ben is setting the burgers in a non-stick pan with a little olive oil, a sprinkle of salt and a few twists of pepper from the giant grinder that sits, like a household god, on the bench. The buns are toasting under the grill and being watched like a hawk; the lettuce, tomatoes, cheese slices and ketchup stand ready. The ketchup glows like a military uniform at Meryton. The necessary colour contrast of militiamen, Irene thinks, as some of the ketchup runs down her chin. She holds the bun tightly with her fingers, like holding down a bonnet, made over, and tied with ribbons.

Later Irene and Sue lounge in easy chairs with mugs of coffee. Elizabeth Bennet always uses courage as a spur to speech, so Irene asks Sue if she has ever been proposed to twice.

'By the same man? Never.'

'Did you ever turn anyone down in no uncertain terms and then receive a second offer?'

'Never. What is this? Forty questions?'

'No, I'm thinking of Mr Darcy and Elizabeth Bennet. "*Let*

me thank you again and again, for that generous compassion which induced you to take so much trouble, and bear so many mortifications . . . " All so he could propose a second time.'

'Extraordinary, I should say. A clear case of being besotted. Perhaps a coup de foudre?'

'No, because he refused to dance. He thought her average, her figure average at first. It was only when she spoke and he saw the connection of a lively mind to lively language.'

'And everyone else was so dull a suitor must come back for more? Not very like real life, is it? I thought I was always pretty animated on a first date. Then or never.'

'Listen to this,' Irene interjects, pulling a crumpled page from her pocket. "*The number 2 is sacred to all female deities, such as Rhea, Isis, Vishnu, the Virgin Mary, as it represents the Mother-force separated from the Father and ever-seeking the union that it may bring forth. It represents all the productive forces in nature, including nature-sounds, voice and speech; for it is through sound that creation is brought forth.*"'

'Writing is a form of sound. Perhaps Jane Austen's life was too orderly. Was she a gardener by any chance?'

'A sort of scientist of language? Professor Mordaunt would like that. Or a mathematician. I'm sure she was good at budgeting.'

'That reminds me. Will you do the shopping next week?'

Walking under the trees in Albert Park, Irene wishes now she had included Elinor and Marianne. Two sisters and two suitors; the spectacular second chance, though different for females, of Anne Elliot and Captain Wentworth. Suddenly it occurs to Irene that the pairs are not perfect at first and adjustments have to be made. Elizabeth (free speech and spirit) must learn sound reasoning and an equally applied imagination to lower Wickham and raise Darcy. This is how the novel moves. Two-ness, adjustment, one-ness. Irene sits under an oak as old as the tree at Lambton and boldly adds to her list:

> 6. Two examples of male foolishness: Mr Bennet (detachment) and Mr Collins (pedantry). Whereas Mr Gardiner combines sense and action.
> 7. Mrs Bennet's character and marriage echoed by Lydia Bennet's marriage to Wickham. Two examples of infatuation yielding to indifference. Genetic?
> 8. Two courses at dinner. Fish? Fowl?
> 9. Wickham has two career options: church and army.
> 10. Both Darcy and Elizabeth have a greatly loved sister: Georgiana and Jane.

But these will not do. Professor Mordaunt will get his teeth into 'two courses for dinner'. You might as well say Kitty trims two bonnets. Or Wickham joins two regiments or rejects two livings. Twice Mr Gardiner visits Pemberley, the second time to fish. Perhaps two and not one trout rise on his perambulation. Then Irene thinks of what she has read of Cassandra's life after Jane died, how withdrawn and private it became, a life of living bereavement. And how Jane, once at Chawton, urgently sent for Cassandra as though engulfed in panic. The cause of the panic was an alteration in family fortunes, the reading of a will.

> 8. (writes Irene, removing two partridges or boiled fowls) The two themes of money and marriage.

THE MATHEMATICS OF JANE AUSTEN

Ben walks rapidly alongside a fence which is too high to jump. Behind him the footsteps, padded, nonchalant, like wolves which delicately advance upon a dead campfire. Ben has seen a film of wolves and their strange hesitancy, as if they bring a mere calling card, when the final advance begins. And last year Sue and Irene had taken him to see real wolves at the zoo. 'Like ladies in fur coats going to the opera,' Irene had laughed, pointing out the too thin legs, but Ben could not take his eyes off their pacing. Only the panthers seemed as restless.

The persecution of Ben had begun slowly enough. Sue and Irene had come to a Home and School evening and to parent interviews together. Ben had wished Irene wouldn't come but she insisted. Fleet had come too, for his night walk. Two women with a red setter between them, striding down the corridor.

The boy at the interview before him had become the ring leader. Soon Ben's lunch was being stolen, his sports gear went missing, a pocket was ripped off a blazer. A project with a relief model was doused with blue-black ink. The final stage was to stalk him. It could only lead to a beating.

But not tonight. Head down in his misery, brain willing his Nikes to move faster, a gradual accumulating speed that might leave his tormentors in his wake, Ben does not see a woman bearing down on him. She is full-busted, narrow-hipped, and has thin legs like a wolf.

'My goodness,' she cries as he slams into her. Then, 'Don't I know you? Haven't I seen you with Irene Fisher?'

I have forgotten Mary Bennet contrasted with Elizabeth Bennet at the pianoforte, Irene thinks as she sits in Professor Mordaunt's room, gazing out at the leaves of an oak tree. But such details will not convince. Professor Mordaunt's countenance is set in an expression so customary to it, a kind of sardonic disdain, a scholarly weariness, that it is impossible to imagine the younger fresh face that once lay beneath. Did he ever — for he was made a full professor very young — bound up the stairs to his room or welcome an importuning student with a show of enthusiasm? Does his condescension to women students date from some miraculous year in which their brains were definitively proved smaller?

'Two balls at Netherfield cannot equal two proposals by Darcy, nor can you prove that Jane Austen was deliberately replicating the elder Bennets' marriage in Lydia and Wickham's set-up. Wickham and Mr Bennet may share some disagreeable characteristics — their judgement of women, for instance — but Mr Bennet remains a gentleman, as Elizabeth is fond of pointing out. I always thought she was clutching at straws. And Mrs Bennet hardly attains the rank of Lady Catherine, whose knowledge of etiquette is profound.'

'Except in her remarks about the Bennets' west-facing sitting room and her trying to extract a denial from Elizabeth,' Irene wants to protest, but she knows it is wiser to remain silent. She thinks of Mary Bennet listening to Mr Collins and perceiving a majesty in the length of word.

'But,' says Professor Mordaunt, perceiving her downcast Mary Bennet face, 'there is enough in your notion to interest me, I think. Provided, and this is a big proviso, you start with the most obvious blocks of resemblance and don't allow yourself to become distracted with feminine fripperies like boiled fowls, two pianos or bonnets in a hat shop.'

'Still they might make an interesting codicil,' Irene offers, recovering something of the spirit of her heroine.

'Run along,' Professor Mordaunt growls, 'before I change my mind. Let me see an introduction in writing.'

THE MATHEMATICS OF JANE AUSTEN

'I think something's bothering Ben,' Sue says to Irene that evening as they are clearing away the supper dishes. 'Do you notice how silent he is lately?'

'He didn't want to go to school this morning. Said he had a stomach ache. Perhaps I was wrong to force him.'

'Tomorrow's Friday. Let's pick him up after school and take him to dinner and a movie.'

Before she sleeps Irene takes up *The Key to the Universe* and some more of the chapter on *The Number 2*.

Let 2 remind you that the great problem of humanity on this globe is the perfect blending and mastery of the positive and negative expressions of the Great Creative Force through its pairs of opposites, the sexes. Then she thinks of Jane Austen in the kitchen at Chawton, chopping suet into flour, pleased to be free of polarities: Elizabeth Bennet and Fitzwilliam Darcy, Elinor and Marianne Dashwood, Emma Woodhouse and Jane Fairfax. And yet she can never be quite free of her characters who keep her company as much as Cassandra does. Is it her own nature she is describing: romantic and worldly, astute and playful, rising to speech like the plentiful trout in the ponds at Pemberley?

Ben's mistake has been in trying to explain he has two mothers. My mother is divorced and lives with a friend. It is a mistake to explain anything. Two mothers, no father, two lesbos, poor little sook. It doesn't matter that one mother works in broadcasting and the other is at university. That he sees about as much of them as two fathers, though they make up for it at weekends. Anyway his mother is quite masculine, good at making decisions. What a rich road he has opened to his tormentors.

Unbeknown to him, the two mothers are now speeding towards

him along Gillies Avenue. Irene is in her tracksuit, as she has just come from the gym; Sue on the other hand is heavily made up: she has had a tryout for television earlier in the afternoon. When the make-up girl hands her a tissue and pushes a pot of cold cream in her direction she decides to leave it on. 'I think I look quite glamorous, if you squint.' Sue is wearing a soft green suit over a black bustier, and very high heels which she kicks off while driving.

They come on the little group of flailing boys by a low stone wall.

'Ben,' shouts Irene, who has the better eyesight. 'Stop the car.'

Sue pulls up on a yellow line and the two women leap out. Sue is barefooted but she clutches one bright red shoe. Irene seizes the largest perpetrator in a head lock; Sue brings the pointed heel down on the base of the neck of another. Inspired by Professor Mordaunt's doubts about two-ness in Jane Austen, Irene lifts an insect-like boy straddling Ben under the armpits and throws him over the stone wall.

'Just don't say we're your mothers,' Sue says as they roar off to avoid an approaching parking warden.

'You're going to have two beautiful black eyes,' Irene remarks admiringly. 'Wear them with pride.'

Then she turns to Sue and murmurs, 'Nice one, Cassandra.'

The Mathematics of Jane Austen
The duality of forces, the two-ness, which occurs sufficiently often in Jane Austen's novels to warrant at least an interest, may be exemplified in Pride and Prejudice. *Other novels in the canon share the characteristic two-ness which is sometimes stated in a title*: Sense and Sensibility, *for example. But the two-ness seems to go deeper, postulating a view of the world in which opposing forces,*

moral, financial, social, attract a counter-poise, so that good strives against evil, probity against falsehood, infatuation against a longer-enduring love. Was Jane Austen a mathematician as much as Stephen Hawking is a cosmologist? Did she view the admittedly narrow world she inhabited as worked by levers?

But this will not do. Irene takes up a red pencil and runs it through all the words that follow 'love'.

&

The Ladies Chatterley's Gardener

IT WAS A STIFLING late February day when they found the young man by the roadside. At first Edwina thought they were looking at a red ball on the yellow grass. The legs in denim and the open shirt seemed detached.

'What is it?' Agnes asked. 'Why are we stopping?'

It was a source of annoyance that Agnes who did not drive presumed to drive metaphorically, like a driving instructor who has various safety devices for braking.

'How do I know?' said Edwina. Their quarrel of the morning was not resolved and she endeavoured to inject frost into each Pass the butter exchange.

Agnes, to show she was making an effort, got out of the ancient Rover and came around to Edwina's side. Together they stood looking down at the young man with the unbelievably red face.

Once, driving in the country, Edwina and Agnes had come upon a bloated cow. Its body was immensely swollen as if a bomb ticked inside; stick legs pointed skywards in a last spasm. They had slowed but not stopped: the grossness, as if the cow was a huge speech balloon, was so startling. The air was chill and there was no putrefying smell.

Whereas this young man, when Edwina bent over in a familiar gardening posture, smelt very odd and dead.

'Has he been drinking, do you think?' Agnes piped, shrinking back.

'Any fool could guess he has been drinking,' Edwina snapped.

'Should we apply mouth to mouth resuscitation?' Agnes called.

'Don't be foolish. He's still breathing.'

Deep stentorian breaths, with a shuddering tendency and a slight twitching of the limbs, were clearly audible.

'Perhaps someone will come by?' Agnes went on.

'We have come by, as you so quaintly put it,' Edwina snapped, regretting her decision to stop the car. Now they had to decide on the Pharisee or the Samaritan.

'Perhaps we could phone a doctor. Or an ambulance?' Agnes's patience too was wearing thin.

'Do you see a phone box? And how far do you imagine the nearest hospital is? Or a house for that matter? For the grass verge on which the young man lay was bordered by a high poplar hedge. And if no one else had stopped, it might have been because his head looked like a pumpkin or some kind of fallen fruit.

'Pull yourself together, Agnes,' Edwina instructed, but what she really meant was, 'Brace yourself'.

Luckily the back seat of the Rover was commodious and there was the travelling rug.

Dove Cottage, though anyone less dove-like than Edwina could scarcely be imagined — perhaps some previous owner had kept doves? — was one of a row of retired cottages, villas and mere baches along the shore of an estuary. Its single-laned road announced its inhospitality by a strategically placed cattlestop and road humps, so joyriders rarely ventured further. Dove Cottage was set well back from the road, with a drive leading to the garage for the Rover. Surrounded by ancient trees, it had a circular rose bed and another cut in the shape of the ace of clubs.

Getting the comatose young man indoors, though the Rover was parked at the end of the drive and screened from view by apple trees, was not easy. Edwina was broad-shouldered and accustomed to digging and wrenching trees, but Agnes could barely manage the feet.

'Shut up,' Edwina said several times, though Agnes was not saying anything, merely panting.

Finally they thought of the wheelbarrow, some planks and a cushion. The young man whose dark face looked even more alarming out of its sylvan setting offered no resistance.

'The colour of a damson plum,' Agnes offered when she could catch her breath.

'The doctor,' Edwina snapped. 'Don't just stand there. See if old Fitz is at home. If not, we'll try Flo.' Flo, the district nurse, was frequently bandaging ulcers in the area.

Dr Fitzwilliam was in and he arrived in his old Ford within quarter of an hour. His fluffy moustache, an RAF relic, was soothing and compensated for failing to be entirely up-to-date. 'We can only be up-to-date, as you put it, for a very short time,' he was fond of booming. 'Like fashion.' Since most of his patients had abandoned any contest with fashion decades ago, he was rarely challenged.

But even Dr Fitz seemed nonplussed by the young man who continued to snore on the divan bed in the verandah room.

'Well, well, what have we here . . .' died on his lips as he bent forward to sniff the breath from the partly open mouth. 'Whisky,' he pronounced, 'and lots of it. But I don't like his colour, I don't like it at all.'

'Well, we're not moving him again,' snapped Edwina, who was now thoroughly out of countenance with the Good Samaritan. She intended to have words with the vicar about ramifications.

'I'll have to give him an injection,' Fitz stated, opening his ancient Gladstone bag in a motion that resembled Moses at the Red Sea.

'What for?' Edwina asked. She considered Fitz needle-happy.

'Pain, discomfort. Shock particularly. He'll be in considerable shock when he comes round.'

'Why is he that awful colour?' Agnes asked. 'A sort of port wine.'

'The severest kind of sunburn. I'll have to get Flo to call every day.'

'Should we keep the blinds closed?' Agnes asked, looking doubtfully at the rolled bamboo blinds.

'Only if you want to hide the fact that you've kidnapped a young stud. Quite handsome under all that high colour, I imagine. . .'

When Dr Fitz had gone and the young man showed no signs of waking, Edwina and Agnes retired to the kitchen and drank tea. Lapsang Souchong was Edwina's favourite, but today she would not have minded the sort served in railway cups in which spoons were reported to stand unaided. What had they got themselves into? Flo, the district nurse, was engaged to call at the end of her day's rounds; that at least was a comfort. But when the young man woke, what were they going to say? Had they broken any law, like the law of trespass? Vague ideas of bodysnatchers went through Edwina's head, for she was only dominant in outer layers, her certainties, like Rome, built on a swamp. Then she remembered that bodysnatchers operated by night, the darker and foggier the better. They carried sacks and tools and lanterns held high over their grisly work.

'We'd better have an explanation ready,' Agnes said, breaking the silence. 'I mean about our motives.'

'The first thing we'll do, after explaining how we found him by the side of the road, is let him use the telephone to contact his parents. Or if they are not on the phone I shall write a letter. That way no one can accuse us of kidnapping.'

Then, since the young man had not stirred, they both went into the garden.

Flo got to Dove Cottage around 5.30 p.m. Her knocking at the front door went unanswered, so she went around to the back. At the scrubbed table in the long kitchen a young man with a hideously discoloured face sat between Edwina and Agnes, drinking homemade ginger beer.

Edwina shot her a warning look but Flo knew better than to comment on anyone's appearance. Hadn't she been undressing and bathing Eddie Syzmanowski for years and always finding him at the end of the week wearing seven pairs of socks?

'Not as bad as it was,' Agnes volunteered. 'But we thought you might have some advice, Flo. Or better, some creams.'

'Gus,' the young man said, extending a fairly reddened hand. 'I'm mighty grateful to Miss Agnes and Miss Edwina here for picking me up. I might have been staked out by Indians otherwise.'

'Have you contacted your parents, Gus?' Flo asked, though she was itching to do something to the poor face. Perhaps Edwina had denied him a mirror. Then she recollected that mirrors were in short supply at Dove Cottage.

'They're overseas,' Gus replied. 'Round-the-world air tickets. Said if they didn't go now it'd be too late.'

'I see,' said Flo, though she didn't. Perhaps Gus was in charge of the family home, a watchdog?

'Gus has been flatting,' Agnes volunteered. 'A big old house with a lot of young people.'

'Rats from a sinking ship, if you ask me,' Edwina interjected 'I suppose rats don't notice if one of their fellows is missing.'

How *do* rats leave a sinking ship? Flo had often wondered. Berthed, they might run down the long ropes tied to bollards. Perhaps they ran down the anchor cable and then swam. Later she managed to entice Gus to sit on the edge of the day bed so she could anoint his face.

'Does it hurt?' she asked, applying calamine lotion with cotton balls as gently as she could.

'I feel as though I've been skinned, but it's a new feeling. A bit like the phoenix rising out of the ashes. Or Icarus.'

'I guess Icarus did get pretty well broiled before he came down,' Flo agreed. 'They usually only mention the wings melting. Lucky for you Agnes and Edwina came along. Though they did say you had the shade of a high hedge.' Flo put the used cotton balls in a small plastic bag. 'I'll come back tomorrow,' she said. 'Don't go anywhere near the sun. Even if it looks overcast. Keep a hat on if you're outdoors.'

'Yes M'am, thank you M'am,' said Gus. Then, in a lower tone, so Flo only half-heard, he added, 'It's nice here though.'

Gus's red face, now he had sighted it, unbeknown to Edwina or Agnes, in kitchen knife blades, the backs of well-polished soup spoons and finally a small pocket mirror at the back of the bathroom cabinet, perfectly echoed his inner state. Before he had passed out he had been spurned in love. His abandonment was surely connected to the dreadful scene he had caused at his girlfriend's flat. Though flat was the wrong word, for Lise lived in the same kind of accommodation as himself. The two decrepit old houses, on the way to being squats, could have been the houses of the Montagues and Capulets.

Fridays were a heavy night for the Capulets and Montagues. In groups they trailed from pub to pub, nightclub to nightclub, conversing in some, dancing in others to wear off the effects of alcohol. They ate fast foods, some of which ended up in the gutters; they rinsed their mouths with more beer. Though hardly a ringleader, Gus liked the feeling of loping along in a group, a grey wolf pack. Then, later in the early hours of the morning, 'One is one and all alone.' It was not Gus's night to drive, though they had his car: he could drink until he passed out. But still he wanted to see Lise. Recently they had been quarrelling and once she had called him a 'mere male'. Some half-romantic notion of climbing up the fire escape: Lise was on the second floor of the Capulets in a long narrow room converted from a passageway, the window blocked by a huge Norfolk pine.

The Caped Crusader, he thought.

'Take the Batmobile home for me, will you?' he said to one of the gang. Splitting off from the group, a gliding motion, though his limbs didn't get the message, felt fine too. The cooler morning air fanned his face and he slicked his hair back. Up the fire escape, barking his shins and once nearly falling. Then before he could tap on the window it was flung open, and there was Lise wrapped in a sheet swearing at him to Piss off and never show his face again, to go and drown himself for all she cared.

Edwina wanted the apple trees pruned, and on the fourth day Gus, still pink as a Halloween lantern, was standing on a ladder, ineffectually supported by Agnes, when Flo called. Edwina could never bear idle hands, even if they were attached to wounded faces, and Gus in any case was feeling his idleness. The apple trees were as decrepit as the two women, but they were spirited too, refusing to let the moss clinging to their spindly branches deter them from sending out a few blossoms and eventually even fewer small hard fruit.

'A good shakeup is what they need,' said Edwina. 'Something to bring them to their senses.'

Still Gus came obediently down to have his face examined. Flo was pleased to see he was wearing one of Agnes's straw hats.

'You're going a nice tomato colour now,' Flo remarked. 'Won't you be going back to your job?'

'I've resigned,' Gus replied. 'It was only selling insurance. I rang and told them I didn't think I was suited and they agreed. I tried selling Edwina a life policy and she just snorted. Agnes thinks I should go to varsity in March.'

'She would,' said Flo ominously

The previous evening Agnes had got down an ancient and thin volume about beekeeping and translated some of it:

They know a native country, are sure of heart and home.
Aware that winter is coming, they use the summer days
For work, and put their winnings into a common pool.

But Edwina preferred

Unbounded then is the rage of the bees, provoked they breathe
Venom into their stabs, they cling to your veins and bury
Their stings — oh yes, they put their whole souls into the wound

Then she turned to Gus and asked him how he liked the image of the self-immolating bee.

'Sparta, that's what it reminds me of,' piped up Agnes before Gus could think of a reply.

'It has nothing to do with Sparta, nothing at all. No one could call a bee Spartan,' snapped Edwina.

'Do you mean it has to do with my sunburn?' Gus asked.

'In a way, yes. A necessary suffering. A turning point. For

the bee I've always felt it was a decision. To sting *and* die.'

'Float like a butterfly, sting like a bee,' quoted Gus, contributing at last.

After the apple trees Gus started on the borders, forking out couch grass, plunging the tines in a circumference around the old roses, then kneeling to fine-weed in the gloves forced on him by Edwina. The backs of his hands were a fading pink and had been anointed as often as his face. Sometimes Gus felt he had received the last rites of some primitive religion or that his proud and swollen flesh was actually a mask behind which he was being reborn. Like any pupa he felt vulnerable and uncertain if the next stage in his development would occur. Sometimes he forced his mind to go back over his sighting of Lise to try to figure out if there was another sheet-shrouded figure behind. Her aggression still seared him and he wondered why he had accepted it as a command. For surely he had been on his way to the sea when he collapsed? A vague memory of drinking in several bars en route, of being thrown viciously out of one, of a hot-dog stand somewhere, faintly stirred.

'How's it going?' Agnes called. 'Could you handle another muffin?'

Gus's parents were in Florence, visiting the Uffizi Gallery. Their room in the Hotel La Scarletta overlooked the Boboli Gardens. The tour they had chosen — off-season, good hotels, short day tours and evenings free to dine — was proving ideal. So far the highlight for Gus's mother, Joy, had been a ride in a gondola with a singing gondolier. The way the gondolier braced himself seemed the very epitome of manhood, though she refrained from commenting to her husband. Adrian Fancourt was running to fat around the middle and she doubted he could keep his balance in a gondola. Instead she talked longingly of the funeral gondolas that carried the swathed coffin across the lagoon to the burial island, San Michele. Adrian was amazed at such a wish, which in any case was impossible.

They had five days in Venice and Joy showed every sign of health. They ate at poky little trattoria and walked single-file through the narrow streets in which the agile Venetians passed like cats.

'Promise me, when I die, you'll do something stylish, even if I can't have a gondola.'

'Venetian music? Mandolins?' Adrian called as Joy strolled ahead. Perhaps at the conclusion of the service someone saying: 'Joy's best time was in Venice and she wanted to go out to some Venetian music. A glass of vino for anyone who likes will be served at 49 Mulholland Drive.'

So it was with something of deflation that they read Gus's postcard handed to them at the Fermo Posta.

> *Dear Olds,*
> *Broken off with Lise and left job. Got a bit sunburnt but recovering with two old ducks. Nothing to worry about. How's the winter of your lives going?*
> *Gus*
> *PS Wouldn't mind a decent camera.*

When Gus made no attempt to move on, Edwina and Agnes held a conference. This was Edwina's word for sitting at the cleared dining-room table without the distraction of coffee or biscuits. Agnes had once protested the word 'conference', saying it implied far more participants, but Edwina said Agnes knew what she meant. Both sat with their hands clasped.

'Do you think Gus is a ne'er do well?' was Edwina's first question.

Agnes, resenting the fact there were not two hundred other delegates to raise their hands, did not reply.

'Come on,' Edwina snapped. 'You must have an opinion.'

But there were so many subjects on which Agnes had no opinion at all, or a scarcely formed one. The beginning of an opinion does not necessarily warrant speech.

'He's been good in the garden,' Agnes offered finally. 'The apple trees are a revelation.'

'But why doesn't he want to move on?' Edwina asked. 'He has to support himself somehow. He's earning his keep here, certainly . . .'

But Edwina too seemed at a loss. Was Gus addicted to cinnamon and apple muffins, was he working his way through some private grief, did he imagine himself the gardener to two old Lady Chatterleys?

'We must have it out with him,' Edwina decided, pushing her chair back. 'We should have included him in this conversation.'

But Gus did not come when Edwina called from the kitchen window and Agnes walked through the apple orchard, which was how she now thought of it. Even the moss seemed to be receding along the truncated limbs.

Gus in fact was walking along the shoreline where a stone wall separated a narrow, shell-encrusted ribbon of sand from lush grass. Sitting with his back against the wall he knew he was invisible to the two old dears, who were probably summoning him to yet another muffin. If only he hadn't overpraised the first offering.

Edwina and Agnes would have been surprised to learn that Gus hardly differentiated between them, seeing them as a species, like dinosaurs. He was glad of their shelter of course and had become uncommonly fond of his small verandah bedroom at the back of the house. Its walls were an unusual soft shade of green, like the leaves of the lasiandra tree, and with branches waving against his windows he felt enclosed and protected.

But now, looking across the bay, admittedly tame, he knew he must make plans. For a wild moment he toyed with evicting the tenants in his parents' gracious home and doing their garden in repayment. Then he reflected they probably had some watertight contract. Or he could dress himself up as a tramp and knock at the back door and ask for victuals. Perhaps they'd offer him a slice of bread from the kauri breadbin with its rolled top like a writing desk. Would Towser, the family dog, recognise him though? The new tenants were in love with Towser, his mother wrote, so they had not sent him to kennels.

Why are you mourning so much? an inner voice asked, and he knew — watching a family laden with hampers, fishing rods, life jackets, clamber aboard a launch — that to be the crux. He watched the little dinghy bobbing behind, trying to make out what it meant, until it and the launch were out of sight.

I'll give myself a month, he thought, watching another boat come in, as if to replace the one that had just embarked. Again the tiny dinghy bobbed behind, like an offering to the sea, for surely it could not carry the two huge men who leapt into the shallow water. Lise was such a boat. A boat that passed in the night, he thought wryly. It was not Lise so much, though he could still smell her hair, tinged with a faintly astringent piney shampoo, and its contrast with the damp dough-like smell of their bodies as they lay tangled in sheets twisted like corkscrews. But bed sheets brought back a memory that still felt like a blow. Only the fists were growing smaller and the derisive voice was being lost on the wind.

Digging what was to be the kitchen garden, though up until now neither Edwina nor Agnes had possessed such a thing, took up most of a day. Agnes brought him a muffin on a tray and a mug of coffee.

'Where does "kitchen garden" come from?' she mused.

'From the Middle Ages, I expect,' Gus replied. 'Wherever there was a kitchen window to open and bellow for turnips.'

'And the herb garden, that would be further away?'

'More like a field.' The conversation was ludicrous because neither knew anything. 'You wouldn't like this bed raised?' Gus went on. 'It would be much easier for you and Edwina after I've gone. It would save a lot of bending.'

'Oh, you're not thinking of leaving,' Agnes said. 'Not soon, I hope.'

And Edwina, who had joined them, quite forgot the conference and mentioned taking out some rose bushes. She had read in a book borrowed from the library that the life of a rose bush may be as short as ten years.

Autumn was coming, and for Gus's parents, now in Vienna, signs of spring amid the chocolate shops, the chilly terraces on which they sipped coffee with kirsch. Daffodils and chocolates are natural bedfellows, Joy thought: they are both too rich to digest.

'Should we offer Gus his room back?' she asked Adrian as they walked arm in arm in the Prater.

'We should have brought Towser,' he said, as they passed wealthy Viennese women tugging small dogs in liveried coats. 'No, Gus must make his own way in the world. Besides, I thought you liked having another guest room?'

'I do,' said Joy. 'And it's not as if he can't call on us in an emergency, is it?'

When Adrian didn't reply she slipped a hand into his coat pocket, plunging it down until it reached the lining where her fingers located a button, a dry-cleaning stub and a single foil-wrapped square of Toblerone.

Agnes had sewn curtains for the verandah room, thinking such an area of glass needed insulation. She had taken pains with the fabric: a green not quite identical to the walls — Agnes in her youth had been a promising watercolourist and knew the behaviours of colours. She lined the curtains with calico and hung them while Gus was visiting Flo.

Flo too was concerned at the young man's seeming reluctance to move on.

'Perhaps he'd just like to stay for the winter,' Agnes suggested. 'While he gets himself together.'

Edwina had just snorted at this unaccustomed jargon but she took the precaution of drawing up a list of outdoor chores, including the ambitious one of building a new garden shed.

Dr Fitz had called and summed up the situation in a practical fashion: 'What used to be a term of bed rest or a sanatorium. Only now it's called time out.' Still he cautioned Edwina, whom he credited with having the most marbles, to set some unstated limit. 'Autumn leads to winter,' he said, standing at the kitchen bench, like some Roman poet.

'So you think spring,' said Edwina.

'No later than spring.'

'Care to put it on a prescription, Fitz?'

'No, just a word to the wise.'

Flo, undoubtedly briefed, offered her camellia hedge to trim. At first Gus demurred: he liked camellias. Fitz's lawnmower needed attention.

The Labours of Gus Edwina wrote, and pinned them by the

fridge. And Agnes got out Virgil again and left a charm under Gus's pillow.

O formose puer, nimium ne crede colori.*

His fresh face, new-skinned, was fortunate in being shielded from the moon.

---

* *Don't bank too much on your complexion, lovely boy.*
Virgil (Publius Vergilius Maro) 70–19 BC. Eclogues no. 2, l.60

&
Big Bertha

WIMP. THE WORD sounds in Bertha's head and then, like a splinter of bamboo inserted into food, it goes further. It penetrates her blood stream, it cruises dangerously close to her heart. She can feel her heart beating, taking on another word burden. *I don't love you, I wish you'd get off my case, out of my face, get a life.* And now *wimp*. Not a crisp word, Bertha decides. Or if it has any backbone in it, it's like one of those fried noodles, stiffened by immersion in hot oil. *You don't drive any more, you can't fix a fuse, you're scared to get up on the roof, you take taxis. Wimp*: the worm that gives up and dies.

But Bertha does rescue worms. Sometimes she thinks that her salvation — if any such exists — may depend on it. A worm will tip the scales. A worm resting on her naked palm and wiggling and tickling, or warmed by a woollen glove. Worms flushed onto concrete from grass verges, worms trying to fit their soft selves to the jet-like brilliance of the wet macadam. Last week she picked up one that wiggled so much against her palm and poked its snout between her fingers that she had to release it under a bush in a neighbour's garden. But normally she gets home, lifts the dried fern that forms a protective cover around her special bulbs and slips the worm under that. No, Bertha is decidedly not a wimp with worms.

Bertha goes to the bookshelf and gets out the dictionary she bought last month, *Collins Concise Dictionary, the only dictionary you will ever need*. It cost $39.95 on special and until now she has considered it a bargain. Hasn't she found in it *John of Gaunt* and *gallimaufry*, Jane Austen's birthdate. She has flicked through her favourite letter, *z*, and touched a finger to *zambuck* and *zeugma*, *Zeuxis*, a Greek painter, *ziggurat* and the last word of all *zymurgy = the branch of chemistry concerned with fermentation processes in brewing*.

But now she turns slowly to *wimp = a feeble ineffective person* and its children *wimpish* or *wimpy*. Her eye slides down past *wimple = a piece of cloth draped around the head to frame the face, worn by women in the Middle Ages and still worn by some nuns* to *wimp out = to fail to do or complete something through fear or lack of conviction*. It's as if, for a short space, the dictionary itself is in a funk.

Why be upset by a word, Bertha tells herself, when there are so many? Not all words are created equal; some have distasteful burdens which they wish other words would carry. A sweet sound cannot compensate for a sour meaning; a harsh sound may hide pure gold. But she felt her son's word was chosen, as if he had quickly scoured an inventory — limited as that might be, for Paul was no reader — and scored a bullseye. For once Paul had found the right word. *You don't drive any more, you can't fix a fuse, you're scared to get up on the roof, you take taxis . . .* these were Paul's definitions. No, she would not consider each of them in turn, recognising them as feebler, ill-sorted, hardly illustrating his point. *A feeble ineffective person* was what she had to deal with.

Bertha took herself out into the garden, leaving the dishes in the sink. Her hands shook a little and were consoled by the feel of her dirt-encrusted plastic-sprigged gloves. She remembered the hollyhocks she had inserted her fingers into as a child playing on their farm. One hollyhock sheath for each finger. How silky they felt sliding on. One day she would go to dances and wear long evening gloves.

But that was a time when she believed in fairies and rings of toadstools, in presences that vanished in a puff of dust, as when you trod on a puffball. She saw herself, unsentimentally, holding a dandelion clock close to her face, blowing and counting.

In reality Bertha Billington was a dumpy full-breasted woman like a little pigeon. She was strong, firm for all her plumpness and, except when she lapsed into foxgloves, realistic.

So what had gone wrong? She tried to think about it as she weeded a segment of her herbaceous border, lifting oxalis from the base of an azalea and filling her gloves with dead leaves. Why should her son, for whom she had laboured on kindergarten committees, Home and School, even the board of his high school, suddenly regard her as a wimp?

It was true she had not replaced her car after a bad accident and a defensive driving course had left her uneasy. 'I'll walk,' she decided. She was thinking of her figure, frightened she might turn out like her aunts who in their fifties had thickened into a strange sexlessness like slab cake.

But in fact Bertha had become used to taking taxis. She liked the idea of someone being at her beck and call; she liked chattering to the driver or alternately sitting in silence as though some great sorrow preoccupied her. 'Have a good evening,' they would say as she got out, and she would return the wish to them, knowing her evening would be sedate. In fact Bertha hardly had evenings at all. She had bed and a fat book, at least five hundred pages, to last a week. No matter if she fell asleep in the middle of it, since such books were always overwritten. After a time Bertha did not think of replacing her car at all. 'Home?'

the taxi despatcher would say, and Bertha would respond with a laugh, 'Yes, home.'

And when it came to holidays Bertha was likewise stymied. It was strange that the garden brought these truths to mind, as if the soil yielded them. Her job at the Education Centre now entitled her to a month's leave a year. Teachers came and went like swallows on the first day of summer break or even, pleading extenuating circumstances, a few days before. They went to India, the Andes, carnival in Rio; they backpacked like nostalgic hippies through the youth hostels of Europe. Even the quietest went to the Lake District or joined a Vampire tour of London.

'Give my regards to Dijon,' Bertha would call. 'Drink some Beaujolais nouveau for me.' She had been to London once and seen the posters announcing the new vintage, though she didn't try it.

Sometimes Bertha pored over snapshots: Miss Foley and Miss Filbee in front of the Leaning Tower of Pisa, Miss Filbee attempting a lean in the same direction, Miss Foley laughing and clutching a straw hat as if she expected the breeze to be oddly angled. Or Dr Wunsch's beautifully focused and crystal-clear shots of alpine flowers for which Bertha knew he crawled on his stomach and made a frame with his hands.

Bertha's own holidays, which did not coincide with the teachers', for the Centre remained open all year, were spent in a small private hotel in Auckland. At least they had been spent that way for eight years until one morning, returning to her accustomed room to collect an umbrella, she overheard one of the chambermaids refer to her as an old bag. 'I can't think why the old bag comes, can you?' a voice called to someone bent over the basin giving it a quick wipe.

Bertha had paused in the doorway and then gone resolutely in. At least the chambermaid, for whom Bertha always left a generous tip taped to the mirror, had the grace to blush. She left the same tip that year, at the end of her week, but she never returned. The following year, when a note came from the manager, she didn't reply.

After that Bertha began to go to conferences associated with her work. She could not abide a holiday without a purpose. She joined Miss Foley and Miss Filbee at a Drama in the School Curriculum conference and wondered if she could dramatise her own staid job. Miss Filbee started waving her hands about more as she spoke. Bertha went to night classes on Chaucer and the Elizabethans. She felt consoled to learn that life expectancy in the Middle Ages was twenty-eight years for women.

All these thoughts go through Bertha's head as she weeds. She thinks she can perceive a wimpishness: the not returning to the hotel or replying to the manager, the taxis that had replaced a private car, the conferences, the classes. But the seeds of wimpishness go back far further, into her widowhood and her solitary failed affair. It was even there in the financial lectures she had given her son, 'laying her cards on the table', as she called it, when economies were necessary. For was she not really saying 'Protect me'? And his taunt of wimpishness, might it not have arisen then?

Bertha goes inside and runs a hot deep bath. On an impulse she empties a sachet of Epsom salts into the steaming water, said to be good for removing impurities.

In the weeks following, Bertha consulted brochures. Ballooning, whitewater rafting, bungy jumping, abseiling, walking tours with rudimentary accommodation. She watched a television programme in which a person was lowered into an inaccessible valley on a long rope. The guide descended as well, parallel, so they could chat. The valley was of an extraordinary beauty, a

Garden of Eden. How the guide and the abseiler got out was not explained. Perhaps, thought Bertha, they picnicked together or went into the woods to make love. Ballooning appealed more, but only the week before a balloon had come down in the sea and a young woman drowned. Yards of golden silk spread out on the water and the rescuers battled with it like dressmakers. Whitewater rafting depended on an ability to have the face immersed, and Bertha always swam with her head out, a breaststroker pose attached to a crawl. And if the raft suddenly flipped, which seemed all too likely, the scramble in the rushing torrent would be formidable.

Once, at a conference in which she had skipped a session, Bertha had witnessed a crowded jetboat skirling about a jetty accompanied by screams and laughter. The pilot had raised his fist in a salute, and the boat had pivoted like a dancer and rushed back up the river, charging at and just avoiding the banks. Bertha stood with a cameraman attired in the company uniform, who handed her his card. Then he leapt into his car and rushed off to get the films developed.

And bungy jumping. The very thought makes Bertha shiver. Trussed by the ankles, then flung down and out into space, back snapping like a wet flag, eyeballs straining from their sockets, arms flung out in a diving position or an Olympian's salute. And afterwards the amazement, the emblazoned tee shirt, the miraculous garrulous confidence. Bertha had read that you could be photographed there as well, in the last seconds like a condemned man, then flying into space like a bird. Could anyone be a wimp if they bungy jumped?

A fat worm wiggles on Bertha's palm as she quickens her pace up the hill. She looks for a patch of earth into which to place it, but the nearest garden is edged with concrete terraces. Resolutely she goes on, dropping her bags on the path and lifting a leaf to place it under. Bertha always thinks ahead, to the watchful bird spying from a tree: the leaf is a roof and a chance to burrow. Just the same this worm has caused Bertha to shiver slightly. She picks up her bags and goes inside to wash her hands and make a cup of tea.

Today, instead of the dictionary, Bertha picks up a volume of the Everyman encyclopaedia. Unwittingly she has selected the volume that contains Bertha, if any Berthas worthy of containment exist. *Bertha, Big*, she reads, *see Big Bertha. Big Bertha, nickname given to the specially prepared long-range German naval gun (or guns) which fired on Paris from the neighbourhood of Coucy a distance of 75 miles during the First World War.*

Bertha pours more tea and imagines herself shot from the mouth of a cannon. Bertha and Big Bertha. The cannon would need a wide mouth and its barrel would have to conceal substantial curves. Bertha's hips are wide and she could easily become stuck. The lighting of the fuse and the spectacular bang, Bertha surmises, are a ruse. It is one of those events where the landing is never shown, only the trajectory. Her white spangled outfit, body-hugging, her tiny starfish-shaped hands, rigidly pointed in prayerful flight. But where does she land?

Bertha consults Miss Foley and Miss Filbee about their August holidays. They are going to Italy. Rome, Perugia, Florence. 'See Naples and die?' queries Bertha, but no, not Naples. Too poor, too much washing strung out between the tenements. Miss Foley has never got used to capacious knickers waving in the breeze for all the world to see.

'I think I might go on a walking holiday,' Bertha offers, though neither Miss Foley nor Miss Filbee enquires. 'Something a bit rugged, good for the figure.'

Neither Miss Foley nor Miss Filbee responds. It's as though they haven't heard.

Now the words are out, Bertha spends part of her lunch break at a travel agent. She had not realised there are so many alternatives. For is not walking a simple activity? There are tours where the participants are as laden as packhorses and probably barely able to raise their heads, where they sleep in communal huts with the cold ashes of someone else's fire and where the tin opener does not work. Then there are the moderately civilised: hard walking by day with aching feet and smelly socks but a guesthouse to stay in with clean sheets and a substantial breakfast to start the day. Finally there are the glamour tours: easy strolls in the bush, a little gentle climbing and the luggage carried forward by launch. And at the end of the day a lovely hotel, someone's private mansion with white verandahs and sloping lawns, rose bushes and individual bedrooms. Bertha sees this hotel quite clearly; she sees herself reaching down to unlace her boots and to feel her feet gingerly for blisters. Of course muddied boots will not be permitted in such a house; there will be an annexe for wet-weather gear and light packs. And on the morrow, mysteriously, the packs will be filled with a delicious lunch.

Bertha selects a tour to the Sounds that includes moderately demanding walks with a guide, a comfortable bed and hot dinner at night, generous showering and laundry facilities, plain but well-maintained accommodation.

'I hope it's not too Spartan,' she says to the travel agent. 'Not that I want to be a wimp.'

'I understand it's very pleasant,' the girl replies, but then perhaps she says that about Naples or Calcutta.

'I want to stretch myself a little,' says Bertha, aware of the contradiction of her figure, the hips that have grown more box-like over the winter, the bosom that is winning its wish to roll over like a fully broken wave. 'I wish to lose a few pounds.'

The young woman looks at her sceptically, thinking of the muscles tautened by tramping boots and weighing more, of the hearty appetite stirred by modest rigours. The meals at the lodges would feed an All Black. Or so she has heard. A sort of Brueghelish feasting. 'I could eat a boot.'

'I'm sure you'll enjoy it,' she repeats, pressing leaflets on Bertha of connecting flights, alternatives such as transference to a four-star hotel if the tramper breaks down. In the small print there is something about Search and Rescue and helicopter standby. The leader will carry a first-aid kit and is fully trained.

'It is important to have good socks,' she counsels Bertha finally. 'So many trampers just splash out on the boots.'

Bertha's holiday is not until September. In the intervening months she sets herself some small exercises. She goes for longer than usual walks and she searches for streets that are steep. She suspects that 'moderately demanding' is an understatement, applied by someone who has climbed Everest. She tries on tramping boots in her lunch hour and consults a colleague, Peter van Dillen. Peter has long soft girlish hair and a nose stud but his body is like hard wood. He reminds Bertha of a centaur.

In the privacy of her bedroom Bertha does knee bends, stretches and touches her toes. She raises her hands to the ceiling, feeling her bust lift on underutilised muscles. The XBX Plan lies on the bedspread. She turns the little bedside radio to a music station as she jumps and runs on the spot. She finishes off with some half-remembered yoga exercises from three winters ago: the pose of the hero, the tree. Finally she lies flat on the floor, breathing diaphragmatically, feeling her breath like speech: statement and response, a choir inside a ribcage. Paul comes home and finds her in the corpse pose and she has to spring to her feet to prevent him dialing 111.

Now that her son has calmed himself and departed, Bertha takes out the book she has borrowed from the library on the Krupps. She is curious about the woman who gave her name to the gun, Bertha Krupp von Bohlen und Halbach. There is a photo of Bertha in the book: she stands at a slight angle to the photographer so one arm is hidden. An ostrich-feather boa conceals the elbow of the arm that curves against her stomach. Her face tends to length, her eyes are serious and deep, her nose a little large, her mouth soft but fuzzed. Her bust, Bertha notes with sympathy, is full and deep and accentuated by a crossover sash.

Clearly Bertha Krupp is voluptuous. She is also very good, because the final chapter contains a tribute to her character. *The way in which she performed her duties as wife and mother appealed to the workers at Krupps. Even those who had never seen her in her domestic environment knew what a good manager she must be and were sure that she remembered where every stick of furniture was, that she went from one of the many rooms to another carrying her bunch of keys . . .* There is no mention of a gun being named after her. Was it a name applied by enemies, the recipients of the 200-lb shells?

Bertha goes to the wardrobe and takes out the new tracksuit she has bought for the tramping trip. She runs her hands down her ribcage where she can still feel bone; she takes a deep swelling breath and her bosom strains like a ship stuck on a bar. Her hips cause her hands to change direction: her hips posit the horizontal. Bertha cannot get a good view of her back, which is a mercy. She will buy another tracksuit to complement this. Suddenly she thinks Bertha Krupp might have been the victim of cartoons.

BIG BERTHA

On the first evening of the tramp Bertha sinks into a comfortable narrow bed in a tiny room at the Bushwalkers' Rest. Her pack and boots, cleaned and freshly packed, lie at the foot of the bed, her socks hang over the radiator. Bertha, when she booked, paid extra for a single room. She curls under the duvet and pulls her long flannelette nightdress, two sizes larger than Bertha, around her toes. The hotel is eerily still after the various door-shuttings and coughs and gurgles of running water have died away. Just before she sleeps Bertha remembers something about Bertha von Krupp. In the year of her wedding her mother had said to her: *The fear that all this may one day collapse oppresses me like a nightmare. But I believe that I have brought up my daughters in such a way that they will be able to withstand the hardest blows of fate.* Bertha stretches her legs inside their cocoon of flannelette and thinks she will survive tomorrow, which includes 'an ascent moderately taxing but with splendid views and more rest stops'.

The next morning they wake to a grey drizzle. Bertha sips her tea and wishes she could sink back, wimp-like, against the pillows. Could she plead a headache? Or send herself a fake telegram: URGENT MATTERS REQUIRE YOUR ATTENTION. PLEASE RETURN IMMEDIATELY. But there is no telegraph office in the bush, only these nightly hamlets, well lit and smelling of soup and roast meat.

Bertha has attached herself to a solitary man in the group; the rest are couples, ranging from honeymooners to a pair celebrating their silver wedding anniversary. The honeymooners bound ahead, giving the first intelligence of a lookout or the next guesthouse. Bertha and the wiry taciturn man bring up the rear. As they tramp along there is the accompanying sound of a river somewhere below, and Bertha's thoughts turn to worms.

'I rescue worms,' she confides to her companion whose gaze is straight ahead. He hardly ever speaks.

When he doesn't respond she describes the feeling of a worm on her palm and how she hastens up the street, thinking of a burial place. 'I think of them as submarines,' Bertha says. 'Diving for safety before the birds come.'

In the evening Bertha addresses a card to Miss Foley and Miss Filbee. *Today's tramp was harder*, she writes, *but I feel fitter. Almost attached now to my tramping boots and wet socks. Tomorrow will be mainly descent: new muscles to ache. I believe descent is harder.* Bertha marvels that walking has so concentrated her egotism. Will the Misses F retaliate with *Today we walked from the Trevi Fountain to the Forum.*

Bertha's room this evening is larger, with a faded chintz bedspread and a wicker chair. Her book, *The Blessings of a Good Thick Skirt: women travellers and their world*, lies at the foot of her bed, unopened. She thinks of the pleasurable ache in her muscles and the stretches the team leader leads them in each morning before they shoulder their packs. Yesterday they did these stretches on the gravel driveway, making crunching sounds like the cracking of bones. And Bertha had evaded the silent man and walked all day with two married couples. For a few hours she concentrated happily on her own increased vigour and the scenery, each item of which, seen with lifted head – massive tree, ridge, or glimpse of lake water — has contributed to it. You can't eat scenery, a voice says in her head, but another voice answers: You can. Scenery is fuel.

On the last day of the tramp, before the group breaks up and is dispersed by strategically placed cars or more plebian buses, they come to a great viaduct. It arches above a deep green river. So far above that the river seems the width of a ribbon.

'Shall we take a look?' the guide asks. 'We're making exceptional progress today.'

BIG BERTHA

On top of the viaduct Bertha can see small figures. Others notice them too. Then suddenly a cotton thread shoots out and hovers on the air, before tightening itself into a plumb line. There is a weight at the end like a sack.

'Bungy jumping,' the guide says. 'The most exhilarating experience on the planet.'

The little group follows him up a disused road. So the prisoners march to their execution, Bertha thinks. The climb is steeper than any they have tackled, and the viaduct disappears, then comes into sight again, closer and larger. Another figure, briefly cosseted, falls, and a scream echoes and dies.

Bertha is walking behind the honeymooners whose arms automatically entwine. She doesn't know why she keeps close to them unless love is a protection of some kind. They climb a final ridge and here straight ahead is the bridge with real-sized people, more than appeared at a distance: there even seems to be a queue. And the next victim is definitely being consoled and led back from the edge, sobbing because her nerve has deserted her.

'Let's do it,' Bertha hears the honeymooners say. 'Let's do it together.'

And now the failed girl is standing on the little platform again, tears dried, face set like flint.

'The jump master,' one of the honeymooners whispers.

'Keep your eyes on the horizon. I'm going to count you down. On the word *Bungy* let yourself fall into a dive.'

The little group of trampers stands silently at the bridge's approach, pressed behind the male honeymooner. Horatio at the bridge.

'5,4,3,2,1,' the watchers chant, and on the word *Bungy* the young girl falls, arms flung out, hopelessly unable to touch the horizon, crying at the impossibility of it. At least Bertha thinks she hears a cry, sucked riverwards by the wind. The rope twists on the air like a knotted gut. Peering cautiously down, Bertha can see the rubber dinghy and a man standing up in it. The body bounces up before it makes contact with his stretching hands.

The little group on the bridge breaks into applause. Below in the green ribbon, inside the yellow boat, the young girl seems to be raising her arms. The two honeymooners approach the tour guide and ask if there is time for them to jump.

'Only if we can do it in tandem though.'

Tweedledum and Tweedledee, thinks Bertha. Then: *One is one and one all alone and ever more shall be so.*

'Me too,' she hears herself saying. 'I'd like to bungy as well.'

One of the honeymooners twines an outside arm around Bertha's shoulders.

'Do you want to go first or second?'

Wimp Bertha thinks to herself. And *Bertha von Krupp, Big Bertha*, the gun that pounded Paris, she'll be flying 75 miles. She thinks of her advantages of heavy bust, belljar hips. She doesn't speak to the jump master or say a single word after claiming a place. She thinks *God speed* as the honeymooners fall together, eyes and ankles secured, each other's beating heart a spar. Bertha doesn't hear the terms that are meant to console: Calibration set, Karabiner locked on, Top systems check, Rigging check, Jump systems are secure. To each question of the jump master she nods, with compressed lips. She checks her cheeks are truly flint that the wind shall force further against bone. She steps onto the little platform, holds the far cliff and skyline as if it is a tightrope. Worm is her last word.

At the bottom of the boat Bertha lies like a deflated parcel. But her mouth grins and her eyes sparkle.

'You jumped well,' says the young man who undoes the harness. 'You really launched yourself like a bird.'

'Or a jet plane,' says Bertha, wonderingly, as they help her up.

The honeymooners are sitting on the grass, sharing a flask. They beckon Bertha over.

'There'll be a photo,' they tell her. 'So you can prove it.'

That night, the last of her holiday, Bertha sleeps in a little attic room. A vast lawn stretches in front of the old house, the verandahs are coiled with budding wisteria vines. Even the silent man has gone out of his way to speak to Bertha; the guide insists she sit by him at dinner. But when she is questioned about it, Bertha lowers her eyes. *The life she had was never an easy one. It was no pleasure to her to have to provide for guests every day, even to have to play with her children with one eye on the clock and to try to fit in a little time to herself among her endless social duties. It was only an unusual facility for self-denial that enabled her in such circumstances to reduce inevitable friction to a minimum.*

When she is finally alone, and has evaded the silent man's offer of a nightcap, Bertha re-lives the moment in the jump when she had lost all control. It was before she bounced up again as though plucked by a string. It was true she had sailed at first, an orderly shape. She had nothing to lose by leaping out. But she fell into fear and that fear lasted an interminable time. She had to submit to it: there was nothing else to do. Then, upside down, she looked into the glassy surface of the river and saw the dinghy. She had the photos to prove it in her handbag for Paul.

As Bertha sleeps, something like a declension goes through her mind to be translated into dreams: Fall, Fear, Held.

&

The Pulley

THE COSTUMES FOR Annie Pigtails and Falldown were hanging at the end of a rack in the ballet dressing room which was a long low room under the orchestra pit. Two girls' sailor suits with huge piped collars and dark blue calf-length pleated skirts under which dark stockings and black ballet shoes peeked out. Eloise's own pigtails were too short, so each evening, not trusting the dresser who was a harried woman, she had her mother entwine the artificial pigtails, stiffened with wire, into her own thick flaxen ones. Or to be correct, one, for Eloise's hair was parted unevenly into one fat substantial plait and one thin. But it was as useless trying to change the lie of her hair as expecting grass to grow at a different angle.

Eloise had no idea she was going to be Annie Pigtails, a cameo dance role warranting her name on the programme: she was part of the ballet. It was the producer, the formidable Miss Isadora Valavil, who had plucked her from there during rehearsals simply by pointing a long white finger in the manner of a witchdoctor. It was a day on which Eloise was in a dream. They were dancing in a circle, twirling and tossing their heads and looking over their shoulders. Over her shoulder Eloise glimpsed a steely dark eye fastened for a second on hers.

The dancer chosen to be Falldown was signally displeased

and protested, but Eloise lowered her eyes modestly when it was explained to her that she would have a small part.

'But I can still dance in the ballet?' she wanted to know.

'Of course. Except you'll have a few more costume changes, that's all.'

Dancing in the ballet was not proving as pleasurable as she expected: there were lifts required from males who had never danced before and themselves been press-ganged from the chorus. Eloise's partner, Hans, was Dutch, and his feet seemed to end in clogs. They disliked one another from the start. At the end of one number with the whole company on stage Eloise was expected to be lifted onto his shoulder and doubted they would make it. Every time she expected them to crash to the floor.

But as Annie Pigtails, spared from competition from Falldown who invariably fell before she could create any impression, Eloise had a perfect little character role. That it made no sense for a full-grown cowboy to be stirred by a pair of pubescent sailor girls who were precocious flirts hardly mattered. Annie and Falldown were simply satellites, like the moons of Jupiter. 'Like a pair of eye dogs,' was her brother's comment after the first night and Eloise, whose flirting had improved, aimed a fist at him, the fist she regularly shook at the luckless Hans.

During her two weeks, extended to three by popular demand, Eloise fell in love with the theatre. Not the rehearsal rooms which resembled a church hall and gave no impression of how each segment would look on a real stage, but the venerable old theatre in the town's centre, overdue for refurbishment but still complete like a child's elaborate toy. The great wide and deep stage on which she and Hans might crash among the flats; the massive moth-eaten curtain in burnished gold with bobbles; the sinister fire curtain behind it; finally, looking up, as if into constellations, a towering space of pulleys and iron rungs where, most miraculously of all, awaited the scenes to come. Eloise could distinguish a wide cornfield — 'the corn is as high as an elephant's eye'; the front of a cute little house with roses twining on the verandah; a picnic site with a barn, an outdoor stage and a drawn-up wagon.

It was the smell of the theatre though that impressed most. Dust, aeons of dust, it seemed, and electrifying tension that waited in the wings, the clopping of pointe shoes as they rattled up the wooden stairs to be inserted ceremoniously in the resin box. The glimpses inside dressing rooms where greasepaint wafted out, temperaments were frayed and a row of hot lights illuminated every pore. Lines of chorus faces being worked over by a make-up team, the frantic running with needle and thread. The nerves infected by other nerves, the lucky rabbit's paw, the bottle of brandy stashed in a hatbox: Eloise loved it all.

Best of all was the spotlight. It trained on Annie and Falldown as they sidled in from stage right, walking on the balls of their feet like poodles, not flirting yet but looking as if they might at any moment. The spot beamed down on them, heavenly . . .

> *When God at first made man,*
> *Having a glass of blessings standing by;*
> *Let us (said he) poure on him all we can:*
> *Let the worlds riches, which dispersed lie,*
> *Contract into a span.*

Eloise's family came to the first night: mother, father, brother. She begged them not to, but they considered she needed support. She dreaded the remarks of her brother, who was studying agriculture. He might say something like, 'I've seen a better-looking sheep.' The leading lady had tight woolly curls. Or make some remarks about the cowboys, most of whom were bank clerks or builders. But as she stood in the wings with Falldown, who was nursing a sore ankle — falling down was not as easy as it looked — Eloise reflected that the faces in the audience were only a blur: a dark grey amorphous mass to be wooed. And once you were on stage, to be overlooked in favour of eyes and expression directed towards the gods. 'Eyes toward the gods,' Miss Valavil had commanded at rehearsal. 'Lift your heads.' Eloise kept her head lifted extra high that night so if her brother saw anything it would be the underside of her chin.

'Little snot face,' he said afterwards. 'The world's haughtiest midget.'

By the middle of the first week Eloise felt she had lived in the theatre all her life. Each evening, after a light snack prepared by her mother and with an apple and barley sugars packed into her little suitcase, she entered the theatre by an alley lit by a single bulb. That the alley was practically invisible to the ordinary passerby gave Eloise an odd pleasure. So must secret societies and hooded figures vanish through walls. Once inside an equally unpromising door which led up to the stage or down to the dressing rooms she breathed in deeply as if the air was perfumed. She hung her coat on a peg and seated herself in front of a dressing-room mirror to examine her face. The strong naked bulbs cast no fear as they did for some ladies of the chorus. The bland surface of Eloise's face, outlined by a headband, awaited her ministrations with cold cream, no. 5 and no. 9, carmine and loose powder. Under and above each eyelid a black line appeared, while in the corner of the eye a red dot was fastened with a matchstick. By the time Falldown appeared — she was always late — to share the other half of the mirror, Eloise alias Annie was almost done.

Then Eloise would go and sit in the greenroom where the chorus were milling about and infuriated cries and tantrums could be heard from doors to which a paper star was stuck. The leading lady demanded someone else to do her make-up; a costume whose lining was full of shark-like tucks split and had to be hastily repaired. Eloise's next costume when she was part of the ballet hung ready on a peg: a soft blue scooped-neck dress with matching bonnet with tulle and ribbons. Or she might creep up the stairs and stand in the wings watching the lighting crew or the scene shifters or props with their table laid out with a birdcage and stuffed bird, a parasol, a pistol, a lariat. The call boys rushed about importantly with their lists, banging on doors from which issued groans. Sometimes an understudy had to be called upon, but that was rare: a star meant star quality. And Eloise, at a certain point in the evening, tried to think herself into the part of Annie Pigtails: a girl she saw as vivacious and daring, a natural-born flirt but a conservative who would probably grow up to be just like her mother.

From the moment they sidled on, giggling together, and the spotlight took them up as if to say, 'Here's where the action is, folks, something's going to happen here,' they became part of the great design of the story. Richard Rodgers and Oscar Hammerstein II must have bent over their piano and pencil and said: What we need here are two little pubescent flirts. Make that sailor costumes, like young women who are dressed as girls by their mothers. A lot of men go for that sort of thing. Will Parker probably doesn't know he does. Ado Annie will suss it right away. It's a family show, so one of them can fall down, showing that a grown man in love won't buy it. And Rodgers would have struck a few notes on the piano and Hammerstein struck his teeth with a yellow pencil and another page would have got done.

'Annie, Will and Falldown centre stage,' Miss Valavil commanded, viewing them through her eyeglass. 'He's only a country boy. Try to drive him distracted.'

So strength first made a way;
Then beautie flow'd, then wisdome, honour, pleasure:
When almost all was out, God made a stay,
Perceiving that alone of all his treasure
Rest in the bottome lay.

Up in the gods, unknown to Eloise, her father looked down on his miraculously transformed child. Relaxed in the presence of only strangers, she seemed to him transformed: flirtatious but airy, dancing in the spotlight as if she were in repose.

It was not in Eloise's father's nature to praise, so she had no idea he had been a second time to the theatre, this time sitting in the front row of the gods, leaning over the rails and surveying the stage like an eagle. He could see Eloise as she waited in the wings, saw her clench her fists as she had from birth: she was clench-fisted in baby photos. He felt she was not in her part, however much she imagined she was; that all her imagining deserted her at a moment of entry. Falldown at her side was fretting about her first fall. Eloise had listened, quite sympathetically, while Falldown explained she was not a natural faller and had to count the falls in her head, hardly hearing the laughter that followed each one. Because of this Falldown was not nervous in the same way. Whereas Eloise, for a few frightening moments, doubted everything: the void into which she must step, her very existence. If someone had asked her what character she was playing she wouldn't have known the name. *What am I to Annie Pigtails and what is Annie Pigtails to me?*

'You'd think she was wearing the spotlight like a gold dress,' Eloise's father said to her mother, making Eloise's mother, who had had a tiring day, think of a siren in gold lamé.

'It's gone to her head, you mean? I always had my doubts about whether it was a good idea.'

'No, I think she is perfectly unaware of it. More like someone raising their face to the sun. Someone at the beach . . .'

But Eloise's mother was not mollified and was sharp with Eloise about her chores. Only two days later when Eloise was voluntarily cleaning her mother's shoes was it mentioned. And Eloise's reaction was strange too.

'She acted as though she'd been caught out,' Eloise's mother explained as she brushed her hair at her dressing table. 'Almost like a burglar.'

'I should have told her myself,' her husband replied.

> *For if I should (said he)*
> *Bestow this jewell also on my creature,*
> *He would adore my gifts in stead of me,*
> *And rest in Nature, not the God of Nature.*
> *So both should losers be.*

The next night Eloise performed very self-consciously. Even Falldown, timing her falls exceptionally and adding a tiny element of deprecation, noticed.

'I thought I was better than you tonight,' she said as they sat plunging their fingers into pots of cold cream in the dressing room.

'You were,' replied Eloise, knowing Falldown was without malice. She had felt herself grimacing not flirting with Will Parker, the tall gangling cowboy who wrapped his arms around Falldown and herself as if they were parcels. And instead of loving the spotlight as a space traveller might love an encasing beam that transports him from one world to the next, it had felt like an interrogator's lamp.

'Never mind,' said Falldown, buttoning her coat and preparing to leave. 'Tomorrow's another night.'

'Thanks,' said Eloise.

'See you, then.'

Eloise walked down the darkened alley where her father's car awaited. Night after night he came to collect her. She felt a sudden pity for him, forced to collect an actress who had failed.

> *Yet let him keep the rest,*
> *But keep them with repining restlessnesse:*
> *Let him be rich and wearie, that at least,*
> *If goodnesse leade him not, yet wearinesse*
>   *May tosse him to my breast.*

Eloise lay in her bed, face turned to the wall.

'Lie down for an hour,' her mother suggested. Eloise had eaten nothing and her head felt hot.

'A touch of temperament,' her brother murmured.

Is this how actresses feel in the middle of a run, she wondered. Seeing the nights stretching ahead of them, ceasing to believe or care. She could never be Annie Pigtails again, the pubescent flirt twirling the pleats of her sailor skirt at a cowboy grateful for any distraction. Annie who was undermined in her ambition to be a woman by Falldown in the way a melody is undermined by a bum note. Pity for poor set-up Annie caused a tear to run down Eloise's cheek.

Still, when her mother called, she got up and bathed her face in cold water and patted her eyes with a towel.

'I've put in a cake of chocolate,' her mother said.

In the car she sat silently beside her father, staring straight ahead.

'You're quiet tonight,' he said. 'Everything all right?'

'I'll be glad when it's over,' Eloise said. 'I'm getting sick of it.'

'You didn't look sick of it on Wednesday night. I thought you were wonderful. Not a child of mine, I thought. You were special on Wednesday, Eloise.'

'It's Friday,' Eloise said, looking at her hands, traditionally clenched. 'Why didn't you say?'

'I suppose I thought you'd get swollen headed. But I can see it's not that at all.'

'Ado Annie got swollen headed and lost her voice. She sang some of the songs at a café and got told off by Miss Valavil. They had an understudy for two nights.'

'But you're not Ado Annie. You're . . .'

'Annie Pigtails. You've forgotten my name already . . .'

But both knew that was false and they were protecting one another.

The car drew into the kerb, the light over the stage door beckoned, and still Eloise sat, watching a droplet of water run down the car windscreen.

'You won't get wet if you go quickly.'

A hand covered her fist and then she was gone. What was the saying: *Coming out into the spotlight, going home in the rain.*

That night Falldown almost lost her fall counts because beside her blazed the kind of pert seductive schoolgirl that almost caused Will Parker second thoughts.

&

Genealogy

NO ONE SAYS: Jane Austen, your face is turning blue, black, but your novels will grow more popular with each century and in one sample year there will be three films. Or: John Keats, you are indeed among the English poets.

Instead we go back, abandoning our own hopeful work, to ferret, generation by generation, in dust. We start with the handkerchief over the discoloured face, the lungs that dissolved. We deny that they were looking forward at all. Wilfully, as if in the presence of royalty, we walk backwards. How softly the foot slides back and the heel descends. But in this posture we face backwards too. Beginning at the deaths of others, we die in our own lives. Behind our heels we pray the door is open.

A young man came into the Genealogy and Reference Room looking for his mother. He was tall, bony, pink-skinned. His ears looked as if they were coming to a decision about their placement on his head. One was slightly higher than the other. His hands and feet knew no such inhibitions: they had steamed ahead and were enormous.

The Reference Room was glassed in and held cabinets of books, some the colour of honeycomb and very battered. The young man — his name was Clarence Downer and his age nineteen — was vaguely comforted by their appearance, sensing a value beyond battering, things written down worthy of being clasped. It was a Monday night and outside the long windows the night was blue.

'I'm trying to find my mother,' Clarence said to the librarian, who was looking at papers on her desk. She had a steady gaze designed to keep at bay thoughts of Oscar Wilde and babies left in portmanteaux at railway stations. He was too old to be a lost child, she thought, though perhaps there was no limit on maternal deprivation.

'When you say "lost" . . .'

'I'm adopted,' Clarence said, swallowing, drawing attention to his Adam's apple.

'Do your step-parents not have any information? Have they not explained?'

'They didn't want me to know I was adopted even. My stepmother's really angry. She says it's on my own head.'

That he was adopted had never occurred to Clarence Downer until the fateful day, 30 August 1982 to be precise, he received a letter. Letters were few and far between in the Downer household: an endless procession of bills had given Emily Downer an antipathy to the mail. And this letter was in a fine deckle envelope, pale blue. Emily handed it to him gingerly as if it were a discus she was about to throw. It seemed only right then to open it in front of her whose status would change in an instant.

Dear Son,
I have Parkinson's disease but before I rattle to pieces I would like us to meet. Just one meeting will suffice. The progress of the disease though slow is inexorable so do not delay too long. I . . .

Clarence lifted his eyes at this point and encountered Emily, his mother. 'Son?' he said. 'What does the old biddy mean?' For a wild second he prayed the writer of the letter was addressing the Sun, easer of aches and warmer of the afflicted.

The librarian, Alice Gray, who had been filing inserts in the *Index to the New Zealand Statutes*, gave Clarence a steady softcop gaze. It was only by keeping her eyes firmly fixed on an enquirer that she could prevent their heads turning, to the ceiling, the floor, out the window, while they murmured their request.

'Do you have your mother's date of birth?' she asked when Clarence finally settled on her face. When he looked bewildered she prompted, 'But you know your own date of birth?'

'February 11th 1967.'

'And your mother was how old when you were born?'

'I don't know,' Clarence almost wailed. 'I didn't know until yesterday that I had two mothers. I always thought the one I had was my mother. Then this letter came. Now all hell's broken loose.'

'Well it hasn't broken loose in here, not as far as I know. But you'll need to do a little detective work. I take it you have a surname.'

Yes, he had that. Bachour. Emily Downer had practically spat it at him. 'Don't ask me for more,' she warned. 'I've said too much already.'

The surname on the letter had been hard to read. The writing looked affected too, spiky and swift, as if any communication, however careless, were to be treasured. Alice Gray could have told him that such peremptory self-confidence was common to letters requesting genealogical information. Most looked as though they had seized the pen in a lover's fit. *My great-great grandfather sailed from Gravesend on the Red Rover in 1867. I wish to know at which port he disembarked. By 1888 he was rumoured to be residing in New Plymouth.* Or, *My great grandmother, nee Fawcett, related to the Fawcetts of Somerford Keynes . . .* It was the presumption of interest that unnerved and angered Alice, though she wrote back politely enough. *I regret an examination of the shipping arrivals for 1867 and 1868 does not mention your relative,* or *Miss Adeline Fawcett and Mr Thomas Edgecumbe Esquire were married at St Mary's church on 14 September 1872. I enclose a copy of the wedding notice from the Taranaki Herald.* Secretly Alice longed to scrawl in a clotting clerkish hand: *Gone no trace. Vanished from the face of the earth. Gone to ground.* Or to affix official stamps like the embarkation labels on cabin trunks. *Southampton to New Zealand. Not wanted on voyage.*

There was something about Clarence Downer, though, that attracted exasperation and compassion in equal quantities. You longed to seize his collar and pat him down, to make him tea and recommend something improving to read. To point out if he didn't take himself in hand there was the embroidered sampler of the Workhouse. Emily Downer felt this, and Alice Gray bending over *Births 1941–1948* felt it too.

Emily Downer had been more thrown by the letter in the blue envelope than she cared to admit. The scrawling signature, the looping *ll*s, overburdened with air and importance: Emily thought she could trace a trembling in the upstrokes. She went into Clarence's room and touched the few possessions on his dresser. No silver-backed brushes, no neatly folded monogrammed handkerchiefs, no shirts ordered six at a time. Her hand stroked the stained, unevenly varnished wood, lifted a box of tissues, a pair of crumpled socks which she held instinctively to her nose.

She sat on the narrow bed that Clarence had occupied for

seventeen years, straight after the cot they had made for him. Before that it had been a wide deep drawer. Looking back, Emily wonders if the drawer was an act of vengeance on her part. The Bachours would have provided a bassinet with netting and flounces reaching to the floor. Except Clarence was not and never could be a Bachour. Had the oak drawer which she had padded with an old sheet represented a coffin?

Gerry Bachour had been Emily's employer for a week in the big house at Tancred. Gerry was twenty-eight that winter and Emily can still close her eyes and remember the big party for which she had carried tray after tray of delicacies and gathered up glasses to be plunged immediately into hot suds. The silver trays, the lavish food, but the passage to the kitchen silent and cold except for the intermittent rush of feet. There were all sorts of people helping out: ground staff, a boy who delivered groceries, farmers' wives — small farmers, Emily guessed, for the crème of anything were in the long drawing room or out on the verandahs. If it wasn't for Athol Downer, Emily might not have accepted the job at all. They had met at a local dance and thereafter, each Sunday, he took her driving.

Each Sunday he took her to a 'spot', as he called it: it might be a river bank or an elevated view, a grassy knoll where scores of picnickers had embraced in cake crumbs and crushed egg shells. How Athol knew what a 'spot' was Emily never fathomed. On which segment of the road to stop, around which continuity of hills, valley, habitation to place a frame?

Emily, sitting on the edge of her son's bed — he will never be anything but 'son', she thinks angrily, as if the word could be torn out of her with red-hot pincers — looks for the frail thread that began her connection with Gerry. At first she can't remember, and then it comes to her. Athol bending over changing the wheel of a car, so honoured it was a wonder he didn't doff his cap or bow. Damn him, Emily thinks. Damn him. But her heart slides away from the curse as though it's a sloping laundry chute. Without that party there would have been no Clarence, long and gawky, soft-hearted and stubborn as a rabbit. Clarence who is at this moment in the Genealogy and Reference Room bending over a microfiche of Births A-L AAGARD, E.J. to BARLOW, C.M. 1 of 11.

Clarence has worked through 1941, 1942, 1943 and found only a single Bachour: Bachour   Violet Wilhelmina   1329.
'I can't find it,' he says to the librarian who is making passes behind his back with armfuls of books.
Privately Alice Gray thinks the dead should be left in peace. But she bends over the microfiche box and fingers an earlier year. So many of the dead are liars, fudgers, mumblers of certificated details. She can practically see them, shuffling their feet at the registration of a year-old baby as newborn, wilfully obfuscating respect for authority and clerkly skills with a sly game of their own. Only last week two women had approached the desk, faces beaming, at the discovery their mother was illegitimate, thereby releasing another family tree branch to be investigated. The serious researchers carry hardbacked exercise books and files of cards: they approach microfiche, microfilm, cemetery records, militaria, owners of fencible cottages, bankrupts, gazettes, *Journals of the House of Representatives*, old town maps and land transfer titles with the confidence of engineers in the boiler room of a ship. Alice imagines them in overalls, oil-stained and carrying tiny oil cans. Sometimes there is a tiny gasp of pleasure or a groan and Alice raises her eyes. Once she saw two middle-aged women strike their palms together like footballers.
But Clarence, Alice can see, is a novice. Bewildered and

embarrassed that he is uncertain of the alphabet: the alphabet librarians run their eyes over with the speed of blade skaters, the order of words so well ingrained, the position of Mac and Mc, that they can hardly imagine it is not common knowledge. Clarence inserts the microfiche upside down, then he pushes it from side to side like a shopping trolley, looking for the right aisle.

Alice, since there is no one else in the room, takes pity on him and looks over his shoulder.

'You say the first name was Geraldine,' she asks.

'I think the letter was signed Gerry,' Clarence says miserably. 'But not Bachour. Lasc . . . something.' Before Emily snatched it away. He will not pry and she will not produce it: Emily's morals, more faintly echoed in Clarence, are inward-turning. It will be like the letter in the Sherlock Holmes story, concealed in the letter rack while the carpets are lifted and the floorboards raised.

'Keep trying. Bachour is probably the maiden name,' Alice instructs and then, since Clarence looks helpless, she hands him an old catalogue card. 'Then you can write to the Registrar General for your mother's birth certificate.'

She doesn't add that the simplest calculation will give him his mother's age at his birth. Privately she doubts Clarence can subtract.

Emily could tell him that. That he, so rabbit-like, was conceived in a pile of furs at the end of a double bed at Gerry Bachour's twenty-eighth party at Tancred, with fires banked in all the rooms, and the verandahs, like sanatoria, open to the night air. There were men in dinner jackets smoking, Gerry herself flourishing a long ebony cigarette holder bisected by a single pearl.

Gerry's Thunderbird had broken down on the road between Tancred and town. Athol and Emily had come upon her lying by the side of the road, like an accident victim.

'The best way to make you stop,' she cried, gaily getting up and brushing down her tweed skirt. 'I've had a look at the wheel nuts and given up.'

Emily felt at an immediate disadvantage: her face was smudged from tussling with Athol because it was becoming apparent that beauty spots and liberties were inexorably connected — as if by framing some proportion with his hands she could not resist compliance. Her lipstick was smudged from turning her head away from a scene of expectant tranquillity in which an embrace was required; a few yards further on a field was being taken over by gorse: what emotions were required there? Gerry on the other hand looked as composed and at home stretched out on the road as if scenery did not matter to her: she might have been Ophelia in a dry riverbed.

Gerry Bachour's confidence was not limited to her body, the easy way a leg or arm would be flung out, the expansive gestures of her hands: she was instantly on familiar terms with Athol and Emily. When Emily was asked if she would be prepared, for a fairly meagre sum, to assist at a function for which staff were in ghastly short supply, it seemed churlish to refuse. Athol was making eyes at her, perceiving an advantage. Gerry had invited Emily to lie down on the roadside with her — 'It's no use interfering with men, they just want to get on with it' — but Emily had stayed sitting, her knees drawn up and both arms wrapped around them. She had had doubts even then.

Clarence was overawed by the Genealogy and Reference Room, its microfiche and microfilm readers, its drawers labelled Births, Marriages, Deaths, its Laws and Statutes, yearbooks and

GENEALOGY

Parliamentary Debates. Mostly he was in awe of the silence that hung there, the busy competent way other researchers devoted themselves to their task. Still he doggedly visited each Monday evening, attempting to piece together something of his putative mother, Geraldine Fay Sylvie Bachour. He had not replied to her letter, was unable to, since he did not know the address.

'Did you notice the postmark?' the librarian had asked.

'Auckland, I think,' Clarence had responded.

'Well, let's see what you have,' she replied. 'Born in 1935, maiden name Geraldine Fay Sylvie Bachour, married Richard Pember Lascelles in 1968. You were born in 1967. And Richard Lascelles is mentioned in *Who's Who in New Zealand 1980*. Distinguished army record, JP, managing director of a textile firm specialising in school uniforms.'

Alice wonders if Clarence has ever worn one of the uniforms — piped blazers and monogrammed pockets, grey and maroon or royal blue and black — but Clarence does not look as if he attended a private school.

'No issue,' she reads from *Who's Who*. 'So there are no mysterious half-brothers or sisters tucked away.'

'That's a relief,' Clarence replies, thinking of Emily. How is he going to break the news of his researches to her?

'Where are you going?' she asks and he says 'Out,' like a ten-year-old.

Before he leaves he writes down the address from the electoral roll: Lascelles, Geraldine Fay, widow. Widow, he thinks. Serves her right.

But Emily is also a widow. Athol Downer had proved a disappointment. Or Emily had disappointed him, she could never know. The money that came with Clarence's adoption had bought the garage and the house that went with it. The house fought a losing battle with car parts, tools, oil and gasoline.

Emily attempted to wall herself in behind beds of tall sunflowers and sweet-smelling stocks but the garage always won. The cretonne chair arms and backs were grease-stained and Athol smelled of fumes. 'Combustible, do you find me?' he'd mock. 'But then you could do with a bit of revving up yourself.' His manner was sardonic, faintly accusing, though Emily had been the means of his fortune. Perhaps he hoped for a son of his own, more vigorous than Clarence, who was thin and sickly. Was it my fault I witnessed his conception, Emily wondered. Coming into the main bedroom in search of the coat of a departing guest. 'Randy,' thought Emily angrily, though the guest, twined about a man in a dinner suit, had pleaded a headache. And there at the base of the bed in a nest of furs was Gerry, one well-shaped leg flung out (did she wiggle her toes? — Emily certainly got the impression — or wink?), the other leg curved high and pleating an evening shirt. The man's face was invisible, smothered in chinchilla or sable or breast. 'Excuse *me*,' Emily said. Luckily the fur and purse she sought had escaped the deluge.

'So you were there,' Gerry would say later in the nursing home. 'He's as good as yours.' She seemed to think she was conferring a favour, a droit de dame. Then, seeing Emily's recoil — Gerry was a mistress of body language — she added, more soberly, 'There'll be money too. A goodly sum.'

Geraldine Lascelles' address is in the Auckland telephone directory as well as the electoral roll for Mt Eden. Clarence writes in on a used catalogue card. But he will not write a letter. Primitive and simplistic as his reasoning is, it has a clear moral ground. A letter had distressed Emily: another letter would be unthinkable. A telephone call, a visit are his options.

'How are you getting on?' Alice Gray enquires over his

shoulder, and two or three of the lavender-covered electoral rolls crash on to the carpet.

'Fine, thanks,' says Clarence miserably.

Alice observes his misery and associates it with genealogy. The misery of the dead not allowed to lie in peace. Sometimes she thinks of the drowned, dispersed through interminable seas, their bones grist to sand. Then she remembers reading that shipwrecks and downed planes are deadly sources of infection. Is genealogy a pestilence then? She thinks of the middle-aged couple she directed to a tedious and probably fruitless search of a year's shipping intelligence in a period when embarking and disembarking passengers were listed along with pigs and barrels of butter. *We know our relative came here but after that it's a blank.*

Let it remain a blank, Alice almost says. Let him take an impulsive voyage from New Plymouth to Nelson on the *Penguin* along with seven other passengers (two steerage), an American Minstrel Troupe (10), one box books, 30 cattle, one bull, two horses, 5 casks tallow, 44 bales fungus, 70 sacks carrots. It is one of Alice's dreams: to sail on a merchantman and come up the Thames, not Southhampton where the festooned, games-infested, all-friends-together liners berth.

But for Clarence Downer and others like him Alice feels a confused pity. Forced by circumstance to search for knowledge they do not desire: suddenly resurrected parents or unknown siblings. It must be like a van Gogh bedroom of plain bed and dresser, yellow rush-covered chair suddenly dissolving in a hurricane. Clarence's bits of knowledge from microfilm and fiche — a society wedding, on his last visit: *Miss Geraldine Fay Sylvie Bachour to Captain Richard Pember Lascelles, four bridesmaids, three flower girls* — afford him no pleasure. The gushing detailed description isolates him further. Was he perhaps sleeping in the bottom drawer of a wardrobe at the time? Or had a crib come with his dowry, a crib with sides like waterfalls and a veil — surely a mock hint of marriage — over his head?

Emily had assuaged her misery by writing never-to-be-posted letters to Gerry Lascelles. But even these — the first in crude capitals on unlined paper — do not express the messages of her heart. Do I not exist?, she wants to say. Why do you not mention me? To go directly to Clarence as if she has not had his care for a whole nineteen years. More than care since Athol ran off with Sadie, a theatre usherette. At least then she and Clarence had been able to leave the garage and move into town. Emily had gone to work at a railway café, a flat-roofed art deco building by the railway tracks. Its proprietor, Bessie Smith, was a cleanliness fanatic and there was not a scrap of food that was not fresh. Bessie ran her eyes over each morning's consignment of pies from the bakery as if they were troops on parade: little flags indicated their fillings in the warming drawer. Emily found it soothing to clean the Formica tables after each customer, even if they only had a cup of tea. Once a week the artificial flowers that were the centrepiece of each table were dipped in hot suds and left on the draining tray. And the men, truckers, railway workers, the occasional businessman, were so well-behaved. 'Thanks, Bessie,' they'd call, as if they were thanking their mothers for a meal.

I have no issue apart from you, Gerry had written, *and for this reason I should like us to meet. Neither have I issue,* wrote Emily, starting a fresh page, surrounded by balls of screwed-up paper, but she didn't know how to continue. Clarence had been difficult from the start, colicky and restless, balling his fists, stretching and contorting. Athol had not taken to him. 'We should have asked for more,' he said.

I take issue, Emily began a fresh page, *with your tone, as if you had the right, after all these years, to command.* Then she went to the big medical dictionary, its childhood ailments well thumbed, and looked up Parkinson's disease. But even that could not soften her heart towards Gerry Lascelles.

In the Reference and Genealogy Room there is a queue for one of the microfilm readers and at the other a schoolboy has misloaded a spool which has unwound all over the carpet. Now bits of fluff will adhere to the surface, tiny hairs obscure a vital name like a tombstone crack. Alice bites her tongue and does not chide the boy. But a collective sigh goes around the room and a lady at a microfiche reader raises her eyebrows. Alice wishes they would all take themselves off to the Mormon Church archives where if you are lucky a whole spreadsheet of family connections may suddenly appear. And if you are not so blessed a sufficient sea of identical names ought to convince that the dead should be left in peace. For there are so many of these dead. Alice had entered a family name and seen an identically named woman of the fourteenth century, resident of Massachusetts, appear. Alice found herself thinking of the witches of Salem and half-hoping a woman with her great grandmother's name had danced around a fire or shaken a fist at the heavens.

Clarence comes to the desk and stands bashfully looking down. He asks for a map of Auckland. When Alice directs him to the information desk downstairs he mumbles his thanks for her help.

'It was nothing,' she says. 'Very rudimentary. Have you found what you need to know?'

He shakes his head numbly and doesn't answer. He is more terrified than he can admit by the description of his mother's wedding. *The bride looked a picture in her Bachour heirloom wedding dress of lace over silk and a pearl skullcap as she stepped*

THE MATHEMATICS OF JANE AUSTEN

from her father's Rolls Royce Silver Shadow onto a carpet of rose petals. As the happy couple left the church officers of Captain Lascelles' regiment formed a guard of honour with drawn swords.

Grande Vue Drive is a short rising street on the flanks of an extinct volcano and Clarence, as he climbs, peering at the numbers which are oddly erratic, feels perspiration on his neck and brow. He peers up a steep driveway guarded by a cluster of letterboxes, one a replica of a house.

In the end he had compromised and sent a postcard. *I will call at 10.30am on Friday 5th. Please notify me at work if this is not convenient.* He was pleased with 'notify'. He had overheard the librarian use it in the Genealogy Room. 'I'll notify this correspondent who seems to have a connection to your family tree and then you may be able to get in touch.' Clarence had written the postcard on his last evening, wondering what excuse he could have for coming again, unless, as he saw others, he simply took some books from the shelves and sat at a table and read. But there had been no confirmation, no response of any kind. Perhaps she simply took him at his word.

The drive skirts three houses before Clarence reaches number 9. There are various notices: NO PARKING. THIS IS A PRIVATE ROAD. NO ACCESS. A smaller one, stuck into what seems a communal herbaceous border: PLEASE DO NOT TAKE CUTTINGS. Clarence's hand snakes out and he fingers a leaf. He decides he will pick a leaf on the way back.

He steps onto a wide verandah and confronts a door knocker, an electric bell and swaying wind chimes. He chooses the electric bell, and musical chimes sound inside the house: Clarence imagines the notes spreading along the hallway and into the room where his mother is waiting. He feels chilled, sweaty, tongue-tied. There is a long pause and then, just as he reaches for the illuminated bell again, the sound of a stick striking bare wood. Long John Silver or Blind Pew.

The face that stares out at Clarence is prematurely aged and finely wrinkled, an evenness of wrinkles like a furrowing. In certain lights, Clarence thinks irrelevantly, it must be cruel, in others kind. But the eyes are piercing and seem to glitter, and the quivering hand that grips the walking stick is laden with rings.

'So . . .' says a rasping voice, and when Clarence fails to respond, 'Follow me, follow me.'

There is room for both in the large hallway but Clarence keeps to the long port-wine carpet runner as if he is afraid of falling off. They come to a small sitting room with a gas fire and a table with a tapestry cloth piled with books and tea things, a bowl of potpourri and a glass decanter.

'Mildred will make the tea,' Geraldine Lascelles says and she lifts a bell from behind a pile of novels. 'But I wanted the walk to the door for myself. Walking's good for me. I walk and quake and feel like a volcano.'

'Mum thinks you are a volcano,' Clarence finds himself saying.

'She always did,' Geraldine laughs. 'I'll never forget her face the night you were conceived. If I have the correct father in mind. But it was a rather lean period, romantically speaking, and I think my calculations were correct. Are you very good at mathematics, Clarence?'

'Not very.'

'A pity. I could have passed it on. Captain Lascelles was a bit of a wastrel; I had to act as paymaster. Still I have some stocks for you, later on.'

They sit in two wing chairs on either side of the hissing

gas fire with its fake clouds, and Clarence imagines it is companionable: himself and this prematurely aged woman. 'Sharp as a tack,' he will report to Emily, 'but ugly.' Then he recollects that Emily does not know he is here, on part of his annual holiday.

Geraldine is scrutinising him closely and she is not pleased with what she sees.

'You're a bit of a rabbit, I think. The White Rabbit, only elongated. As if you've been pegged out by the ears.' A fit of coughing and a violent tremor follow this bit of malice. Clarence says nothing. He can see the russet foliage of a plum tree through the window. He realises he is no longer afraid.

'Did you want to see me for any particular reason?'

'Only the once-over,' Geraldine replies, one hand like a claw over her mouth. 'As you were the once-over yourself.'

Alice Gray closes the venetians in the Genealogy and Reference room and looks out on the wet street. She shelves the books left on tables, straightens chairs and switches off the photocopier. She sends the PCs into darkness, returns the screen on her desk to Program Manager. She straightens the boxes of microfiche above the newspaper microfilm drawers, the leaflets of the local Genealogical Society who have never heard of Jean-Paul Sartre's words: *Man's self is nothing except what he has become at any given moment.* Let them rest in peace, she thinks, as the last blind closes off the last chink of light.

&

Money

THE MADRAS SHORTS, in two patterns of stripe, are just $4.95. Emma's hand hovers over them, then inserts itself to feel inside the waistbands, searching for the size. She holds a pair against her waist, checking the length. But they do not quite cover the knee which has been in purdah for some time. Still, she turns and looks back at them as she walks down the aisle towards the checkout, imprinting them on her memory, just in case.

Emma Woodhouse is adept at stretching her money, squeezing from its margins, like those roadside verges grazed by cattle in a drought, small unexpected treats. Only the day before, in a ridiculous shop that sells nothing over $2, she had located a small necklace with three pewter fish separated by beads and tied with thick white cotton strands. The fact that the fish leave black smears on her throat doesn't really spoil the find. It is admired by people wearing 22-carat chains.

On the way to the bus stop Emma purchases a small bag of firm tomatoes ($1.20) and two avocados ($1.50). Since her big fright the year before, Emma has become thrifty. She has fought her instincts and won like *The Man Who Shot Liberty Valance* or Gary Cooper in *High Noon*. In *High Noon* it was the stationmaster's clock which was the frightener. For Emma it was 1/3/94, the day her insurances, mortgage, electricity, phone, rates all fell due, like the train with the huge smokestack pulling into the station at Hadleyville.

Maxine Mazengarb uses her credit card like a weapon. Its fine-honed edges remind her of razor blades; when she hands it to a shop assistant it is handled as delicately, with the fingertips, as an artifact. A secret understanding flows between them: they are speaking in code, far from the vulgarity of money. Maxine's nails are painted a red called Vamp: it makes the handling of anything analogous to those curators of fine art who wear soft cotton gloves. The card could be a little gold chip, a miniature wall safe hidden behind a watercolour.

'Do you think I am made of money?' Paul, Maxine's husband, will wail, as he always does, at the end of the month.

'No, but this card is,' she replies.

Today she has clocked up: one lilac silk shirt with tails, one side-fastening taupe gaberdine wrap skirt, a complete set of Elizabeth Arden Flawless Finish with free tote bag, a pair of blue suede pumps with square toes and an intimation of platform soles to come. In spite of all this Maxine does not feel satisfied. She partakes of a bowl of café latte and a pumpernickel open sandwich at a trendy brasserie and then, as a peace offering, she has the waitress pack a custard caramel square ($3.50) for Paul's supper. The combination of caramel, custard and wholemeal sends a mixed message which finally causes her to smile. The wholemeal base is the earning capacity; custard and caramel the rewards we hand to others, the rich outpouring of largesse.

Uptown, at 1.30 p.m., Tim Blackadder and Paul Mazengarb have risen hastily to their feet to murmur regrets, promises to keep in touch, thanks for the opportunity, to a client, their prey, who has escaped thanks to his pager. The message on the pager is concealed by a large hand but Tim suspects it is some kind of war code: THE WHITE RABBIT NEEDS TO FLEE THE HUTCH; THE WHITE RABBIT'S PARACHUTE HAS FAILED TO OPEN. Nonetheless Bruno Sturzaker was a fast eater, like a buck rabbit, and has got through entrée, entrecôte and profiteroles and most of a bottle of Goldwater Waiheke Island Merlot, necessitating Tim and Paul's beckoning for another bottle and secretly grinding their teeth.

The two portable phones rest on the tablecloth but only Sturzaker's had rung, just as Tim was broaching the sales pitch. They had had quite a discussion at the office about where to insert their undoubted abilities, their style and flair, and their so far rather slim but well-satisfied list of clients. Whether they should mention a trendy political party was anxious to recruit them, having heard of their talent at Art School? 'Perhaps we should present ourselves as the Split Enz of advertising,' Paul mused. But how to fit all this into a luncheon, to get the balance right for the expenditure? The casualness — both Tim and Paul wear trendy new suits, a recognised outlay — the air of dining at *La Coupole* every day? Obviously it should not be as difficult as Melanie Griffith's and Harrison Ford's machinations in *Working Girl*. Gatecrashing family weddings and taking over your boss's identity are not necessary in Auckland yet, but Paul thought he could see why Melanie and Harrison talked very fast in tandem. Somehow he felt they had been outwitted. The only bright note was that Sturzaker's call had come from a woman, and Sturzaker had coloured slightly and then seemed to lose the thread of what they were saying .

'Well, old cock, what do you think?' remarks Tim, pushing his chair back.

'246.10 all up,' grimaces Paul, pocketing his credit card. 'All down the drain as far as I could tell.'

THE MATHEMATICS OF JANE AUSTEN

Sally Faber drives her immaculately groomed, deodorised and polished Laser Liata towards Helensville with the two American tourists in the back. On the front seat rests a wicker hamper with small checked tablecloth, checked paper napkins, a smoked salmon quiche from a trendy bakery in Ponsonby which Sally is hoping to replicate one day substituting smoked fish, a selection of meat and salad sandwiches, a Russian teacake made by herself and frozen, two cans of Budweiser, two bottles of Chi'i and a bottle of Stoneleigh Chardonnay. Sally wears her new Thornton Hall jacket ($438) and an old but well-preserved pair of black slacks from Warehouse Clothing. One day she will attend to her lower half but the jacket is more visible, like a TV announcer.

Hank and Maisie von Buren sit happily in the back of the car like children on an outing. 'My, what a darling little car,' Maisie von Buren says on first sighting the Liata. 'Isn't it, Hank, just adorable.' Their broad lazy accents include Sally. They drive beside the ocean and Hank von Buren squeezes his wife's hand and talks of the Pacific war. They pass several picnic sites but the von Burens demur. Sally herself is famished. Finally at 2.30 p.m. Hank von Buren confesses to a homesickness that will be assuaged only by a visit to McDonalds.

'I know you'll understand, dear,' says Maisie von Buren. 'We Americans are like this. A couple of cheeseburgers and a Coke will set him right. It's like saluting the flag.'

Sally offers to pay but the von Burens wave her away. The thought of the expensive picnic food brings tears to her eyes and she can hardly choke down her cheeseburger.

At a Table for Eight in a discreet grey and pink restaurant with hovering waiters who seem prepared to pitch themselves into the halting conversation, Simon Maxwell and Laura Penn quickly size one another up as the best prospects. They do not sit together until dessert and are separated again for coffee and liqueurs. Their eye contact is so intent over the intervening courses, the spoken word seems stilted. The rest of the guests seem so conventional, so obviously in clothes bought for the occasion. Laura wears her little black dress like a second skin.

'Well, hello there,' says Simon.

'A bit like the Lobster Quadrille,' says Laura. She is glad they have dessert: rare steak while eyeing a prospective partner could be unnerving. She recognises Simon's suit as Mr Fish.

'The couch-potato version of the Gay Gordons,' replies Simon. 'Not that I've ever done a Gay Gordons, apart from the gin that is. My mother told me about them. Compulsory meeting dances.'

'Ghastly,' Laura agrees.

'Oh I don't know. That way we'd be stiffly touching shoulders or waists. You'd be able to tell my jacket was minimally padded and my shoulders were my own. I'd be able to tell if you were wearing one of those padded bras. I should rather like being stabbed in the chest.'

Is this the equivalent of dirty talk?, Laura wonders.

'And of course,' Simon goes on, wiping his lips with a pink napkin, 'I could pretend to be uncouth or a poor dancer. I could crush your toes and pull you into my arms.'

Later they recall it is 1995 and exchange business cards and salary brackets. Simon is on 60 thou and Laura a rising 35.

Emma Woodhouse lifts a teabag from a box of 50 Darjeeling and switches on the electric kettle. She reads that *Darjeeling grows among the foothills of the Himalayan Mountains and the exquisite taste was for many years a reserve of the Maharajahs.* She tries to imagine the high mountains and their aromatic foothills. Then, unbidden, she sees the tiny hands of children picking leaf by leaf. Leaf by leaf, coin by coin. There is no concealing the worries of a small and static cash flow. No number of Maharajal cups of tea slowly sipped can disguise the paucity and imbalance of her luxuries. Laura's phone call about meeting a man worth 60 thousand hasn't helped.

'Lucky you,' she says into the phone.

'I'll come over on the way home from work. Anything I can bring?'

'Anything you like and yourself,' Emma replies, hoping she sounds casual. Around her head in a pictorial balloon float olives, Dom Perignon, truffles. She goes into her bedroom and takes her $1 and $2 skirts out of the wardrobe and arranges them on the fading bedcover. The Hero skirt has definitely a look of being discarded. She fetches her nail scissors and angrily begins to unpick the eight belt loops that tie it to the 1980s.

Back in their Ponsonby office Tim and Paul spend what's left of the afternoon catching up. The answerphone is on because Ginette, their secretary, is at the dentist. Tim suggests it is a tryst: Ginette has so many dental appointments and her teeth appear perfect. There is a pile of little messages on each desk. Paul has one from the bank manager about his credit card overdraft. Angrily he phones Maxine and blusters and threatens. As he speaks she kicks the blue suede pumps under the bed where dust will adhere to them and they'll look used.

'Of course I don't think it grows on trees, darling,' she says. 'If it did I'd have a plantation. I'd have them in windowboxes. I'd have one on the dining-room table.' Suddenly she wonders if the clipped ball-like trees in tubs that guard the doors of the better restaurants could be money trees? They look as if they are clipped each morning. Train the tree and put the notes in the microwave.

'I won't want anything much for dinner,' Paul is saying. 'Perhaps we can start economising there.'

Exhausted after her day with the von Burens, Sally can face only a poached egg for her evening meal. She unpacks the cutlery, glasses, napkins from the hamper and puts away the von Burens' cheque to which they have added, over fairly faint protests, an extravagant tip. 'We won't forget your adaptability, little lady,' Hank von Buren says, patting the shoulder of the Thornton Hall jacket. 'Going out of your way for the hamburgers and fries. I intend to recommend you in our company's newsletter.' And Maisie von Buren presses on her a little silver dress pin in the shape of an armadillo. 'To remind you of us and Texas,' she says, leaning forward with a waft of expensive perfume. 'Cute critters,' echoes Hank. 'You'd like them.'

Sally takes the bottle of wine out of the chillybin and puts it in her fridge. Then she thinks of Emma Woodhouse and takes it out again. She gets into the Laser Liata and drives off into the night.

Tim Blackadder's bachelor apartment overlooks the grounds of Old Government House. One of his reasons for paying a substantial deposit and raising a mortgage for the rest is the view of these well-tended but not over-formal gardens ringed with mature trees. When the grounds empty of students at night and only a few visiting professors are in the residential wing of the Staff Club, Tim thinks of walking there. He considers these grounds are the other half of his third-storey apartment whose only greenery is some Virginia creeper and the terracotta pots of the residents. Of these Tim has his share: the balcony ledge and floor are a screen of foliage, flower and herb.

Tonight, Tim does finally cross the road and go for a walk in the university grounds. He opens a small wicket gate and steps onto a path made soft with leaf mulch. He wanders between beds of rhododendrons and azaleas and then on to the soft fine grass in which no weed is permitted. The street lights and the lights of the classical old building enable him to see without straining. It seems absurd, unholy, to think about money in such a setting, but the fear of how committed he is rushes upon him out of the darkness. The disastrous lunch with the slippery client, who surely outwitted them, means his and Paul's salary cheques will be punished and he'll have difficulty making payments on his midi-system and the new refrigerator to replace the old one which was leaking.

He thinks of Paul, whose erratic brilliance will either make or break them. Let it be soon, his heart urges. One way or the other. His future swings between stretch limos and endless eating out or being evicted and scouring the marts for sticks of furniture. But another part of his mind, prompted by the sight of the huge looming building, the light flashing in its lugubrious long panes, knows that money is laboriously hard to acquire and can be dispersed like stardust. He skirts the caretaker's cottage, wreathed in vines like some Victorian hangover, before he turns back.

Burglary, he thinks. But that is not the answer either. Behind his back in the spacious drawing rooms rows and rows of newly upholstered chairs sit waiting for the brains to fill them.

Laura brings a bunch of shaggy chrysanthemums, a box of chocolates and an individual plunger pot: gifts indicating a certain vacillation of mind, Emma senses, though she receives them with practiced gratitude.

'I forgot the ground coffee,' Laura says. 'Next time'.
'So . . .' says Emma. 'Tell me all.'
'Three little words,' says Laura. 'How often it seems to come

down to just three words. I don't know.'

'Describe him then.'

'He seemed so *prepared*. As though he was just waiting to get to me, as though he had singled me out. Not that the company was that thrilling. Anyone with a soupçon of something above niceness would have stood out. In fact I'm wondering if Table for Eight doesn't foment rebellion in at least a pair of members every time it meets.'

'So you're meeting him again?'

'Yes. At his apartment this time.'

'You don't want a chaperone?'

'No, but I thought I might get you to phone during the evening. Just to give me an out if I need one.'

'What time?' says Emma, writing down the phone number.

'Ten-ish? I could say I've got a headache coming on if things are not going very well. Then perhaps you could come by.'

Since her spectacular descent into thrift has had the added effect of marginalising her social life, Emma feels rather pleased. 'Give me the address then,' she says. 'I'll cruise by if you need me.' Though 'cruise' is the wrong word for her Lada. A kangaroo will go past, driven by a woman in dark glasses.

The weight of Maxine's spending lies on Paul's stomach like a suppurating ulcer. That evening he finds a Lladró flying nun hidden under a hat in the wardrobe. The price, $162, is still attached to the box.

'Now you've spoilt it,' complains Maxine, but the coldness in Paul's face prevents full histrionics. 'It was going to be our anniversary present.'

'There won't be an anniversary. There'll be a For Sale sign on the lawn and you'll be shopping at St Vincent de Paul. Or perhaps you could enter a bloody convent and take your credit cards with you. Perhaps they'd accept what's left on them as a dowry.'

'Where are you going?' Maxine asks, watching shirts, slacks, belts, shoes being fired into a suitcase.

'Probably to the nearest brothel. Somewhere where you get value for money. To find someone who can balance the books. A woman with a degree in economics.'

'But Paul . . .' Maxine cries.

'Shut up. You can return that flying nun or take it to bed with you for all I care.'

Simon Maxwell's apartment is on the fourth floor of a stone block opposite the university. Laura Penn stands on a balcony, liberally screened with pot plants and small ornamental trees, including a miniature lemon tree, and thinks she prefers it to Simon. There is something brutal in the way he has wrenched the single lemon from the tiny tree, a fruit that, because of the tree's size, seems like a child. Slices of it adorn her strong glass of gin.

And over dinner — lasagne and salad, fruit salad and yoghurt — Simon has talked incessantly about money. He has asked a great many questions about Laura's personal finances: does she have a portfolio, an investment manager? When she dismisses these things with a laugh his eyes narrow as if he is sizing her up. She tries to recall his conversation at the Table for Eight. Or is this the next step in a process she has not recognised? Chitchat and then finances. To Laura's parents money was a taboo subject, like bed. If you were in financial straits — Laura's chequebook at the moment is a tiny bit overdrawn — that was private. You emulated the Old Testament Jews who hid sorrow under washed faces and clean garments.

They take their coffee on to the balcony and stand looking

out at the park. Simon takes her cup from her hand and twines one arm around her waist. Just why she slaps his face with her palm Laura never knows. Is it the talk of money? Or does he imagine, since she is financially unpromising, she might be good for something else. His voice follows her into the park calling something like bitch, ball-breaker. Bank-breaker, you mean, thinks Laura, walking quickly towards the giant wooden building. She collides with Tim Blackadder who is strolling on the grass, ruminating about his overdraft.

Thanks to the expensive uneaten picnic for the von Burens, Sally Faber has to postpone her purchase of black Jaeger slacks for another month. She has dined on the picnic, eating sandwiches for breakfast and dinner, and the von Burens' tip has not compensated for the humiliation. Yet she cannot afford a caterer. She phones the polytech and asks about personalised catering. She is directed to a course run by a retired chef from the Regent. The fees are steepish but Sally has long followed the adage of invest now, collect later. Except what she has collected thus far is rather small. When she feels low she brushes her Thornton Hall jacket and admires it hanging in the wardrobe, carefully apart from other inferior garments, in an air bath of its own.

The first lesson is hors d'oeuvres and Sally finds her attention wandering. Instead of a tray of asparagus wrapped in prosciutto and skewered tortellini, the image of Hank von Buren eating three cheeseburgers comes into her mind.

'Are you unwell?' the woman next to her asks.

'No, just a memory,' Sally replies.

To prepare the hors d'oeuvres they work in pairs. The woman next to her, Maxine, is surprisingly adept. 'I've been here before,' she explains, carefully arranging red cherry tomatoes stuffed with smoked salmon and cream cheese on a bed of green dill. 'Though it seems another life away.'

Sally doesn't ask why she is taking the course.

'I'm hoping to cut costs in my business,' Sally explains. 'Something I've conspicuously failed to do up to now.'

'Sounds interesting,' Maxine replies. And she proceeds to listen.

Maxine returns the Lladró nun to the shop and cancels her layby on a panne velvet cocktail dress. Paul has not phoned and she is too proud to contact him at work. Then she remembers a movie starring Meryl Streep in a decidedly underprivileged role. Meryl Streep has dry chapped skin and wears fingerless gloves. Her eyes are red-rimmed through malnutrition and lack of sleep, her hair has never seen a salon.

Maxine finds an old stained gaberdine coat in the garage and a pair of down-at-heel shoes in the laundry. She swabs the worst of the stains from the coat because pride does not evaporate and even Meryl Streep made an effort. At 4.30 p.m. she drives her Ford Probe into a parking building two blocks from Blackadder & Mazengarb. Her face is scrubbed of make-up, and as she walks along she bites her lips. Perhaps she should have bitten her fingernails: Maxine seems to recall Meryl Streep's were bitten to the quick. In a doorway she takes a Louis Vuitton scarf, unironed, from her pocket and ties it under her chin like the Queen at Balmoral.

She hasn't prepared a sentence or even a word. Shall she place a hand on his shoulder as Meryl Streep would after yet another job rejection? Insert her roughened hand into his and squeeze? When Paul comes down the stairs at 5.05 p.m. Maxine is nervously biting the well-manicured nail of her index finger.

Tim Blackadder takes Laura back to his apartment, ironically one floor below and directly underneath the apartment she has fled, for coffee and medicinal brandy. Why Laura allows herself to be led back to what she thinks of as 'the scene of crime' she can't imagine. But there is nothing about Tim Blackadder that makes her uneasy. He seems as worried as herself. And when she explains her reason for flight was not seduction but money he seems to understand.

'I've never been good with money,' she says to Tim, as though it is necessary to say this at the beginning. 'I'm not overdrawn or anything, or owe anybody, but I'm not good in the sense I don't treat it with the utmost seriousness.'

'Me neither,' says Tim, thinking of the expense account lunch. 'Me neither.'

'Don't you think we should be buried with it?' Laura goes on, bravely hoping no one is peering down from the balcony above, recognising an improvident voice. 'It should be poured into the graves of those who thought it the most important thing. All they amassed.'

'I've often thought they should be forcibly sent to Bangladesh or Bosnia or Biafra,' Tim says. He notices he is feeling noticeably better. Perhaps he is thinking of Bruno Sturzaker parachuting down over a malaria-ridden swamp without a cellphone.

'There have been cases of people being buried in their cars,' Laura says. 'My car would not be worth it, however.'

Tim nearly asks what sort of car it is, but something in her manner checks him. He senses a need for conversational reform. So they talk about the trees in the park, their probable age, stars and the constellations they can name.

'Do you know what she said?' shouts Paul to the eight sitting around their dining room table. '*Come home, I've got rid of the nun.*'

Maxine looks demurely at her plate, oblivious to the shrieks of laughter. It was all she was able to think of, before Paul escaped. He doesn't recognise her, of course, though he gave her the scarf. People down on their luck have to compensate with directness. It's not the message about the nun that makes him seize her arm and hustle her into a passing taxi but her appearance. The nun is for public consumption. 'God she looked a sight,' Paul hoots. 'I took her for the office cleaner.'

'Meryl Streep,' Maxine protests, but no one hears her in the laughter. 'Meryl Street in *Ironweed*.'

Later when the guests have gone, having dined on a slightly abbreviated menu, slighter cheaper but still very acceptable wines, Paul and Maxine have a serious talk about money.

'The way I look at it,' Paul begins, for he likes, in advertising as well as conversation, to begin with the big picture, 'money is a gauge of behaviour.'

'What did you think of the hors d'oeuvres?' Maxine asks.

'Fine, fine. The dinner party was fine. Can we keep to the subject.'

'Sorry.' The returned Lladró nun still makes her presence felt.

'Try to understand, Max. Money is a signifier of character. Every bit as good as a lie-detector or a fingerprint. And the beauty of it is it's so unconscious.'

'Money talks, you mean?'

'Yes, but not in the obvious way. Not in the way people imagine. Take Tim, for instance, and his new woman, Laura. He's terrified we're going under but he's given her a corsage.'

'Bit extravagant for a Table for Eight at home.'

'It means he's conquered his fears for one evening and relaxed.'

'It could be an investment.'

'No, I think it's more subtle than that. He's realigned his priorities.'

'He'll probably realign them again at the office on Monday.'

'But he's given an indication of his character. When the chips are down . . .'

'So you go around watching people's expenditure.'

'Their attitude to money. Do they stand you a drink, loan you a bus fare, pay for their own movie tickets. Or do they leave their wallet in the glove compartment, carry only parking meter change. I knew a man who carried no cash at all and got all his small expenses, like cups of coffee, paid. Said he got the idea from the Royal family.'

'I think Sally is fairly cautious but is prepared to take a calculated risk.'

'Well sussed, Meryl Streep.'

'I'm thinking of putting my piggybank funds in with hers.'

Paul tries the idea on Tim when they're lunching in a small park with a high tiled wall over which water cascades.

'So you're bringing Max's spending under control,' he says. 'Blinding her with philosophy.'

'Her spending was a comment on me, really. Not that I intend to expound to her on that. What about old Bruno Sturzaker, though? Plenty of scope for analysis there.'

'A lot of effort for a free meal?'

'It'll cost him in the end, though. Now we know he's a skinflint we can mark his card.'

They stroll back to Blackadder & Mazengarb companionably in the sun.

Money is where the heart is. The effort we bring to bear on it, the secrecy we wrap it in, for it is more secret than prayer, Paul thinks. Perhaps he should take a leaf out of Maxine's book and enrol for philosophy. When the chips are down, what we do with it or fail to do with it is what counts. Will Tim re-mortgage his apartment for the sake of the firm? Will Sally build a little empire and employ another driver? Will Maxine revert to imitating Donald Campbell streaking across a white-hot desert after the money-spending record of the world?

Laura Penn, whose method is to hug unhappiness close but to pass happiness on to another as though it is a hot potato, worries about Emma Woodhouse. Tim has repeated to her some of Paul's meanderings about money to which she has hardly listened. But it occurs to her Emma is outside that band, like a radio band that separates paupers and Kerry Packer. Where we live and breathe and have our being. Laura, Sally and Maxine are determined to do something about Emma. Maxine recalls Emma was good at calligraphy at school, Sally thinks she has a flower press, Laura of greeting cards. Sally sees Emma's flower cards on thick recycled paper pressed into the hands of Hank and Maisie von Buren. Otherwise no hamburgers.

Laura Penn and Tim Blackadder walk in the grounds of Old Government House. They hold hands lightly as though their fingers have crept towards each other in the dark. It is a minimal contact which emphasises the gift they intend to give each other. How shall we share our money, Laura wonders. She sees it stretching in front of them, gold and silver coins, banknotes as dark as leaves, where once there were breadcrumbs and intervening doves.

&

Jesu,
Joy of Man's Desiring

THE ZENITH OF confidence, though they are only thirteen and fourteen, primo and secondo, chosen duetists, little Glenn Goulds, though they play with perfectly straight backs and without his grimacing. If their feet feel heavy on the way to the baby grand, confined in their black crotchet-like shoes, the backs of their necks prickle. Eilish is bothered that they appear significantly modest now; Merridee cannot wait to strike the first portentous note.

'A lovely thing,' states Miss Foy as they come into the practice room together. 'Soaring and dipping, spires and valleys. Yet so calm.'

Eilish and Merridee stand before her, puzzled. She is not their choice of music teacher, being scatty and flamboyant.

'Bach,' she goes on, to the two simpletons. Then she realises they hardly know one another, coming from different forms.

'Eilish McBride,' she says, 'and Merridee Walton. And Johann Sebastian Bach. Mighty Bach if you're studying *Under Milk Wood*.' She can't remember if it's the thirds or fourths.

'We are,' says Merridee to break the silence.

'Right. Well we're not aiming at Mighty Bach here. This is the pianoforte not the organ. We're aiming to open Bach up like a watch, take one of his most beautiful tunes and show how it works while keeping the melody ever uppermost. Admiring the watch but never forgetting its function is to tell the time.'

Eilish and Merridee look at their shoes, abashed. Why couldn't they have been allotted Mrs Ramsay who has dark curls and a cat in her room?

Eilish has been given primo, Merridee secondo. Miss Foy's decisions are arbitrary. 'Let me look at your profiles,' she says. 'We need to take the audience into account.' Eilish is shorter and has a retroussé nose. She will probably never be prettier than she is now, with her fluffy cropped curls. Merridee is sallow, her jaw is too strong like a hanging judge. Still, Miss Foy estimates she will grow into it.

Forced into a kind of friendship by Bach and Miss Foy, Eilish and Merridee walk along the corridor of the music annexe where pianos, violins, violas, trumpets, clarinets, flutes, even a piccolo and the occasional triangle articulate behind closed doors. The cacophony, punctuated by sudden silences and exhorting voices with false confidence, thrums like a sick headache. The wood of the corridor is highly varnished like the autumnal gleam of a violin. A small girl passes them, humping a cello like a dressmaker's dummy.

'You'd think they'd have trolleys,' Eilish remarks. 'Like they do at airports.'

The thought sets them giggling as they rush down the concrete steps and up the curved drive to school. The music annexe is in a little valley of its own, one of Bach's dips. It is surrounded by soft feathery trees that act as sound baffles.

JESU, JOY OF MAN'S DESIRING

Miss Foy has folded the corner of the page to be turned into a sharp crease. 'There is plenty of time for Merridee to raise her left hand and turn.' But it doesn't seem so at first. 'Of course Bach knew about page-turning, silly,' Miss Foy goes on, reading her thought.

But Merridee hardly notices; she is in a reverie in which her hand steals out, lightly as a butterfly, finger and thumb lift the page and the endless ticking watch continues. She tries to imagine herself one of the Bach family, perhaps a baby, and this is the first thing she masters, she crawls on her stomach . . . A family so imbued in music it is like breath to them, more than food even. It is employment and life, so they consider nothing else; Bach never has a change of heart.

Miss Foy's voice, raised and peremptory, brings her back to earth.

'Page-turning, however much it amuses you, is not a note, Merridee. You are slowing down. You must keep up the rhythm.'

Merridee resents playing secondo, though she admits Bach does not distinguish, does not divide the world into two: high and low, light and dark, good and evil. Yet secondo always seems to struggle. Is it because the notes are deep, reverberating more slowly, unwilling, unless prodded, to stir themselves from winter sleep? Bach who always insisted his pupils think before they struck a note, plan before attempting composition. She has seen Miss Foy's appraising glance, quickly veiled, which decided Eilish should be visible to more of the audience while Merridee fades into the stage curtain.

But it is not like that when 'Jesu, joy of man's desiring' begins to come together. No one could think of discrimination then. The first sweet line seems to well up and hover, supported on a stem as a flower is. 'Des–ir–ing', Miss Foy chants. 'Desiring goes on for ever, not like desire.' She desires the lesson to be over; she feels the flicker of a migraine. Clearly it is impossible to explain to two little girls who sit so prissily together, two little girls who would scrupulously cut an apple in half or a piece of chocolate. Whereas what they are attempting to play — to peck at — is of a wholeness so blinding, so rudimentary, it seems to bind the whole world together.

Now there are only three weeks to the House competitions in which Eilish and Merridee will represent Batten. Curie, Batten, Melba, Dickinson: outdated exemplars bestowed by the founder. Models surely, but which of the thousand girls will discover radium or fly solo? As it is Miss Foy feels like banging their heads together or at least pressing on their sparrow-thin shoulders.

But at the last a very small part does seem to work: Curie raises a test tube, Batten flies, Melba sings and Emily Dickinson wafts downstairs in a white dress. It is the section that accompanies

With the fire of life impassioned
Striving still to truth unknown

Even the bodies seem to have relaxed a little.

Eilish and Merridee are becoming companionable.

'Sometimes I wish we had a piano each,' Merridee confides. 'Two black pianos, back to back.'

Eilish would prefer white. 'Then we could see each other's eyes and pull faces.'

'Or nod when to start,' Merridee agrees.

This is the alarming part of playing together: even a slight nod, like a Mafia chief giving the go-ahead for an execution, is hard to get right. Is it the moment she starts to nod or when the nod is complete? Should she just say 'Now' under her breath or count to three? And Bach, now they are getting into it, is like getting into a river. Other composers are like the sea with unexpected waves and lulls; Bach is more like inserting a stick or a little boat. You think you will catch it downstream but it takes on a life of its own.

'Will we get a tryout on the baby grand?' Eilish asks Miss Foy.

'Of course,' she says.

She thinks of pupils who, confident enough in the bee-like cells of the music annexe, have hardly been able to locate Middle C.

'Imagine Bach is looking down at you and you are playing for him. It is Bach's music, so it is Bach you must please. Just as Anna Magdalena Bach felt close to him when she played the simple pieces in *Anna Magdalena's Notebook*.'

Miss Foy lifts the bust of Felix Mendelssohn 1809–1847 and sets it on top of the piano. 'Play to the friend of Bach,' she instructs.

Miss Foy has Mendelssohn, and Mrs Ramsay, two doors along, has Schubert.

'When you are on stage forget the audience, be totally unconscious of them. Imagine you are in Anna Magdalena's house; it is evening and the family is gathered in the drawing room. You are two of the Bach children playing together and Johann Sebastian is looking over the top of the piano at you.'

Merridee starts to giggle and puts a hand over her mouth. She is thinking that the noises in the Bach house must be very like the music room.

'Run along then, Catharina Dorothea and Wilhelm Friedemann,' says Miss Foy when their forty minutes is up.

They are glad to. For besides the bust, Miss Foy has suddenly burst into song:

Through the way where hope is guiding
Hear what peaceful music rings

Her voice is light, fluting. It sends shivers down their spines.

Now Miss Foy has started singing, she goes on:

Drawn by Thee, our souls aspiring
Soar to uncreated Light

or

Hark what peaceful music rings
Where the flock in Thee confiding
Drinks of joy from deathless springs

Oddly the effect is to increase the metronomic quality of Eilish and Merridee's playing. They really are playing like a well-adjusted watch. Bach can survive Miss Foy. Determinedly Eilish and Merridee, like Catharina Dorothea and Wilhelm Friedemann, disassociate themselves from the surrounding cacophony. They are a street in Leipzig in which dramas are going on behind closed doors. A woman shrieks from a window, another empties a chamber pot over someone's head; there are fisticuffs and a body is left bleeding in the gutter. But Bach's harmonies override it all, like street sweepers or night carts drawn up under a starry firmament. Miss Foy for a moment becomes Magdalena Wilcke, Bach's second wife, her clear outstanding voice swelling the already-made family.

'Two weeks to go girls,' Miss Foy states as the last syllables of *Into the love of joys unknown* die on her lips. 'I think we are getting there. If I haven't been able to distract you with my singing . . .'

'Are you nervous?' Eilish asks as they pass quietly along the corridor of the music annexe.

'There's two of us,' Merridee replies. 'I'd hate to do a solo.'

'Perhaps we'll infect one another, like plague or fever.' 3 Latin are studying the Black Death, spread from a parcel of clothes charitably sent from London. Probably no one blamed the clothes: they were worn to funerals and while nursing the next victim, the fleas nestling in their folds. Eilish shivers. Sometimes she can feel Merridee shiver beside her. Though the stool is wide she is very conscious of Merridee's body, slow to relax.

'Perhaps we need Miss Foy singing under her breath?' Eilish whispers as they come to the last door behind which a cello is writhing.

'Maybe she'll stand behind the curtain?' Merridee giggles. Then, though Bach is secure and solid, they are running and leaping up the hill.

The competitions will be held in the school assembly hall which is large enough to contain the whole school in long class lines, the teachers down each side and the headmistress — always breathless, always rushing — and her cohorts on stage. Behind the backs of the junior teachers, alert for infringements, rise wall bars, for the assembly hall doubles as a gymnasium.

'May the Lord lift up the light of his countenance upon you and give you peace,' the headmistress intones before going on to the business of the day. Eilish often tries to fit an image to these words but the best she can come up with is the sun rising. In front of her the line undulates like a rope that is not straight. 'Music competitions will commence from Monday next and girls are asked to move quietly in the quadrangle. Notices will be posted outside the doors.'

Merridee looks across at Eilish in 3 Latin and their expressions meet in equal grimaces. Their heads turn aside at the same moment and concentrate on the neck of the girl in front. Left hand and right, left body and right, Catharina Dorothea and Wilhelm Friedemann (there is no help there because Bach had only one daughter): some gap is closing between them. On the long stool each feels the warmth of the other's body; they share the keys that would fail to sound if the other were not present.

Now Miss Foy is driving them on, knowing they have crossed the Rubicon, defended the bridge, circled the earth like Puck. They slide onto the stool like two snakes in the sun, one . . . two . . . three . . . Eilish counts, their hands poised above the first notes, the notes themselves crying out to be released. The white keys leap forward, the gap appears as the finger strikes down — a delicate measured strike, an individual caress — and a little cliff opens on either side. And the velvety black keys — the black cliffs of Dover — whose cliffs are air, wait to be stroked too, their backs as black as voles.

'Jesu, joy of man's des–ir–ing,' sings Miss Foy, lifting Mendelssohn down and replacing him on the side table. Henceforth they will imagine Johann Sebastian Bach. 'Des–ir–ing,' she says, a hand lightly on each air-touching shoulder. 'Desiring. It's all in that word, my angels. Endlessness. You are winning now, you are going to win.'

The day before the competition Eilish and Merridee have a dress rehearsal. They decide who will climb the three steps to the stage first: it would be unthinkable to collide or jostle and start *Jesu, Joy of Man's Desiring* to a backdrop of giggles. Merridee will carry the music and place it on the stand. Eilish goes last, empty-handed, except for the weight of Bach. She feels like Mary Queen of Scots, and the sweet harmonious music to come is her speech. The feeling of being *in* the moment, *being* the moment, almost blinds her so she counts the steps . . . one . . . two . . . and commands herself: Head up . . . best profile . . . take time to get seated . . . imagine you are wearing tails (one of Miss Foy's). Afterwards they practise their bow. Merridee clasps the music in her left hand and they incline forward from the waist. Without a glance they sense one another's movement. They would sense it if there were two baby grands, not one. *Over hill, over dale, thorough bush, thorough briar,* such is the way of duetists.

Seated in the front row with the other performers, Merridee imagines the sea parts for her as she and Eilish climb the steps to the stage. Her forehead feels as massive as Bach's; she glances at Eilish and they exchange the smile of conspirators. Here are Anne Boleyn and Walter Raleigh, passed beyond all tantrums (hasn't Sir Walter asked for a knife to stir his wine?): clear sailing now to the consummation. Haven't they heard from another competitor that Miss Foy thinks they are brilliant, that Bach would be as proud of them as of Anna Magdalena. That they have mastered Bach in a way that is unusual for two so young. And that Miss Foy is certain they will win — or rather Batten House will — which is the same thing, only pleasingly, self-effacingly modest.

> *Desiring man's of joy, Jesu*
> *bright most love, wisdom Holy*
> *aspiring soul's our, Thee by Drawn*
> *light uncreated soar to*
> *fashion'd that flesh our, God of Word*

This is how it comes out. Or worse.

impassion'd of the life fire with
unknown to striving truth still
throne round soaring thy dying

Hideous. Where is the ghostly Bach head on the piano now? Where the indrawn breath of the audience? Is that a titter rising? A gasp from the wings where Miss Foy cannot begin to sing sotto voce, rocking back on her heels in ecstasy of tripartite creation. Hideous, lamentable, undone. Pose that produces nothing, confidence with no ground. The robots coming unprogrammed, publicly. Is it the first note which Merridee, pulse ringing in her ears, cannot distinguish? Even the page is turned at the wrong moment, leaving a little darkness like a dead star. It might as well be the darkness of a coal hole, the cupboard at the bottom of the stairs in which someone is rending their clothes.

Own ever though thine dost lead
unknown of in joys the love

Bach, it seems, attempts to hold something; the structures are not entirely gone. It is only the notes, the cliffs of fall, the dark keys over, that are in the wrong sequence. If you can imagine a fat ungainly trapeze artist in a wig trying with all his might to fix things, at least to untangle the strings. *Jesu, joy of . . .*

How they get off the stage without caterwauling is the miracle.

Miss Foy steps forward smartly as the girls begin to file out, and draws Eilish and Merridee out a side door. Headaches, migraine, both simultaneously afflicted? — she will think of something: duetists are prone to cross-pollination, unless there are two

JESU, JOY OF MAN'S DESIRING

pianos. Even then a sneeze might carry across the raised lids. They walk slowly down the path to the music annexe. Miss Foy had prepared a little victory supper, though of course 'supper' implies evening. There are lemonade and special biscuits, langues de chat: Miss Foy was looking forward to translating that. Still food like music is a need, in triumph or terror. Eilish begins to cry softly. Miss Foy searches her brain for a Bach family story which will illustrate a temporary disaster.

In 1720 when Bach returned from Karlsbad he found his wife, Maria Barbara, dead and buried. Miss Foy is about to mention this, and that Maria Barbara, like herself, was known to sing to Bach's accompaniment, when she reflects it is too huge. It will pass, she thinks, looking down at two crestfallen heads. Langues de chat were a good choice, though: they look like the tongues of bells. Eat, swallow and digest a disaster is the way to do it. Instead she offers, 'No more competitions, until you feel you are ready. Or not at all, if you like.'

'Thanks,' says Eilish, lifting her streaked face.

'Sorry,' says Merridee, secondo underpinning primo.

To other music staff Miss Foy simply remarks, 'I always wondered what Bach would sound like if he came off the rails.'

Thirty years later Eilish Tancred, née McBride, opens an American hymnbook, *Journeysongs*, of which she disapproves, and turns to no. 377. Only a faint memory of the disastrous duet remains, rising lightly. Her lips curve in a faint smile as she remembers the langues de chat the music teacher, name forgotten, had forced on them. Like eating dry piano keys. On the way back to class Merridee had been sick behind a purplish rhododendron.

'Jesu, joy of our desiring', Eilish reads, recognising gender correctness. Thee has become you, Thy your. But there remains a bright tight kernel, a kind of constriction which is odd because the music waves and flows. Eilish does not sing. Instead she ponders the sharpness of 'flesh that fashioned . . . life impassioned', as if the words are steel traps. Yet they do not catch Bach. With what virile strength he rises above them, soaring out of reach. She sees a white mushroom growing between the jaws of an ankle trap under a great oak. Or mist gathering to detach itself from wet fields. She sees her two divorces and shaky third marriage pass through the jaws and soar up on the impulse that propels a fountain. Eilish's eyes ascend to the rose window above the altar, the one that always reminds her of Mackintoshes toffees.

When she gets home she must re-draft her will. It won't be the first time. She shall have 'Jesu, joy of mans's desiring' — she will insist on 'man' — for her funeral's recessional hymn.

&

The Lark Quartet

BEA AND CATHRYN are sitting on high stools in a pizzeria across the street from the little theatre. They are eating entrées only and coffee, since a quartet is something like an execution. Half a chicken for the black man, a whole one for the white who probably burped. Once before Bea has been to a string quartet, a Soviet one, with a stomach full of spaghetti and meatballs, rough red wine. How hard she had tried to emulate the frozen faces in front of her, faces not even the lampshade with its frill, or the music, like streamers against the side of a giant liner, could soften.

The woman next to them is going to the Lark Quartet as well. 'Do you know them?' she says. 'I heard them in New York.'

'No,' say Bea and Cathryn in unison. 'But we're looking forward . . .'

'Absolutely fabulous,' says the woman, consulting a huge wristwatch whose centrepiece is a treble clef.

Then there is just time to run across the street with umbrellas up, queue for a programme, slip out of their coats and stow them under their seats, lean back and begin to be briefed.

'The Lark Quartet,' Cathryn reads, 'is becoming one of the most sought-after string quartets of the younger generation,' but Bea is only half-listening. She is looking around the theatre as if it is a drawing room they have just entered. The Soviet quartet had played on a box-like dais on a flat floor, just large enough to hold them and the ridiculous lamp. Bea had thought the lamp resembled a pair of lady's bloomers. Tonight there is no lamp, only a curving stage, not too high but high enough, decorated on both sides with autumnal arrangements of twigs and berries.

'Shostakovich,' Cathryn reads and Bea gives a little shiver. She hands the programme over and Bea places it on her lap. What is going on behind the blue curtain, she wonders. Is someone looking at a watch or straightening a blouse? Perhaps a grimace is being exchanged. What hotel are they staying in? Or are they staying together? Bea has read that quartet members often stay at separate hotels to create the necessary space between them. The blue velvet seats that curve around the stage are bathed in lowering shades of blue, the voices hush, and on to the stage stride four women in white blouses, black skirts and glowing red, silver and gold cummerbunds.

Then, for a few preparatory moments, it is as though the four women on stage are arranging themselves in a drawing room, pulling a chair closer, adjusting a stand, flicking over pages of music. They seat themselves, ceremoniously, and Cathryn sees that one long black skirt is culottes. Violin, violin, cello, viola. The cello is the mater familias, the ground; sometimes, in the flurry, the leader. The instruments of a quartet must be of the highest calibre. The lightest of tuning is taking place: four good hostesses making sure the cushion is behind your back, the footstool just where you want it. Then there is a little hush and Cathryn wonders which player she will watch most, which fingering, which bowing arm. Or will it be one instrument she will try to follow, as hopelessly as the children lost in the woods tried to follow breadcrumbs. Or a face, the profile of one, the way the hair, swinging in the updraught the music creates, falls against a slender neck. The strength of shoulder into which the gleaming instrument fits as though a Titian-haired child has burrowed there to meet both comfort and a censure.

Bea too is looking for a place to focus. Unknown to Cathryn she has flung herself into her car after a vicious quarrel with her son. She expects to return to the chaos she walked out on, the remains of a meal spoiled by anger: Never talk with your mouth full, never talk at all should be the rule. Her son's mastication will have to be mentioned before he takes his first girl to a restaurant. Then she thinks of his bedroom, mercifully at the farthest end of a long hallway: a chaos centre which only Peter Pan could penetrate. 'Show Tinkerbell your room, dear,' she hears herself saying. 'I know you need space.'

She has not entered Seth's room now for six months and still he shouts abuse about wearing the same screwed-up soiled t-shirt three days in a row, though to her knowledge he has at least five others. Bea's eyes go to the two EXIT signs, glowing like lozenges. Should she have one made to read LAUNDRY? The blouses of the quartet are so fresh. And their hair, each looks as though it has been brushed a hundred times, as though a bow has been passed over it. As she sinks further back into her padded seat Bea pushes Seth away from her like a gargantuan load of dirty washing. Get behind me, Satan, she almost says. No, not Satan. Almost imperceptibly, like the first notes, her spirits begin to lift.

As the first notes of Aaron Jay Kernis's *String Quartet 'musica celestis'* drift over the audience like disturbed dust, Cathryn too has come to a decision. Or is it the light snack, the glass of wine, the coffee settling in her stomach? Never again will she listen as she once listened to the Prague Quartet, the Borodin, the Medici, with her face drained of blood, eyes glistening, neck rigid. Until she felt like an icicle the music would crack. A test of stillness to correspond with the efforts of the musicians. She will give up the notion of self-blame as if quartet-listening is some kind of etiquette. She will think of whatever she likes and the quartet can flow in and out of her. She will be a fish in the sea. Almost instantly she thinks there is something gill-like about the bowing motion of the violinists. Yes, like her, they are breathing!

In fact what Cathryn thinks of is New York. She has never been to New York, but its brownstones, Central Park, SoHo and the glittering needle island of Manhattan are familiar in a secondhand way that resembles a grainy black and white film. The final frame of Woody Allen's *Manhattan* stays in her mind like the upper third of a vast cathedral. She forgets indecisiveness and the slow dining of Woody and Diane Keaton, and sees again the lights of the vast panorama gleaming with fanatical lighted windows. But most of all, as the images come and go, she sees the occurrence of beauty, one frail second among a wagonload of seconds, an angle of light transforming a facade, the hopping of a sparrow. She closes her eyes tight and an image of a fox

Cold, delicately as the dark snow
A fox's nose touches twig, leaf;

appears in the shadow of a stoop. He materialises by a dustbin which he proceeds to inspect. Then he glides away leaving fresh paw prints in the slush.

Bea, who has read the programme, knows the Scherzo is 'made of bits and scraps of things' but there are angels above the roof. The same old world drawn large and deep, deeper than the apple cores and pizza crusts under her son's bed, higher than the stars she looks at before retiring, blinking back the tears. What her son needs to govern him is Beethoven, a masculine presence so huge it can enfold the terrors that lie behind his childishness. When her husband left Bea had envisaged a gentler relationship: she would confide in Seth, not too much, but things like her financial woes. She would explain to him why he could not have Reeboks. Later she would bring him a cutting from *Time* about the actual costs of making a pair of Reeboks in Taiwan. She might even tackle Michael Jordan and his earnings. But she never has. Michael Jordan is not to be shared by a son and mother, and when she mentioned exploitation and huge false advertising there was a blazing row. In the moments when Aaron Jay Kernis seems to hesitate between one emotion, one image and the next, Bea reflects on her failure and feels soothed by such a variety of experience.

Cathryn is thinking of birds. Not birds of elaborate and colourful plumage which makes even fashion models look wan but common sparrows, blackbirds and thrushes. Birds which survive in the unlikeliest environments. Hasn't she read of a bird nesting on top of lights at a football stadium? A large bird, blown off course. She thinks of New York roof gardens, of sparrows pecking between the feet of passersby, or flying up with wisps of cotton from the garment district in their beaks, or hair combings from an apartment window. Hasn't she once seen a white gull carrying an absurd shape in its beak that turned out to be a banana? Concentrate on the music, an inner voice tells her, and she refastens her gaze on the Lark Quartet.

Eva, Astrid, Jennifer, Anna. Cathryn had memorised their names from the programme before she handed it to Bea. Strong direct names, unlikely to be shortened. And the faces, as her eyes linger on each one, drinking in the features — do they find this unbearable, the eyes of hundreds crawling over noses, eyes, jaws, hairlines? — the features are strong too, as though there is an equal drinking in there of the music made with four voices. Such fine brows, such expressive mobile mouths. And though they are watched, examined, every second under the stage lighting, such inward concentration on their instruments. Absurdly Cathryn thinks of a Plunket circle. Four beautiful aristocratic women who have each given birth to a genius and are so confident of their child's merits they are graciously enquiring about the other three.

Aaron Jay Kernis's quartet comes to an end, reminding Bea she has not concentrated properly, or was that part of the composer's intention: to forgive? To allow that melody which we most admire is built from fragments of discord like dust sent flying into the air from a cleaned surface. That we no longer believe, Bea ponders, so we need to see the workings? That if we are honest, at the end of a day we achieve a few seconds or minutes or quarter-hours of real happiness? The lights come up, the quartet leave the stage, and Cathryn and Bea sit on in the blue velvet seats.

Finally they get up and follow the slow procession for coffee. Bea feels she could do with a gin and tonic like the flat gin and tonic with her name on a slip of paper covering the rim at Wyndham's theatre. She and the actress she had gone with had flicked the slips of paper off and taken their gins to a vantage point, superior to those not in the know. To be in the know is the great thing: to know something about Aaron Jay Kernis, for instance, but the programme only says born in 1960– . A fine pale face, somewhat long, Bea decides, with fingers that have not seen the sun. Owner of an apartment or a loft. A huge bare space where crowds assemble for a modern salon. The glasses they sip martinis from are shaped like filters. Or it a brownstone with trash lying about and snow piled up? Is this where Alan Jay gets his inspiration, plodding with his head down, amid the garbage?

'Didn't care much for that, I'll admit,' a voice says in Cathryn's ear.

'Bit of a curate's egg really. Still we always have to have something modern.'

'I suppose it shows off their technique in a way.'

'Be interesting to see what they do with Mozart.'

'Can't stand Shostakovich, can you? Wish it was Borodin. . . one of the nice Russians.'

Cathryn and Bea return their cups to the servery and slink back down the steep steps to the blue seats as if descending into a well.

But when Cathryn decides she is going to concentrate totally on Mozart, *String Quartet in B flat*, K589, it seems she can't. She closes her eyes and concentrates, and all she can think of is wallpaper. Herself lying on top of a huge wardrobe, papering a passageway in a little cob house in Lawrence. A crib was the word for it. A crib to which she had tried to bring a touch of *House and Garden*. Layers of wallpaper had come off, bubbled on the surface, smooth and professional underneath. It was like turning the pages of an old book: each paper darker, more sombre and formal, until the paper Cathryn had chosen, cream with a small forget-me-not pattern, seemed frivolous. She had laughed as she lay on the wardrobe, imagining a guardian angel in a Chagall painting looking down: bright stars in a cerulean blue sky, the pointed roof, herself flattened on the wardrobe, the kitchen table with its rolls of paper and paste pot beyond.

Oh why can't she concentrate?

Mozart is Cathryn's favourite composer. If the world ends tomorrow or lasts for another million years, if there are thousands of brilliant new composers, it will still be Mozart on the winner's podium with the gold medal around his neck. When Desmond leaves the house in the morning Cathryn rushes to put on K504 or K551, the *Prague* or the *Jupiter*. Then, while she cleans and wipes surfaces, she feels her soul being restored. It is not that Mozart is above agony, far from it: he catches at agony and drags it with him; he uses it to make the tempo urgent, for who is so urgent as Mozart? Even Mozart's trills have agony in them, as if he is pressing on a sore spot, staunching the pain and the melody together.

But tonight Mozart himself seems weary. Is it the commission from the King of Prussia who wants to play the cello? Bea can imagine the king in a lemon frockcoat and lace ruffs sitting in a little circlet of gold chairs, his royal elbow sawing at the cello and the sounds being drowned by flattering remarks. And Mozart knowing there would have to be rather a lot of the royal elbow, the royal sawbones. Mozart who is two years from his death, beginning again, as weary as Bea passing down the hallway and averting her eyes from Seth's bedroom door. She *will not* look, but her nose twitches: the miasma of dead apples, mildewed sandwich crusts, bits of burger bun. There will be Coke cans, incompletely drained, with possibly a moth or a fly at the bottom. Try to keep focused, she tells herself, as Mozart kept himself focused on the king.

So Bea focuses on the faces of the four women, whose faces seem to have become naked with so many people examining them. If it is only a desultorily good quartet, if Mozart himself despairs of it, their faces show nothing of this. The four faces wear an attentiveness that is more than musical. Perhaps they are historians too, students of costume and manners; they play as if they are looking down from a great height upon a tableau in which Mozart is dissolving in quicklime in his grave and the king is mopping his forehead with a silk handkerchief. The notes carry Mozart's distaste, his ache for the simplicity he is required to provide, the conversations between cello and first violin he despairs of, but eventually they carry something more. A triumph of spirit, Bea thinks, or imminent death. Or is it just that we all take what we have with us at any time and weave from it like the bower bird? Four beautiful foreheads beam back like beacons, making gold from straw.

Suddenly Cathryn wonders if they have chosen this quartet because they are women. Because they sympathise with Mozart's difficulties and ennui; that they are at home with the need to flatter, to overcome dominance by guile. That they are actually helping Mozart, strengthening him as a nurse strengthens a child. Acknowledging that Frederick William II wanted a large share on the cello, wanted it to dominate the first violin, then the second violin and viola in turn, as if the other instruments were making a court visit. And poor Mozart has had to make the king's bowing look agile and rapid while the notes remain depressingly ordinary. Only women could do this, Bea reflects, watching the four serene faces, faces that beam at a child's drawing, all holes and flat perspectives, giant flowers and stick legs. Not merely beam but act as if the child has brought home a beatitude.

Cathryn believes that melody, like a good moment, comes from its opposite: discord. There is discord, or searching, and then the melody appears like someone arriving at a door and throwing off a cape. Pressing the door bell, setting the shoulders and calling, 'Darlings, I'm here.' But the discord, or neutrality — like Mozart's neutrality and effort to rise above it in K589 —

is part of it. Only rarely does melody spring forth fully fledged. Perhaps it might in a song? But it's not expected in a quartet. How moved Cathryn had been by Isambard Kingdom Brunel's bridge over the Thames with all its workings showing, girder added to girder, rivet to rivet. Gliding under it in the tourist barge, she had hugged herself with pleasure. How I love you. Isambard Kingdom Brunel and Wolfgang Amadeus Mozart. How I love seeing all the parts and how they make a whole. It is as well Cathryn has these thoughts when the Shostakovich begins.

Bea, who did not mind the Mozart, finding its eventual panache uplifting like a moral sampler, is now plunged into doubt. She is back in the Russian film of *Hamlet* where the stage becomes a great steppe. She barely remembers Hamlet's face — except that it is pale and fine-boned — but she sees again the wind disturbing something like chaff. And again this returns her to Seth. Only now his room is swept bare: apple cores, pizza crusts, squashed Cola cans are siphoned up into a deadly tornado. The walls are flattened to the ground, a net curtain dances like a ghost. And Seth seems to be staggering about, clutching himself as though he has suffered a stab wound. His inordinately long arms, accentuated by long sleeves and ruffles, are wound about his body. A terrible fear tightens Bea's chest. She thinks of the young men who die in battle and whose last cries echo their first: Mother, Mama, Maman. To calm herself she tries to locate the eerie sounds in the strings: just above the bare board ground, about the height of a child's torso or an adult's knee. The height of unassuaged misery and clinging. What does it matter that Seth's room is a rococo mess?

Cathryn is thinking about Russian novels, half-forgotten but never entirely erased images of Pierre Bezuhov wandering about the battlefield in *War and Peace*, or a family sitting outside a dacha with packed trunks. Vaguely she thinks of the rows of cots in *Cancer Ward* or a day in the life of Ivan Denisovich. There is a vast sweeping misery against which struggle is useless. Sonya Tolstoy leaps a small hedge as she runs towards Leo, keys clanking at her waist, but years of being amanuensis lead only to a dilapidated railway station, a grave covered by swirling leaves.

As the relentless and pure music fills her heart, Cathryn thinks of her marriage and is frightened by what she foresees. The absences, the courtesy, the passionless habit, what are these intimations of? The dumb animal content of their sex life, like two creatures bundling and bumping together. Will she be left holding a seagull or searching in the snow like Lara? Tears for herself run down Cathryn's cheeks. Desmond does not like string quartets, does not like what he calls the excessive strain of four players aping forty. If he were here, under protest, he would complain at the excessive expressions the four women are wearing. He would feel challenged by gleaming eyes, a unique identification with an instrument, almost an act of lovemaking. The cellist, he would say. Anyone would think it was a man. And the violins babies, mothers with offspring in their arms. And the viola? A beautiful cat, one that perches on a shoulder and purrs.

Suddenly Cathryn realises how much personality it takes to play a quartet, how each is an uncompromising soloist. Even each instrument is carefully chosen for individuality. Where has she read that the tone of the cello is dark and robust, chocolatey? And the second violin is not really 'second' at all but equal, only different, like two friends, herself and Bea. Each of them, at times, has dominated. There has been Bea's moment of triumph as the lead in a stage play, when Cathryn, who thought she knew her friend so well, saw her transformed, taken out of herself, so poised and confident under the spotlight. She had crept backstage with a posy of flowers and imagined, though the theatre was small and very badly served with dressing rooms, the scent of furs, a whiff of expensive perfume, the popping of champagne corks. Then Bea had sunk back, deliberately, modestly, into her daily life. Cathryn's moment had come when her book, *Flower Presses and Pressed Flowers*, was published and she had made an amusing speech about the morality of crushing flowers and preserving them inside books. Now she is thinking she will write something about the meaning of individual flowers, tying them to the books they are inserted in. It will be like someone ransacking a bookcase for banknotes.

We have taken turns, Cathryn reflects. Occasions when one or the other has sat at a kitchen table — in Bea's case the corner of a kitchen table — hands wrapped around a coffee mug, listening to the explication of a bad patch. Why shouldn't the instruments in a quartet be allowed a bad patch, to offer those soothing monosyllables that affirm, one to the other, before being called on for an opinion? How strong and masculine a statement might come from a cello. Or the excitable banter of two equally talented friends die into accord. How useful the differentiating viola.

When the Shostakovich comes to an end Cathryn claps until her palms hurt. She claps for the driving brilliance of the final Allegro, for the glorious spectacle of four souls, bowing arms, instruments united, but most of all for the triumph of melody. She has seen it created in front of her eyes, the labour it requires, the steadfast hopeful heart. As the bows of violinists and violist rise towards the heavens, Cathryn imagines she sees generations of life to come. She turns to Bea and their heads lean together.

THE LARK QUARTET

'Wonderful,' breathes Cathryn.

'Wonderful,' Bea agrees.

Four beautiful brows with their instruments held like trophies — except for the cello which looks as if it is going to do a twirl — bow in unison and then the faces are raised as if they have skimmed through water. Cathryn examines the shoes protruding from skirts and trousers and finds they too are individual. Then the Lark Quartet turns and goes through the curtain. There is a last glorious flash of gold, red and silver cummerbund, a poise of the nape of the neck that is heartstopping, and they are gone.

Bea and Cathryn have clapped until their hands ache. Three times the Lark Quartet has returned as though pulled back on strings, bowed and skipped off. Finally they turn and smile at each other conspiratorially and grant an encore. Neither Bea nor Cathryn hears what this encore is because it is announced from the stage and next day's paper does not mention it, going on instead about how the Larks miss their families and whether they have large phone bills. But this encore is as full of dance and harmony as all three quartets combined. It is perfume extracted from a field of flowers.

Bea and Cathryn cross the street in the rain, searching for a cup of coffee. The shutters of the Pizzeria Napolitana are up and the lamp over the door glows forlornly. Bea remembers a converted bank whose ground floor is a chemist shop. Soon they are seated at a gingham table with a Vat 69 bottle and ossified candle with two espressos and two wedges of Black Forest gateau.

'Was it a good performance, do you think?' Bea asks, stirring sugar crystals into coffee. 'I mean a good performance is unavoidable, but was there something extra tonight?'

Remembering the four triumphant faces, the joyous

congratulatory looks, Cathryn thinks there was. After all, why should a superb performance not occur in a provincial town?

'It could be accidental,' she says, looking out the dark window at glistening streets, a few neons desultorily flashing. 'In the lap of the gods, I mean.'

'Or a good dinner, a better than expected hotel, a shorter journey between towns than anticipated.' How did the Larks travel, come to think of it?

'Not the good dinner,' Cathryn responds, stabbing a large piece of Black Forest and conveying it to her mouth with a bowing arm. 'They always eat after.'

Cathryn imagines a late supper in a hotel room, a trolley with silver dishes, a waiter with an ice bucket. Bea who has a low opinion of provincial sophistication sees the Larks opening the miniature bottles in their mini-fridges and slicing a loaf into jagged door-stoppers.

'Surely a performance like tonight's must make eating seem rather irrelevant?'

'I doubt it,' Bea replies, stealing a corner of her friend's cake. 'They are probably as hungry as horses.'

'Do you think they go to different hotels? I've read some quartets like to.'

'Where would they go? The Regent or the Hyatt? Perhaps they might in a proper city.'

'One or two of the hotels are not bad,' says Cathryn defensively.

'No, it's a cold night. I see them huddling together.'

Bea spears the last piece of Black Forest and thinks how difficult it is to retain one's personality. She could sense the Larks struggling: their superb instruments, the music, themselves. Like falling overboard from a beautiful mahogany-fitted yacht and swimming around it with beautifully executed strokes.

'I expect the married Lark has very high phone bills,' Bea says.

'And the others probably phone their families or partners.' Cathryn cannot bear to think of the Larks not being equal.

'We should have waited by the stage door and thanked them.'

'We could have invited them to autograph our programme.'

'Or invited them home.' But Bea's voice falters. There is not only Seth's room but Seth himself. Probably at this moment the house is rocking to Def Leppard or Motorhead.

'Welcome to the Hotel California,' Bea imagines herself saying as she and Cathryn huddle against the stage door. Beds of flax are snapping in the wind and their umbrellas attempt to fly. Then, naturally, they are walking in single file along the wet street. Cathryn will offer to carry Astrid's cello and be gently rebuffed; she will hold her umbrella over it instead. 'Don't worry,' Astrid says. 'My cello is well protected.'

Up the stairs to the dark little coffee shop with its ornate plaster ceiling and dark panelling. Bea carries plate after plate of Black Forest gateau and asks for bottomless cups of coffee. 'Make mine latte,' says Jennifer.

Then what will they talk about? 'Do your instruments have names?' 'When did you first meet?' 'Here,' says Eva, thrusting the programme under Bea's nose. 'It's all in here.'

Bea shakes herself awake and watches the rain trickling down the glass, the pedestrian crossing globe reflecting in a puddle.

'More coffee, more cake?' she asks her friend.

'I couldn't,' says Cathryn. 'After the music I feel full anyway.'

They walk to the parking lot together, heads bowed under their umbrellas. Bea bows lower than usual, imitating the radiant Anna. But Cathryn, unfurling hers and lifting her face to the rain as she fumbles with the key, is a lark ascending.

&

Abraham, Edward Ernest, Jacob and Nina

Nicholas stands perfectly still as Mary and a live baby (Mrs Pigott's last and latest, Joshua Daniel Pigott, 15lbs 4oz, three months and four days) prepare for the Flight into Egypt. The Church of the Holy Sepulchre is packed and there is an extra hush as Mary, sidesaddle — except there is no saddle, only a shiny cloth — is handed the sleeping child. But even if Joshua Pigott wakes and squalls, Nicholas will not falter. The Flight into Egypt, the Nativity, Palm Sunday with the aisle a carpet of ferns and everyone holding up sprigs of sharp-scented macrocarpa: these are parts of Nicholas's year. Ecumenically, he appears at St Peter Chanel's Catholic Basilica (copes and incense), St Margaret's High Anglican (incense and brass eagle) and the Memorial Children's Hospital (balloons and crayon posters). A donkey is chosen above a horse, and when Nicholas is returned to his field and is not wearing his cover the long cross down his spine and across his shoulders proves it.

Jacob makes his lips into a moue and cautiously touches the top wire of the electric fence. Nothing. It must be the second wire. Now he opens his mouth wider and grasps the top of the white standard which is fastened into the field by a shallow spike. Jacob lifts this high and lets it fall. The wires of one segment crumple, the electrified wire among them. But there is still not quite enough width. Jacob moves down the row and repeats the process with two more standards. Then he stands back and Nina, Abraham, Edward Ernest pour through the gap. The strip of grass they are allowed for the day becomes a meadow with buttercups. There are also the low unfinished branches of the willow.

Jacob was a Christmas donkey and is well behaved except for opening gates. He has the courtliness of a profound thinker, the delicacy of a chess master. He contemplates a latch with a disc that falls in place, and works out a sequence. He would be the perfect accomplice to a safe blower, never panicking, ready to take the bullion on his back. Except Jacob would probably despise a safe blower, so full of adrenalin and fear, just like a horse.

Jacob has undone a lock considered impenetrable and let seven donkeys parked in a field after show day onto the road. This lock has exercised him considerably: it requires an elaborate sequence and the use of lips and teeth. Jacob is both hindered and spurred on by the gallery that stands behind him; one of the donkeys was *Best in Show*. When the lock finally yields with a snap, this is the donkey that leads the donkey caravan first to the rose garden, then the rhododendrons, and finally across the road to a ditch where the grass is long and succulent.

Sometimes, as a respite from thinking, Jacob stretches his neck towards the lowest branches of a young walnut tree. The length of his neck, the stretching of his lips, the delicious leaves weighted by still-held raindrops: he is certain of success here. It is the equivalent of Sherlock Holmes resting with a little violin-playing. When he is really thinking, Jacob stands statue-still.

Nina and Jacob are in the donkey cart together: mother and safe-breaker son. The crosses on their backs disappear under shoulder straps; each forehead sports a brass. Nina is pale milk-chocolate donkey brown; Jacob, like Abraham and Edward Ernest, ghostly grey. Jacob's rump rises higher than Nina's; the traces swell on his flanks like an equator line on a globe. Does he want this outing, down the sealed country road, turning into traffic for a few hundred yards, feeling Nina's fear of the white road markings, pulling her slightly towards the centre? Then they will be on the long stretch home, another long road with wide verges and houses with driveways and wagon wheels embedded. Ernest Edward and Abraham will bray their delight as they pass and stick their long necks over the fence. There will be an armful of hay for each, an apple and a piece of licorice. On the home turn Jacob will pull twice as hard for Nina; he will play the devoted son.

Edward Ernest hardly goes in the donkey cart now, unless it is a team. Edward Ernest has begun to stall at bridges. It began on the quietest, most familiar bridge, over little more than a dry ditch. As if some memory struck then, some association that cannot be countermanded, a solid block of image corresponding to the interruption to the road. Sweet words and fingers inserted inside the long ears to rub and caress — as if ears are very long foxgloves — make no difference. Was it the brutal farmer Edward Ernest was sold to by the vicar, a man who considered donkeys like women and walnut trees to be beaten? Edward Ernest had borne his blows and curses in the time-honoured fashion as if the perpetrator was merely human, a cross in itself. But at the sight of those he loved and had never forgotten, he practically bounded into the horse float. His old field was paradise regained. Nina escorted him around its borders and soon Abraham, who

ABRAHAM, EDWARD ERNEST, JACOB AND NINA

was well disposed, greeted him nose to nose. As for Nina and Jacob and Edward Ernest, they twined and nuzzled in the longest pash session on record. Someone who observed it said the twining necks were like swans.

Abraham takes Edward Ernest under his wing. Is it simpatico because Abraham was not quite fearless enough to separate bulls, to kick out ferociously with hooves and voice, and was going to be shot? If Edward Ernest has an unresolvable trauma, Abraham has the clash of combat ringing in his long ears, a desire to charge, obliterating fear in an instant, delivering blows to the air, to anywhere. But with Edward Ernest, Abraham becomes gentle. They stand together at the fence, press against one another in their canvas coats. Or they face one another in the shed which is open on both sides: two grey ghosts, little ghost and larger, as if by sharing the watches of their sleep, bulls and bridges are neutralised.

Nina falls in love easily. She is in love with Jacob her son as they trot or walk together in the pony cart. She leans towards him for reassurance about a passing car and also on the country road with grass verges. And it is noticeable when he undoes a gate or lowers the electric fence he allows Nina precedent. Nina has produced five offspring: Nicholas, in spite of his short stature and religious affiliations, was highly sexed. Without her two sons and Abraham, Nina would fall in love with a sheep or a goat.

Nina and Jacob, turning the donkey cart into the last long stretch, sight the horses grazing. Young girls loosely hold the leading reins. A palpable unease travels the space between them, as if an electric storm hovers. Under their loose covers the horses quiver and twitch; heads rear and hooves threaten to drum.

Finally the horses are dragged up a long drive, skirts flapping as in a joust; one, breaking loose, tramples a rose bed. The air seals itself over the road, calm resumes, and Nina and Jacob's jingling rhythm starts up again, the harness alive on their backs, the cart issuing creaks. A little white dog follows at a discreet distance, making no sound at all.

In the morning there is bread: two bread rolls each, sometimes with poppy or sesame seeds. The electric fence is moved a yard or so further into the field, the standards reinserted with a warning glare to Jacob who looks innocent though he is probably doing calculus, and Abraham, Edward Ernest, Jacob and Nina move forward onto the fresh grass uncovered. Behind them the donkey droppings are being forked into buckets to prevent the spread of worms. There are no humans in this story, only hands. Hands carrying hay at night, hands throwing covers over backs when the weather changes, hands opening with religious solemnity to reveal a piece of licorice.

Edmund Leach in a famous essay, 'Anthropological aspects of language: animal categories and verbal abuse', sets our relationship to animals like the standards of the electric fence —

Self . . . Pet . . . Livestock . . . 'Game' . . . Wild Animal

and the donkey's *Ee-yaw* among the words of baby language, along with *baa-lamb* and *moo-cow*. That Ee-yaw or Hee-haw is on this list is a safeguard, for the sound that Abraham, Edward Ernest, Jacob and Nina make as the hands assemble the bread rolls from the supermarket bag is hardly suitable for tender ears. Maybe it is closest to the bagpipes, a sound that seizes landscape and all its dire history into its throat. It seizes too a stillness, as if the world was once very different, a paradise, so a wail is incorporated, a pain that cannot be staunched. It saws the air and rises, unsuitable for church. But if the sound is harsh, the fact that 'ass' has been replaced by 'donkey' is due to its being included on the list of affectionately-regarded, thereby sacred and taboo animals. For the standards of the electric fence which Jacob is now nudging with his nose . . . *Self* . . . *Pet* . . . *Livestock* . . . *'Game'* . . . *Wild Animal* . . . hide a sinister gradation.

'Pet' is safe and 'Livestock' may be reasonably treated, though they end up on the table, but 'Game' and 'Wild Animal' are slurs. No treatment can be guaranteed for them: beaten fields, baiting with dogs, an extreme cruelty masked by ritualistic red coats and stirrup cups. Poor 'fox' whose name is 'dog' (for the male fox) must be suppressed. 'Dog' cannot even be permitted for the pursuing animals: they become 'hounds'. The only way the English could be turned from fox hunting would be to establish the fox as a species of dog. Or breed a dog-fox and show it at Crufts.

If I can enter, just once, as Self, I once climbed to the attic room of a farmhouse set in hedgerow-denuded fields — or vaster fields than there once were — and was surprised by the galloping of horses and the blowing of a horn. Peering out at a line of riders, including some quite ridiculous Thelwell ponies with little girls bringing up the rear, the words 'beating the bounds' shot into my head, though they were quite foreign to my experience. Over the newly ploughed fields the red-coated riders crashed and bugled, the pack of hounds bayed, and a terrible fear descended on field, house, and myself. I felt a blazing like fire, a martyr's anguish, the walk to the scaffold, the hostile crowd to the last speech. I, Self, categoriser through language of animals, can feel it still and summon it at any moment. All Self can say is that the landscape and all living creatures in it dissolved in the fear of what lay in store.

Tiny Nicholas died of skin cancer and was not considered suitable for pet food. Pale-skinned donkeys, those who are put down, or nearly put down, like Abraham, for not kicking vigorously enough at bulls or carrying loads like towers of Babel, are debarred from becoming food for dogs or cats. Nicholas's end, by veterinary intervention, is unknown to Nina, Edward Ernest and Jacob; his existence unknown to Abraham who was well into his apprenticeship as bull kicker. Edward Ernest was not yet sold to the Anglican vicar with the donkey-beater lying in wait. All these things are to be borne as tonight the wind reaches the pitch where it can whistle. Inside their shed Edward Ernest stands alongside and slightly lower than Nina; she keeps the breezes from him. Abraham and Jacob, brawn and brain, stand facing them as in a chess game. From the distance of the house, where at dawn the bread rolls will re-emerge, the scene is that of a manger.

In the summer months Abraham, Edward Ernest, Jacob and Nina are much in demand for children's parties. The houses they go to have long driveways and sweeping lawns, avoiding the necessity to take the cart onto the highway. Sometimes but not often the donkeys compete with a clown who is the indoor entertainment. Specially groomed and stoically still, Nina and Jacob (the usual two) stand on the gravel drive while the cart fills up with eager little bodies, shouting and waving to those left behind, some in tears at the thought of the donkeys being dismissed before they get a turn. Children's parties have a tumultuous air about them: tantrums hover like a dark cloud in an otherwise clear sky. Round and round go Nina and Jacob or Nina and Abraham or Nina and Edward Ernest before signs of his breakdown become apparent.

Scores of soft little hands are laid on Jacob's and Nina's

muzzles; tiny fingers stroke the long soft ears; the tufts of longer hair between the ears are marvelled at as if they are some springy crop. The children not riding in the cart break their queue and run alongside; occasionally there is a teasing boy who picks up a stone to throw but is caught in time. But eventually the clown calls, and the groaning table and the indoor games, including perhaps Pin the Tail on the Donkey. The donkey cart turns into the main road and Nina and Jacob — Jacob especially — are glad to feel the air on their flanks, the breeze parting around their muzzles, the simple scents of grass and earth instead of overheated children.

Were you ever in Quebec
Stowing logs upon the deck

— that might be the amble of the cart, the slight rocking from side to side —

Where there's a King with a Golden Crown
Riding on a donkey.

Then, finally, they turn into the home straight and here is the letterbox, especially commissioned, with geese on one side and donkeys on the other —

Heigh ho and away we go
Donkey riding, donkey riding
Heigh ho and away we go
Riding on a donkey.

Training to go in the donkey cart took months. Nicholas and Nina with long reins, no cart and a crowd of children — those who come to pat and admire — circle the largest field until they are walking like a wedding procession. Nina is pregnant with her fifth, Jacob; Neddy, the father, seems diminished, though this would be a false impression. The field is full of buttercups and daisies. The air of a great project, the Bolshoi Ballet choreographing a new work, or the Moscow Circus, hangs over the field and is sensed by the children who skip and call encouraging words. *Come on, Neddy. Good girl, Nina. Super, Neddy. Clever Nina.*

When the cart is added to the shaft, Nina and Neddy are a unit. Their initial unwillingness is drowned by a great cheer. Around and around the driveway — for the field is too uneven — they walk on, stop, walk on. White lines and bridges wait in the future; Nina's swollen belly will produce a saviour.

'Broadly speaking,' writes Edmund Leach, 'the language of obscenity falls into three categories: (1) dirty words — usually referring to sex and excretion; (2) blasphemy and profanity; (3) animal abuse — in which a human being is equated with an animal of another species. Why,' he asks himself, 'should expressions like "you son of a bitch" or "you swine" carry the connotations they do when "you son of a kangaroo" or "you polar bear" have no meaning whatsoever?'

Ass and *arse* or *ass* meaning *arse*, a word, according to Partridge, considered almost unprintable between 1700 and 1930 though Webster considered *arse* the politer spelling. *Ass* (animal) and *arse* (buttocks). Not to mention rectum, buttocks and vagina. Kangaroo and polar bear have nothing yet to fear, though their day may come, but ass is elevated to the sacred and taboo. And elevated again, into the clear air where kangaroo and polar bear sport, by being taken on as a baby word, a kind of cooing. *Bow wow, Doggy, Pussy, Quack-quack, Ee-yaw*, an escape in the nick of time from ass to donkey, from buttocks to Eeyore, to Robert Louis Stevenson's Modestine taking bread from his hand and behaving more nobly than he did. Abraham, Edward Ernest, Jacob, Nicholas, Nina, saved from words they have no cognisance of, preferring the words for *licorice, Oddfellows* (mints) and, in lower regard: *covers, hay, It's showtime, kids.*

'Can we come and pet the donkeys?' a little piping voice asks on the phone, and a time is agreed. 'Can we bring apples?'

Two small or one large apple per donkey are permitted, so the children have stolen four large Pacific Rose apples from the dining table and lean over the fence which is turned off. Three grey woolly heads and one brown line up. Halves of Pacific Rose crash down on to the grass; in Nina's case it is three-quarters. The juice flies out and foams on the lips like cider. Soon the grass is clear again and Abraham advances his rear quarters to have the backs of his knees scratched. Two obedient pairs of little hands set to work: an ecstatic overlapping pattern that, unseen to the masseuses, causes Abraham's mouth to fall open. Something between a sigh and a groan escapes. Nina, Edward Ernest and Jacob look stolidly ahead. Perhaps it is genetic, or simple reassurance after each bull-kicking session that his knees still work? Jacob is aware the fence is off and may, when the children depart, be forgotten. But figures are moving in the house: Jacob goes instead to measure the growth on the walnut tree, to check the size of the budding fruit.

'Ass' is an insult, along with bitch, cat, pig, swine, goat and cur. 'When an animal name is used in this way, as an imprecation, it indicates that the name itself is credited with potency. It clearly indicates that the animal category is in some way taboo and sacred. And whatever is taboo is a focus not only of special interest but also of anxiety'.

Edward Ernest, when he lived with the Anglican vicar, also took part in the liturgical year; in other seasons handicapped children were lifted onto his back and he walked slowly around the vicar's acre. Many of these children laid their heads against his mane or twined fingers in the tufts between his ears. At Christmas the vicar, who had Romish leanings and a fondness for incense, had Edward Ernest and a black sheep represent the animals at Christ's birth. The Three Kings, Caspar, Melchior and Balthazar, processed up the aisle in gaudy robes made from velvet and curtains. On their heads they wore high turbans studded with fake jewels. Caspar's face was blackened: his teeth shone out, causing Edward Ernest to start, though he soon recovered himself. The baby was a large porcelain doll. Edward Ernest's downcast eyes, a picture of animal modesty, and his tall ears made him the star of the show, eclipsing Mary. As for Joseph, made up to show age-lines on forehead and cheeks, the stepfather of God draped an arm over Edward Ernest's back as if for support.

'The gap between this world and the other world is filled with tabooed ambiguity', Edmund Leach observes. 'These magical ambiguous creatures, e.g. the donkey, are specifically credited with the power of mediating between gods and men'. Edward Ernest that night dined on carrots, apples and a slice of madeira cake.

Self . . . Pet . . . Livestock . . . 'Game' . . . goes the donkey cart, the reins slipping like water over the backs of Abraham and Jacob, courageous and wily one together. Self seems ablaze now as fields are passed and horses stare or skitter, cars courteously slow and are acknowledged by a wave of the whip. Sky and birds and grass verges, individual seed heads. White clouds and a circle of white geese in a field like a little white pond. Holding the centre

ABRAHAM, EDWARD ERNEST, JACOB AND NINA

of the road as time slows around them and something like a cupping glass descends. You can almost feel the immaculate transfer, the transubstantiation: *ass* into donkey, real presence. Another car slows and then slowly overtakes, children's faces grin against the glass.

'If you left home in a bad mood or had just quarrelled,' one of the presences on the cart speaks over Abraham and Jacob's heads, 'wouldn't this wash it all away? By the time you arrived at your destination . . .'

The backs of Abraham's knees itch; he longs to back up to anything, a human, a post. And Jacob . . . Jacob, dreaming of another gate, will have his 'far fierce hour and sweet'.

Milly-Molly-Mandy

IT MUST HAVE begun on a little shelf above a cradle. It had been prepared, together with the little shelf, with toys, some soft and one with a key, a mechanical bear that banged a drum. It was not opened above the cradle any more than the toy with the protruding key was let down for a small fist that sent everything towards an orifice. Though the parents can hardly be blamed. They thought no more highly of it than *The Water Babies* or *The Wind in the Willows*. No one they knew had their trousers tied up with twine or made a virtue out of rolling pastry. No child of theirs — their child had a fuzz of auburn hair — was going to develop boot-black bangs like Milly-Molly-Mandy.

If only they had intervened then, before it came time to move to the smallest size of bed — the mattress was known as Baby Princess — and thrown the book out the window.

The fuzz-haired baby grew into a serious little girl. The Titian hair thickened until it was like sheep's wool: it sprang up from the pillow like a particularly strong kind of grass.

'Darling hair,' her mother said, meaning, unlike herself, she would always look good in the mornings.

A light dusting of freckles bridged her nose from cheek to cheek: she was urged to regard them as kisses.

The books on the shelf expanded each year: there were books

for birthdays and Christmas and unbirthdays, a family joke, since the child's birthday — I had better tell you her name, Alice — was on St Nicholas' Eve. There was *Alice in Wonderland* and *Alice Through the Looking Glass*: Alice felt no consanguinity there, and she was alarmed at her namesake's changes in size. It was Milly-Molly-Mandy she latched on to from the beginning.

As Alice grew her parents marvelled that she read so much. They tried to entice her into the garden where the air was fresher but when enticed she often concealed a small book in her pinafore. She climbed the pear tree and lay along its branches like the Cheshire cat. Attached to the tree was a rope swing. At the point where the swing juddered and shook as though it was about to metamorphose into something else, Alice leapt and landed with her knees in a deep curtsy and her knuckles touching the grass. For a few seconds she was winded like a squashed paper bag.

But mostly she sat in her room on scatter cushions. It was her room now, painted to her design, with a blackboard screwed to one wall where she charted her homework and the number of hours it would take.

The slim volumes of Milly-Molly-Mandy — *Milly-Molly-Mandy Again, More of Milly-Molly-Mandy, Further Doings of Milly-Molly-Mandy* — had belonged first to Alice's mother, Eugenia. On her they had had no effect whatsoever. But on Alice, seated on her cushions, the effect was quite different. She was drawn to Milly-Molly-Mandy the way iron filings are drawn towards a magnet. Though there was no obvious physical resemblance, it was a meeting of heart to heart, almost soul to soul.

MMM in her thatched-roof cottage was not a frequenter of parties, and Alice perceived she went to them as reluctantly as herself. Eugenia and Chas were great party-givers and Alice was expected to put in an appearance. MMM was fitted out in a dress made from a white silk scarf with a pink sash, red shoes and a coral necklace; Alice had a series of elaborately frilled party dresses. She was expected to carry canapés. 'Smile, doll,' her father said. A doll had caused trouble for MMM, a horrid stiff lacquered doll like the one Alice had received for her last birthday. It had come in a long box tied with a ribbon. It was the deadliest thing Alice had ever seen; she hardly cared to lift it out.

For each of Alice's birthdays there was a party: dozens of little boys and girls clasping small presents which were thrust forward. The agony of opening them and thinking of something to say to the giver almost paralysed Alice, who hated most of the contents on sight. Garish poppit beads, handkerchiefs with her initial or arranged in a fan, lace-top socks, hair clasps, since her hair was frequently discussed. 'Alice the sheep,' her enemies called her behind her back.

Then there were games: Hunt the Thimble, Pin the Tail on the Donkey, Pass the Parcel, Musical Chairs for which Eugenia thumped on the piano. By supper time nerves were strained and those who had not won equally ghastly gifts as prizes were well on the way to dyspepsia. The end could not come soon enough for Alice.

She hung up her hated dress, pink with wide collars like Gainsborough's *Blue Boy*; cleaned her teeth; got into her nightgown and took MMM down from the shelf. After a party she always opened it at the illustration of MMM standing on the rug having her frock fitted.

Milly-Molly-Mandy, in the course of party games, had had her heart set on a *funny little white cotton-wool rabbit with a pointed hat on his head*. There was something about the placing of the button eyes or the stitching of the mouth: MMM found herself overcome with a passion to possess. The fairy doll was conspicuously on display for the child who won the most games; the rabbit awaited the booby. Unaccustomed to being a booby at anything — the word was unknown in MMM's household — she thought only to do her darndest.

Alice understood MMM's dilemma as well as the subtle pleasures of competitiveness. How often had she tried to beat some other child by memorising the items on a tray: pencil, nail scissors, paper clip . . . MMM's dark head bent over each challenge with a will. Sometimes Alice even wondered if MMM had supper.

The awful moment when the platinum-haired doll was presented to her, the blushes rising to her cheeks like two little red apples, the collapse of the real booby-brained child . . . Alice went over and over the scene, holding it frozen. How could MMM the winner transform herself into the loser?

Alice had all of the social temerity that Milly-Molly-Mandy conspicuously lacked. Alice would not be deterred by swapping a prize: after her own parties she distributed disliked presents to some child who wasn't invited. It was the attraction of oddness that began to fascinate her, the positioning of an eye, a felt nose not exactly centre. She could see it in windows full of toys: the same genus of toy, some prettier and regular, some more desirous of loving. *The most perfect beauty has some irregularity in it.*

If MMM was derailed on this occasion, there was no reason to think she went permanently off the rails. Her dough-rolling mother, gardening father, would have exclaimed over any prize she brought home. They too might have considered the fairy doll extravagant. The booby rabbit went upstairs and onto the pillow and at night MMM held it over her heart. Forget prizes, forget the booby, but Alice couldn't. She began to look for things that were aslant, askew. *Dappled pied beauty.*

Alice's parents were very conventional though they took care, as many do, to hide it. In Eugenia it concealed itself under darting repartee, fashionable clothes carelessly worn, a fast scan of news bulletins, book lists, theatre programmes. She advanced towards each new opinion as though it was a challenge. Once Alice overheard two men in the hallway refer to her as a 'cock-teaser'. She had no idea what this might be: a bird, a cock chaffinch? Her father put his effort and his languor — he was very good at slow deliberate movement — into being 'a man in the know'. The way he reached across his desk for a cigar or fingered a silver-framed photograph of Alice — some found these movements full of menace. Alice could see he was simply playing for time.

Inspired by boobiness, Alice began a collection of oddities which she kept on her bedside table. There was a fledgling's skeleton, so soft it hardly qualified as bone; a heart-shaped stone from the shingle coverlet of a child's grave; photographs of Marcel Marceau holding a flower as though it was the Holy Grail and the Elephant Man with his head in a bag. When these objects took on the appearance of an altar, Eugenia objected. Alice had taken two silver candlesticks from the dining room which were needed for a dinner party.

'Why these odd things?' she demanded, meeting Alice's cool eyes which looked as if they might discover a smut on her cheek or a crumb at the side of her mouth.

'Because odd things are best!'

When she went to university to major in the works of Wallace Stevens, particularly the influence of French symbolism and its effect on virtuosity, Alice had a series of affairs. Alice at nineteen was five foot seven but looked taller. Her spine was very straight, as straight as Wallace Stevens' might be considered languid:

perhaps she had been drawn to him by the similarly slow movements of her father. Not that she knew for sure that Wallace Stevens was slow-moving, but there was something in the poems that suggested it: thick, well-manicured fingers with rings pushing a poem under a pile of insurance papers.

If just above her head there hung,
Suspended in air, the slightest crown
Of Gothic prong and practick bright,

The young men chosen by Alice were sometimes taken home for a visit and sometimes not. She took them home not to meet her parents, but to use the swimming pool.

The suspension, as in solid space
The suspending hand withdrawn, would be
An invisible gesture. Let this be called

'I can't think where she picks them up,' Eugenia complained to Chas.

'They look like victims of Belsen, most of them,' Chas agreed.

There had been one very fat boy, but by tacit agreement they never mentioned him. He came from Uganda and was black.

Projection B. To get at the thing
Without gestures is to get at it as
Idea. She floats in the contention, the flux

Daudi, the Ugandan, was considerably stricken with Alice. He loved to run his fingers though her hair and feel her tickling curls under his chin. 'Golden Fleece' he called her and assured her she would be considered a prize by his tribe, the Baganda. But Alice was fast losing interest in Daudi. He, spurred by the love of her, was on a crash diet and becoming handsomer by the week. He identified the pangs of hunger from giving up

McDonalds, doner kebabs and Coca Cola with the pangs of love. Whereas Alice had been drawn to him by the tightness and straining of his black skin and a certain fatal melancholia. Alice thought there might be some depth of perversion in him, a depth to which she was prepared to accede, but he told her he preferred the missionary position. Then he went into a long explanation of the history of Uganda and its Christian missionaries. 'You no heard of de pure black boy,' he cried, clutching his chest and showing the whites of his eyes in mock anguish. Alice thought he looked like the Mock Turtle and decided to drop him.

Unknown to her, Daudi frequented brothels where his tastes were not so Christian. He enjoyed dusting and being spanked. A tiny frilly apron glowed miraculously against his ebony skin as he flicked a duster and trembled to be reprimanded. Not that dust mattered in the room he was in. Downstairs was a massage parlour and there was a great deal of giggling on the stairs.

'Well, Daudi Dowdiness.' A stern voice behind him made him realise his attention had wandered. 'I don't think this looks up to standard.'

The voice issued from quite a small woman who had to make a conscious effort to lower it. After Daudi left she often complained of laryngitis.

Alice graduated *summa cum laude* for her thesis, *Fanciful Flights and Solid Certainties in the works of Wallace Stevens,* in which interest was shown by an American publisher. Eugenia and Chas bought her an around-the-world air ticket and urged her to look up the publisher in Boston.

Alice had other plans. After Wallace Stevens, *A most inappropriate man In a most inappropriate place*, she needed a rest. She would definitely not be visiting Florida or any place with palms and ice-cream sellers in boater hats.

All thoughts of Milly-Molly-Mandy had long faded — indeed it is doubtful if Alice knew their influence — but at last she had time for MMM's other component: the pursuit of excellence. It was not the wistful-eyed rabbit so much but the effort that led to its acquisition. MMM had wanted to win something small: to this end her effort had been stupendous. Alice's attempted relationships with boobies had failed because her focus had been too narrow. A limp, a squint, a physiognomy at odds with itself were not sufficient. *I am the necessary angel of earth, Since in my sight, you see the earth again.*

Then she remembered Daudi had told her about his visits to the brothel in a final attempt to elicit sympathy.

After Europe, Alice went to South America. She transformed herself into a backpacker, staying at cheap hotels and travelling on rickety buses with poultry and produce. Emboldened by her new freedom she penetrated areas of cities previously unimagined by her. Her shabby clothes, her remarkable hair, so like the aureole of a crudely-painted saint, seemed to protect her. She was jostled and pinched and had her wallet stolen — her passport and extra banknotes she wore in a moneybelt — but nothing worse befell her. The slant-eyed slums became as familiar and predictable in their way as the great avenues named after generals and revolutions.

Eugenia and Chas were very surprised on Alice's return to learn that she intended to settle in a very rough inner-city suburb.

Natives of poverty, children of malheur,
The gaiety of language is our seigneur.

They pleaded with her to take over part of the family home. The swimming pool had long since been filled in and made into lawn.

In Alice's street there were nightly brawls, and police cars cruised past like swimmers doing laps. But what pleased her most was that hardly anyone looked normal. Grossly overweight women pushed shopping carts; children whose faces never achieved total cleanliness sucked sticky lollipops. No one had a proper silhouette like the outline lined up for police marksmen. Was this what the cruising cars were looking for? There was one street of ethnic restaurants: converted shop fronts with tables poked into them and wobbly unmatching chairs. A few neon signs flashed and enterprising children guarded cars for a fee.

When Eugenia and Charles paid their one and only visit the windscreen wipers were torn off the Volvo. Alice did not improve matters by suggesting the damage was light. 'You should be grateful your tyres are intact,' she observed.

'Never again,' said Eugenia as they drove off. 'She can come for Christmas if she likes or we'll send her present over. I wouldn't even risk the Mini.'

'I can't think what's got into her,' Chas said for the hundredth time. 'It's like batting your head against a brick wall.'

'Why does she want to associate with such people?' Eugenia demanded, and it sounded like a wail. 'It's not as if she hasn't been brought up properly.'

'You're exaggerating, Jeanie,' Chas said, almost angrily. 'They were the same types, the same boobies even then. It wasn't a bloody swimming pool at all. More like the River Ganges.'

It was not a pleasant thought. Besides he didn't mean the khaki-coloured holy river but the pool in the Bible where the lame and palsied were brought. Stirred in its depths or by a wind. Luckily there was no one else at dinner that night, no fresh candidate for his daughter's compassion, interest, exploitation, whatever it was.

The Volvo shook off the last tawdry streets and accelerated into avenues bordered by plane trees. Outside Alice's house, where the air seemed too heavy to stir, a car body was being scratched by a penknife and a bottle was travelling towards a bay window.

When, that Christmas, Alice came for dinner, she wore dark glasses and a heavy layer of make-up. Chas guessed at once she had been beaten and was attempting to cover the traces. No amount of eyeshadow and underlining could conceal the bruise developing around one eye. She wore a loose long-sleeved shirt and Chinese mandarin pants.

'I don't know why you don't bind your feet and be done with it,' her mother cried in anguish.

Christmas dinner was a disaster. Alice insisted on leaving her glasses on. She drank glass after glass of sherry and then brandy.

'Come home,' her father pleaded as, risking the Volvo, he drove her back. But she shook her head and went in through the unhinged gate without a backward glance.

The following year Alice's thesis was published to considerable notice in academic journals — '*Recreates some of the elegance of Stevens, an exemplar of: The poem is its style*' — and she was offered a junior lectureship. To her parents' amazement she accepted. A few months later she put the house on the market and moved to an inner-city apartment. And she began to see a counsellor.

The counsellor's office was sub-let from a legal firm. The decor was brown varnish and Alice sat on a brown leather chair. Battered filing cabinets stood against the walls and Alice wondered if they were full of client files or bequeathed.

At first Alice and James Pettigrew sparred and circled one another like two sailors who have fallen overboard from a boat. The circling reminded her of Wallace Stevens: the weather, the palm trees, the *idea* of a place were so much a part of his work.

Something minute and particular might have a hurricane brewing offshore.

'Many people are drawn to oddities,' James Pettigrew said on the fourth session, placing his fingertips together so fingernail rested delicately on fingernail. They were hardly used fingertips, Alice thought scornfully. Just like Wallace Stevens'. 'However you seem to have been drawn in a manner that suggests an obsession. Buried,' he hastened to add, to counteract Alice's expression, which looked threatening. 'Can you think of anything that might have given you a desire for oddities plus a drive for excellence?'

But Alice could think of nothing. Her father, *Call the roller of big cigars, the muscular one*, was a deceptively ruthless businessman; her mother, *Serve the rouged fruits in early snow*, overly conscious of proprieties. Alice could admit no similarities in temperament.

'There always are,' James Pettigrew said kindly. 'Similarities, I mean. Though the gene factor favours a closer resemblance further back.'

Let be be the finale of seem.
The only emperor is the emperor of ice-cream.

That night it came to Alice in a dream. It was not a dream brightly coloured, vivid with characters or menace. It was a taste of something long remembered that vanished mockingly as she woke. Alice's nightgown clung to her, yet she did not recall any fear. Whatever the taste was, it had made her small again and vulnerable. She knew she had been reading a book.

James Pettigrew and Alice went over *Milly-Molly-Mandy Goes to a Party* on the seventh and final visit.

'How innocuous it is really,' Alice remarked. And it was true the prose seemed transparent, deathless, preserved in amber. *So Milly-Molly-Mandy ran up to the lady who had given the prizes, and asked if she and Miss Muggins' Jilly might exchange prizes, and the lady said "Yes, of course."'*

'All for *a little cotton-wool rabbit with sad beady eyes*,' said James Pettigrew, joining in with enthusiasm (it was not often one got such a quick diagnosis), running his pink fingertip with its straight-clipped nail down the page.

'*Do you love the fairy doll more than the booby rabbit?*' read Alice. She couldn't quite laugh yet.

'Lust and Milly-Molly-Mandy,' said James Pettigrew, sensing despondency. 'You'll be free now, Alice.'

One walks easily
The unpainted shore, accepts the world
As anything but sculpture. Good-bye
Mrs Pappadopoulos, and thanks.

Then to break the mood and restore the elements the dream had lacked he read in a kind of coda: '*So Milly-Molly-Mandy and the booby rabbit went home together to the nice white cottage with the thatched roof, and . . .*'

&

Six Sisters from Ouse

I COULD NEVER get the name out before the laughter started. Ouse, ooze, frog slime. A bog house, the walls crumpling in on a wave from a risen river. Or a house reduced to an ache, no longer a home. At the end of a long hall with a carpet runner a mouth open in a scream or, if the time for screaming was past, opening and closing as silently as a goldfish. Didn't Mary Queen of Scots' mouth open and close for quarter of an hour after her beheading? Wasn't her little dog that went with her, under her claret-red petticoat, washed and washed but refused to eat? There was a flood actually, in Ouse, in my grandmother's house, and afterwards the house was as thoroughly scoured as the execution dais of the dead queen.

But if you can't get past a name, a geographical name, how can you begin any story at all? How can you find those few geographic images and reminiscences that might hold a foot to the ground, a curtain to a window, a change purse to the hand of a provider? The purpose of cleansing the queen's scaffold was to forestall martyr's relics: the little ailing dog might have its fur plucked out for being closest to the event. Not a splash of blood must remain. Certainly no lady-in-waiting to dip a handkerchief.

Ouse, now I think about it, runs, oozes away from me too: its faint scoured description could describe a dozen ill-favoured towns whose purpose is to straddle a highway that disdains them, where travellers might stop for a cup of tea or, on the other hand, press on. There are little towns that achieve a sense of self-regard in new paint and imported awnings, flowers artfully arranged in sawn-off barrels. Ouse was defined by its curve of road at one end and the hill up which it disappeared at the other. This highway, along whose borders I walked as a child, was the liveliest thing about it. Its curve seemed more energetic than the town itself, like a strong arm flung over it. And where the road raced skywards it left what little history Ouse possessed — the graveyard, the church, the school house — behind. As if resenting this, and attempting to have some defining boundary of its own, Ouse possessed, at its other border, a river and a bridge. The River Ouse. 'You've heard of the River Ouse,' I'd say, inserting this into the laughter. 'The famous river that runs through York.' A bridge, I didn't add, decorated with heraldic shields, beautifully and lushly painted, beneath which pleasure craft and barges nestled and willows trailed in the water. The trouble with Ouse was you had to get the name out first, then tone it down. It was a name that hadn't travelled well.

But even York did not work on some of these debunkers, for they could not visualise the city with walls as thick as marzipan, the great Minster and other little churches. If I went on I hastily described Ouse, Tasmania, in ways that denigrated it further: its neither fertile nor scrubby landscape, its run-of-the-period architecture, the general store, my aunt's, set at an odd angle to the road like those bookshelves designed to give an illusion of curving ends. Yet my grandmother's house, Wilga, though plain, stood between two elegant houses that might have graced inner Melbourne.

Wilga had a long hallway like the alimentary canal that bisected the house, leaving the long kitchen at the back gasping.

There was a carpet runner, a brass pot on a hallstand, a shadowy front room where a cream froth of lace made a surprising wave in the dim light. It was down the hallway that the River Ouse made an entrance, forewarned, Shakespearian-fashion, by a flustered policeman on a bicycle. Without that hallway the river would have behaved differently, woven from side to side like the cornered snake one of my aunts dispatched with a broom handle.

    I used to stand outside in the evening admiring the two houses next door. My grandmother's house was wooden but these were soft creamy stone: two storeys as neat as a single block sliced by a stone mason. They had balconies and shutters. The creamiest, richest curtains were nothing to them. They could save Ouse from obscurity.

My grandmother, Alice Bowerman, lived at Wilga with one of her daughters, Eileen. She was in her nineties but still able to use an electrified treadle machine and walk to church on Sundays. A tall wiry woman, her figure and posture held a severe grace. Her face was deeply lined and browned by the sun, for she would have scorned the idea of preserved white ladies who carried parasols and whose skins were a moral reproach to uncouth natives. Not that there were any natives, only convict descendants filled with a vast rock-bottom pride. 'The only way to go is up' was written on their genes. Besides, their inherited crimes were petty and grew more preposterous by the year: a strangled rabbit, a trout, a loaf of bread, a handkerchief of less value than five shillings. My grandmother, summing up the situation of the new land, acted as if she too had stolen a pie from a windowsill or fruit from a barrow. She put aside those artistic parts of her nature: the deep reading; the reflective walks, except to church; the delicate watercolours. She sewed endlessly, six dresses with different details and hem lengths. The six sisters went to sleep with the hum of the Singer sewing machine in their ears.

There were thirteen children in the family, eight girls. The eldest and youngest were girls with six sisters and one brother in the middle. One brother died in a fire when he was a baby; another had a scalded arm with a hot-looking scar; one was angelically simple, conceived while my grandmother was in shock over the fire. Two very hearty, strong ones were teasers but softhearted and as easily led by women as bulls with nose rings. The eldest daughter, Agnes, became Mrs Echo like a bell fading away on the horizon. And the youngest, Sophie, was too young to tag along: the six sisters who had done sterling work as child minders and brother managers handed her back to my grandmother as though she was a porcelain doll. They felt themselves to be a group. There was Mrs Echo, married and inclined to be condescending; and there was Sophie, tumbling about and indulged, for she was the thankful last, at the foot of their mother.

The six sisters in the middle had alliances, of course, allegiances which changed from day to day. The Bowermans were not quarrelsome, but from both parents they inherited a dislike of dissembling — except in the case of Kib, whose saintly demeanour and endless patience would have tried the patience of a saint. Something had been burnt out of him, was the view: he knew neither troughs nor heights but a curious delight in everything — a flower, a kitten, a meal. Nonetheless there was a division of temperament in the sisters: Jane, Ismay and Rose were placid and slowly aroused to anger, which resembled their mother. The other three, Eileen, Irene, Ada, were like their father, who could rise to a rage in a moment and then have it drain away, leaving him forgetful, half ashamed, mildly amused at being so shaken. He held on to something, a gatepost, a tree, when one of these passions overcame him — it might be an injured animal maimed by a stone-thrower, a fence deliberately cut, an instance of bullying — waiting for the rage to drain away. No one who knew him could fear it in him and he didn't fear it himself: it flamed so intensely and was over so quickly he would hardly have had time to raise a fist. Then he would set about tackling the culprit, mending the fence, applying a salve, fuelled like a rocket booster.

In the small house the chores, thanks to their mother, rotated like clockwork. The boys dug the garden, chopped wood, whistled the dogs for milking, mended gates. The girls baked bread, legs of mutton, shortbread; washed curtains, smoothed beds, swept floors, ensured the larder was full. They cooled bottles in the creek, supported by a ring of stones; picked apronsful of fruit for pies; stirred great cauldrons of jam; whipped cream so thick it could be cut with a knife. Each of the sisters had a speciality: Jane's was bread, Ada's pickled walnuts, Eileen's strawberry jam, Irene's fudge, Ismay's an apple tart with crossover strips of pastry, Rose's a facility to put in sleeves. Their mother's was generalship or foresight: she could see the next Sunday's visit to church and its baked meats as an artist in the background of a religious scene makes tiny pilgrims and laden donkeys vanish behind a little hill. And their father? His task was to be one of the Greek gods, a Bacchus, smear-lipped, sated and fuzzy of flesh (from work, not love, though he loved hugely in what there was of his time). His emotions brought dark and light into their lives, mystery and passion and music.

Mrs Echo, Adeline, had married money and swooped on them from time to time with gifts from Hobart. Her dresses were the latest fashion, her hats sumptuous. Her only son, Basil, was clean and scrubbed and already trained to carry parcels. But Jane, Ada, Ismay, Irene, Rose, Eileen did not regard her as a sister: she belonged to an age of elegance they might have encountered in a book borrowed from Miss Swann, the greatest reader in the district. A book about the coming of the automobile or rich families at Nantucket. Rich the Bowermans were not, but it seemed they could produce richness.

Of the six sisters Jane was the first to marry. The romantic brothers had long since taken wives: slim, effacing women. Robert's wife, Clarissa, was withdrawn, Eileen thought, to the point of stupor. Around her Robert laughed, whistled, sang, played the accordion, like a giant dog. With all his personality to end up with someone like Clarissa! Edward's wife, Veronica, was hardly more visible. And Jane's husband, Horace, didn't seem a catch either. Years later, when he confided to one of the husbands, Ada's, that he had had the Bowerman girls on a list and intended to propose to them in order of preference, there was a great outcry.

'Who'd want to be on the list of that odious man?' Rose cried, aware that she, for all her beauty, was fourth. And why should the plainest, Jane, be at the top? The answer was only too obvious. Horace was lazy and enjoyed his comforts. Jane was strong, self-effacing and capable. What stubbornness she had was applied mainly to her estimate of doing things well. On only a few occasions in their married life was it applied to Horace. Ada thought Horace regarded Jane as a Clydesdale, one of those beautiful gentle horses who use their strength of character and limb so lightly no thoroughbred can match them.

As if influenced by Horace and his 'list', the five remaining sisters left for Melbourne. They went in pairs: Eileen and Irene first. They worked as housemaid and cook (Eileen cooked) in a society doctor's house in Little Collins Street. Rose became a lady's companion. Ismay, stung by their letters, answered an advertisement requiring a nanny to accompany a child to

Malaysia. Ada, preparing to pack, was courted by one of Ouse's few desirable bachelors, who managed a general store. He saw he must prevail against the glamour of the mainland and promised her a honeymoon in Sydney and Melbourne. They walked on the hills around Ouse and, as Bill explained the business to her and the range of its stock, she allowed it to be built into a false glamour: the world of layers which in fact it was, for rabbit traps and rifles hung from the ceiling while soft flowered dresses and children's party frocks were shrouded on a rail not far from the bacon-slicer.

Nonetheless, when four sisters returned from the mainland — only Ismay on a passenger liner passing through the Straits of Malacca with her charge, an American boy, Chester, was absent — Ada sensed their superiority. That their jobs — chambermaid, cook, lady's companion, nanny — were not glamorous didn't count, since they were conducted in such surroundings. How plain the Bowerman house seemed, with every bedroom doing triple duty. And though Ada looked beautiful and dignified in satin and guipure lace, they couldn't help regaling her with their own uniforms. Irene was now at Government House where her forearms had been examined by Jessie, the formidable Scottish housekeeper, whose reservations were overcome when someone passed a remark about 'the smallest ones being the best workers'. Her dress for tiptoeing down ninety-eight steps at 5 a.m., lest the lift wake the Governor, was full-skirted black with a frilled white apron and cap, though for blacking fireplaces they wore an apron that covered most of the dress. Kneeling in vast rooms with the other maids, Irene could watch the dawn light glow beneath the long windows' elaborate swags.

To compensate, Ada and Bill came to Melbourne on their honeymoon but first they went to Sydney and, after Melbourne, Alice Springs. This way the lives of the other sisters were sandwiched in a wider world, but Ada had memories that could not be gainsaid. In later years she could talk of Alice Springs and how it made her begin to long for Ouse, which seemed fertile in comparison. Ada, serving in the store or bent over account books for which she showed a facility, was not good at idleness and she was grateful to Alice Springs for making this clear to her. Nonetheless, Irene, Eileen, Rose took gleeful pleasure in surrounding her and the gangling Bill as they walked down Collins Street. Forgotten were the more timid walks they took on their own: eyes downcast, cloche hats firmly rammed down, a walk identical to the one they used — purposeful, swift — in the long corridors of Government House or the passages of private mansions. 'How quick all you Bowerman girls are,' mused Mrs Doctor Fitzgerald, who had employed Eileen, Irene and Rose in sequence and sometimes two at a time. 'I've never seen anyone glide like Eileen does with the soup.'

Only Ismay, gliding over the waves to Malaysia, was absent. A letter from Ada with a postscript, 'I am so glad you are my sister — one among many!', awaited her at a poste restante. Her charge, the American boy, Chester, was no trouble except for his loquacity and his direct way of asking questions. 'Will you get married, Miss Bowerman?' 'Would you like to have a little boy like me?' Ismay, looking over the rail, assured him she would, but his childish solicitude made her feel like an orphan. She brushed a tear from her cheek.

'Are you crying, Miss Ismay?'

'No, it's the spray.'

When Ada and Bill returned to Ouse and Best's General Store, Ada set to and scrubbed all the shelves with carbolic soap. Eileen, Irene and Rose resumed their more cautious lives, rising in the dawn and finishing late, hoarding their days off for cinema visits or saving to go to Gladys Moncrieff. Dr and Mrs Fitzgerald had departed one night in opera cape and furs. Even Eileen, who had socialist principles, was unable to suppress a gasp of admiration as Mrs Dr Fitz in silver and sable pulled on long silver gloves. Dr Fitz's opera cape was lined in glorious flashing red satin. Eileen handed him his cane and top hat and barely resisted a curtsy.

'It's all right, Eileen. I'll be back to a pumpkin in the morning.'

'Never, sir.'

'Don't wait up now.'

Three nights later they were up in the gods in the self-same theatre, peering down at a stage bathed in bosky light where a plump but beautifully draped and corseted figure sang like a nightingale.

'I got carried away,' Dr Fitzgerald said as he beheaded his breakfast egg. 'Forgot all about measles and mumps and the unemployed knocking on the door.' (When they asked for gardening jobs Eileen was instructed to say they had no vacancy but offer a meal.)

Irene was too shy to venture to dances or the cinema alone but she agreed to a blind date with another Government House maid, Minnie, and her fiancé, Ernest. Ernest was an excessively shy young man, which may have reassured since no best friend of his could be boisterous. Teddy was so quiet he hardly said a word, apart from enquiring about Minnie and Ernest's plans, which Minnie provided at great length, but he gazed at Irene and apologised when his shoe touched hers under the table. The tables were very close together and the cups and plates had blue rings. They had two cups of coffee and Minnie complained that now they would never be able to sleep.

'Good thing,' said Ernest. 'It means you'll be thinking of me.'

They walked back to Government House along a Collins Street bathed in blue light. Ada was right, it could be Paris, or as close to Paris as they could come, but to know that and enjoy it was something worthwhile. It was like Irene's reading: when she got to a memorable passage in a book she inserted her hand between the pages and lightly closed it, to savour it. Still a gaze, even a furtive one, can lead somewhere, and it soon became a fixed thing for Minnie, Irene, Ernest and Teddy to meet on Friday nights. The café led on to the cinema, the music hall, the Easter Show. And eventually a very small registered parcel with a note that read 'The best things come in small parcels' — a reference to height and tiny wrists — was handed to Irene by Jessie. She opened it, in spite of pleas for public disclosure, in her room. Inside a velvet box lay a ring with three diamonds. Then she recollected Minnie had pressed her to try on her engagement ring the week before.

Ismay, in Kuala Lumpur at the Shangri-La with Chester Cabot Jnr, received news of her sisters sporadically. Irene's letter of engagement arrived by the same post as one describing a theatre foursome and the hint of an admirer. 'Nothing serious,' Irene had written, 'though it's a relief to have an escort.' Ismay shared the fear: her life was luxurious, easy, but solitary. She talked to the manservant who brought her hot water but he was obviously longing to exit backwards from the room. Her last vision of him was his turban trying to touch the floor. There were rides in the park with Chester: an old-fashioned barouche met them at the door and they sat covered with rugs. But instead of looking from left to right like royalty, Ismay found herself focused on the horse's glossy black mane, thinking of Dobbin the old farm horse at Ouse who patiently bore them all on his back, their short legs hanging down like centipedes. Chester, obedient, prematurely adult, kept up an endless barrage of questions. 'Do you like palm trees?' 'Would you live in a country with crocodiles?' 'Do you think rich people have better manners?'

To a selective few of these enquiries Ismay responded, monosyllabically, except where she felt a short moral comment was required. 'Rich people should have better manners,' she suggested, 'since they are not subject to the same strains as poor people. And you, Chester, are a well-mannered young man.' How could she say that in even the nice manners of the wealthy there was a condescension that prickled the skins of those who had to pile their small change up in little tottering towers? Or that hand-me-down clothes, finer than any expectation, offhandedly, sensitively given, still left a crumb of resentment. But Chester had already moved on to trishaws and whether they would work in Melbourne or be best kept to public parks. Ismay straightened the rug over their knees and forced herself to admire bustle, buildings, pagodas, markets.

Eileen had had one failed romance and did not think she would have another. She had chosen a mother's boy and an only son, a combination whose potency would recur during her years of spinsterhood. She was five foot ten, a product of her mother's genes: 'long tall Eye', her father called her. Frederick, the young man in question, was five foot six, and Eileen was careful to match her stride to his and stoop to his kisses. If she wondered whether all men kissed so wetly, she had no way of knowing. The formidable mother, limping on two sticks and from time to time drawing in deep irregular breaths that no one could fail to hear, was icily polite. Eventually she convinced her son that while Eileen's housekeeping skills were not in doubt, she lacked the ease of a hostess and consort. Frederick, who worked in a bank, agreed. But he lacked the courage to tell her, cancelling his visits only at the last moment, passing on a message to Mrs Doctor Fitzgerald who offered to find Eileen. Eileen was too proud to call at the bank or phone. 'Write and ask him to make his intentions clear,' Mrs Dr Fitz urged. 'I'll give you some of Dr Fitzgerald's notepaper.' So the blow fell like a slow vibration, as if every atom shook and finally dissolved into stillness.

Irene's wedding was to be held at Ouse, and Teddy was brought to meet the family during a break between shearing, train driving and apple picking, which was then the method in which he passed his year. He was received easily by the Bowermans, to whom an addition was nothing more than an extra dinner guest: as children grouped around the long table they had grown used to their mother averring she was not really hungry and passing her plate to a last-minute caller. Or she took a fresh plate from the dresser and went around the table, robbing a potato from one, a slice of meat from another. Ouse, through Teddy's eyes, was reclaimed: the sinking feeling it gave the mainland Bowermans overcome by his willingness to swear the wrought iron work on one or two of the balconies as good as St Kilda; to find the cemetery where Death, like a ringmaster, was edging Catholic and Protestant together, charming; even its valedictory hill proper in the landscape.

The night before her wedding, James Bowerman handed Irene the life insurance policy he had taken out for her when she was twelve. She was now twenty-eight. She weighed seven and a half stone and her wedding dress, sewn by Lady Huntingdon's own Government House dressmaker, was close-fitting cream silk with a mandarin collar. Her bouquet was enormous; she might have been carrying a cabbage. Ismay had sent an ivory fan from Kuala Lumpur. Ada was matron of honour, a role she played in a queenly fashion, and the bridesmaid was Gussie, another maid from Government House. Eileen, too tall to be considered, had requested only that the bouquet not be thrown in her direction. Irene had a mischievous look in her eye. When the photographer vanished under his black cloth like the rear of a pantomime horse, Eileen edged herself out of the frame.

Unlike Ada and Bill, Irene and Teddy honeymooned in Ouse. 'An impossibility, I should have thought,' Ada remarked. They repaired to a bed and breakfast establishment and spent days at the family farm, riding Dobbin's successor with Irene in front and Teddy's arm lightly circling her waist. Teddy was a New Zealander, a Southlander, and keeping close to the home paddock was his way of proving himself.

Then just before they departed for Melbourne, Ismay arrived home unexpectedly. Her American employers had suffered a bereavement and returned to Philadelphia; Ismay, handsomely remunerated and with an envelope of glowing references, had decided to have a holiday. She had taken a flying boat from Melbourne to Hobart. On the last day of Irene and Teddy's visit, she was introduced to a tall swarthy man with penetrating dark eyes. Teddy had met him in the Ouse hotel and, in the bonhomie of new happiness, approached him. The stranger was peering into the depths of his glass as if expecting beer to gush forth like oil; Teddy offered a refill. *The Man from Snowy River*, he thought: he wasn't thinking clearly or he might have taken in something closed about the countenance, an ease with long silences which even the shy would find unnerving. Ismay, so cut off from a life of her own, attentive to her charges, alert to the rumblings of her employers, had hardly formed a single judgement on her own behalf. Without knowing it she looked upon the stranger whose name was Rudolph — a seduction in itself — as a nurse looks at a patient. That his silences intimidated others and might be considered weapons, that he was undoubtedly secretive, attracted Ismay who hardly knew she had a heart. Ada and Eileen were alarmed and tried to intervene; even Teddy, perceiving what he may have started, had a warning word. 'Moody men are so difficult for women,' he cautioned. Irene was too caught in her own happiness. But opposition and silences seemed to join forces to form a wall, one of those walls of artfully placed stones that endure against the extremest weather. When Rudolph produced a black stallion named Rajah which no one else could approach and which could be seen snorting and rearing in its field, Ismay was lost. 'She's a goner,' Robert agreed on one of his rare visits, nervous wife in train, literally three steps behind. But he said it with the complaisance he showed when reaching for his harmonica, not caring if anyone wanted music or not. Even Eileen couldn't help admiring Rajah, standing by the fence with Ismay. Eileen was trying, tall as she was, to be a guardian angel.

Rudolph was an itinerant worker but he had capital and his aim was to buy into a property. The large sheep stations around Ouse struck him as ideal. His stallion, his long sweeping oilskin coat which flapped as he walked, the endless cheroots which, of an evening, he lit from a kerosene lantern, were only a disguise. 'I wouldn't be surprised if when they cut him open he has a black heart,' Ada said bitterly. Bill was in the cottage hospital with a bout of pleurisy and her evenings were devoted to bookkeeping. She had already adopted the policy of asking the rich for cash and allowing the improvident credit, which was to make her known as a local Robin Hood. She was a good manager, however: charitable but firm. No one could consider her a soft touch.

Irene and Teddy were back in Melbourne when the news of Ismay's secret wedding to Rudolph came. Teddy was shearing in a huge station called Randwick Downs and Irene involved in the preparations for the wedding of Lord and Lady Huntingdon's second daughter, Gwendoline. Irene recalled Ada's remark about the black heart and shivered while her mouth held a line of pins.

'Dear Irene and Teddy,' Eileen wrote, mindful of her sister's status, though wishing to write to her alone. 'I fear Ismay is lost. How can it have happened? We know her temperament is so sweet and self-effacing. But is it allied with an awful stubbornness?' Eileen was hardening her heart against stubbornness. She remembered Stonewall Jackson, from school. Stone wall she thought. The desire to turn into a wall. But could that apply to bones and flesh? I blame the horse, she thought, remembering Ismay's loving care of Dobbin, the endless brushing and rubbing of liniment. No one suspected that Ismay in all her years of pampered servitude — coal carried for the fire by a manservant in livery, afternoon tea served by a frill-capped maid — was resentful at a lack of drama. She had seized the risk of Rudolph in both hands.

'All we can do is wait,' James Bowerman said. He meant wait and pray. He was unfailingly polite to Rudolph on his rare visits, laying in a supply of cheroots. 'We were too tame for her,' he told his wife. Perhaps if his own bursts of rage and passion had been longer lasting: did quicksilver equal nothing?

But James Bowerman died before the mystery of his one wayward daughter came to a head. On his deathbed, regretting this mystery like a good story he would not read the end of, he held her hands and whispered, 'Do what you have to do,' trying to make it sound like a blessing.

A week later Ismay packed a small suitcase with broken locks, secured by a leather strap, and trudged the dusty road between Torhill and Ouse. Tears ran down her face but she let them dry in the sun. She thought of salt and whether it would leave a crust. She sees herself at her father's grave and wonders that she can still produce tears. Mrs Echo's huge hat with black swan's feathers cast a shadow over her like an umbrella tree; she feels her eldest sister's fingers dig into her shoulders. 'I always wished I could have given you a life insurance policy, Iz,' her father had whispered, straining away his last precious words, 'but the money ran out with Irene.' She thinks of her sisters — the six, *Les Six*, as Ada had called them once. They felt like six stones.

At Ada and Bill's, a wedding anniversary dinner was in progress. A lace cloth, a rare bottle of pink wine the colour of rabbits' eyes, a pink candle. They pulled up a chair for her, set a place with the best silver. Ada had seized the shabby case and stowed it in the spare bedroom.

'Let me wash first,' Ismay pleaded.

That night she slept in a bedroom whose window opened directly on to the boardwalk. It was a narrow window with a heavy sash, too small for a body to enter, safely screened with the thickest of lace curtains. But still there was enough breeze for the curtains to move and the sweet, soft, faintly dust-scented and rain-refreshed air to enter. Lying back on pillows with hand-crocheted borders, Ismay felt the little breeze mould her face with the lightest of touches, like soft hands dipped in water.

Would Rudolph appear on the boardwalk, his worn boots ringing like fire, leading Rajah, the deepest bond they now shared? Would he offer to buy her a dress, any dress, as he had once before? Would he sign a paper saying he would speak more than one sentence a day? The air moved over her, body and face, like the wind on the heath in *Lavengro,* a book they had read as children.

'Take it to the top of a hill,' Rose had instructed.

So they had climbed up the hill behind the school with a

picnic basket.

'Which way is the wind blowing?' Ismay asked. 'If only the boys were here.'

'Don't be feeble,' Ada said. 'Wet a finger and hold it up.'

Eileen stood tall on top of the hill and read Jasper's speech: 'There's night and day, sisters, both sweet things; sun, moon, and stars, sisters, all sweet things; there's likewise a wind on the heath. Life is very sweet, sisters, who would wish to die?'

At that moment a little breeze blew up, lifting the hairs of their heads, Jane's fringe and Rose's ringlets.

Near dawn, watching light flash in the over-large mirror on the dresser, Ismay felt she had measured all the softness in the world and found it equal to the pain. She had come to a decision: she would stay a few days. And once a year she would visit each of her five sisters. Rudolph could pay for the whole six sisters from Ouse.

&

Acknowledgements

Some of the stories in this collection have already been published: 'Cricket' and 'Money' first appeared in Metro; 'A Turkish Proverb' in Landfall; 'Rose Madder' in the London Magazine and Metro; 'Rose Madder & 10 poems' is the title of a small book to be published by Alyscamps Press, Paris, in 1997. Slightly edited versions of 'Big Bertha', 'Jesu, Joy of Man's Desiring', 'The Ladies Chatterley's Gardener' and 'The Lark Quartet' were broadcast by Radio New Zealand.